KU-377-441

THE CODES OF LOVE

Hannah Persaud

MUSWELL
PRESS

First published by Muswell Press in 2020

Typeset by M Rules

Copyright © Hannah Persaud 2020

Hannah Persaud has asserted her right
to be identified as the author of this work in accordance
with under the Copyright, Designs and Patents Act, 1988

*This book is a work of fiction and, except in the case
of historical fact, any resemblance to actual persons,
living or dead, is purely coincidental*

A CIP catalogue record for this book is
available from the British Library

ISBN: 9781999313531

Muswell Press
London N6 5HQ
www.muswell-press.co.uk

All rights reserved;
no part of this publication may be reproduced, stored in
a retrieval system, or transmitted in any form or by any means, electronic,
mechanical, photocopying, recording, or otherwise without the prior
written permission of the Publisher. This book may not be lent, resold,
hired out or otherwise disposed of by way of trade in any form of
binding or cover other than that in which it is published,
without the prior written consent of the Publisher.

No responsibility for loss occasioned to any person or corporate
body acting or refraining to act as a result of reading material in
the book can be accepted by the Publisher, by the Author,
or by the employer of the Author.

For Arv, for everything x

Love one another, but make not a bond of love:
Let it rather be a moving sea between the shores of
your souls.

Kahlil Gibran, 'On Marriage'

Rules of an open marriage #1:

Never sleep with the same person more than once

'Ambitious,' she is saying, 'to wear shorts in Wales.'

The clouds hang low as rain canvases against the windscreen and Ryan struggles to keep the car steady as it is buffeted by the wind. A steady trickle of water runs down the join between door and window and drips onto his knee, pooling in between his toes. The sole of his foot slips against the rubber of his flip-flops as he accelerates.

When he'd opened the curtains of the room at their B & B this morning, sunlight slipped through a crevice in the clouds and streamed in through the window. As he watched Ada sleeping in the shaft of light, he'd taken it as a sign. He'd had a good feeling about today.

Now he's not so sure it was sensible to make this trip out to the Cregennan Lakes. As soon as they got into the car the weather turned. Today would have been the perfect excuse to stay in bed, windows fastened. The most fleeting of decisions gather volume when inspected later, but for now the cottage is undiscovered. Hindsight is everything.

Ada's warm skin distracts him from the road. He moves his left hand to rest upon her thigh and feels her shift into his fingers.

'Careful,' she says as the chassis of the car crashes against the tarmac in between the potholes. Whose idea was it to bring this ridiculous excuse of a car anyway, little more than a tin can on wheels, not even watertight? She lifts his hand from her leg and places it back on the steering wheel. 'Later.'

She smiles and turns up the music, singing along tunelessly. They could have brought the Audi, or the Range Rover, the Range Rover the obvious choice for a trip like this, but she'd insisted on this car she'd learned to drive in twenty years ago. Emotional about so little, she surprises him with these nods to sentiment.

'We must be nearly there.' He slows to peer through the water sluicing down the windows. 'We've been driving for at least an hour.'

'I'll check,' she says, reaching for her phone. 'It said twenty minutes from Dolgellau this morning.' Opening the window, she extends her arm out, phone to the sky. 'Crap. No reception.'

'Great,' he sighs and pulls over to the side of the road, startling a buzzard that is picking at a carcass.

'Isn't this what we wanted?' She leans over and kisses his cheek. 'A break from everything, total focus on ourselves?' Despite his frustration at the road and the gnawing hunger in his stomach, the car is fogging up and it's exciting being lost among the mountains. They are playing at being free. When she slides his chair backwards and straddles him he worries briefly about being spotted by passing cars; then she becomes everything.

Eyes bright and face flushed, she manoeuvres herself back into her chair and rolls the window down. The cold air slaps them in their faces.

'So.' She turns to him.

'So.' He turns the collar of his inadequate sweater up and runs his hand through his hair. 'You looked gorgeous the other night at the members' club, by the way,' he says. 'I love that dress. Wear it again for me some time?'

'Sure,' she laughs and kisses him on the lips. It's incongruous, her laugh that is so much lower than her voice.

'I can't believe you're not bored of me yet,' she says.

'Never.' He leans over and cups her face in his palms, the gear stick intruding awkwardly between them.

Two hours later they've abandoned their search for the lakes and devoured the remainder of the packed lunch prepared for them at their B & B. His legs are numb and covered in mud from scrambling up steep paths, emerging finally and triumphantly through the cloud cover at the summit of Penygader. For miles around all they can see is a white bed of cloud below them, the sky a clear perfect blue above. It's magical but something feels wrong.

'Who would have thought we'd find this, here?' She gestures to the sun, squinting. She throws herself down on the ground, stretching her legs out. 'It's glorious,' she says, closing her eyes. 'The best sun is unexpected.'

It was chance that led them up here – the OS map is sodden and torn, their phones left in the car for safety from the rain. The path wound its way ever upwards, slippery in the mist. Bare feet would have been more suitable than flip-flops, each smooth rock a slip hazard for his flimsy rubber soles. In a landscape punctuated only by heathers and bilberry, they could have been the only people alive. But she'd remembered something from a brochure she'd read about this mountain, and finding it just metres from where they'd abandoned their journey, it had seemed foolish to not seize the opportunity, with the small wooden sign indicating that Cadair Idris was just ahead.

The light's fading.

'We should go down,' he says, bending and grasping her

hand, pulling her to her feet. She stands beside him and rests her chin on his shoulder, face tilted towards the patchwork sky, her eyes mirroring the blue.

'I wish we could stay,' she says, nuzzling her face into his neck. In the fog and dewy mist that's turning fast to sleet, he understands her longing for anonymity, a cloak of a kind.

Going down is quicker, more sliding then walking. The rain is coming faster, great pear-shaped drops that land heavily on his bare legs. She smiles and opens her mouth wide, sticking out her tongue so that she can catch them. 'Here,' she pulls closer to his face and brushes her tongue against his parted lips, 'for you.' A fork confuses him; he remembers telling himself to always head left but now he can't be sure. He pauses for a moment to think, but Ada rushes ahead.

'It's this way, I'm sure,' she says, walking ahead of him, her frame silhouetted against a murky tide of cloud. She hums a tune he doesn't recognise and stray notes travel back to him, fragmented. He rushes to keep up; she's fit and fearless, confident. But half an hour in and an unrecognisable moonscape confronts them; he's put too much faith in her. He considers the risks that they have taken by coming up here, and imagines them requiring rescue by helicopter or worse. He thinks of the bollocking he would give the boys if they got themselves into a similar predicament, but the reality is they probably wouldn't after all the years they spent doing the Duke of Edinburgh's Award. It's not the first time in recent weeks where he's felt foolishly reckless.

'Come on, keep going.' She grabs his hand. She seems unaware of the hazards of their situation and what earlier felt liberating now seems naïve.

'Wait.' He stops and pulls out the sodden Ordnance Survey map. Lowering himself onto his knees, he shields it with his torso. It's little more than papier-mâché now, but their only

4

hope. In between the contours, half rubbed out, he makes out the letters P E N Y. The compass has fared better against the storm and he angles it to the map. 'We came the wrong way,' he says quietly. It's not her fault; he didn't disagree with her choices. He regrets his willingness to be led. He wrings the map out in his hands and feels it twist into pieces. He walks to her side and places an arm around her waist, although the action costs him precious body heat.

'We'll be fine, back up and fork right, there's still some light.' It's not long, though, before that fades, replaced by inky darkness. No lights in the distance, no telltale signs of life. He focuses on putting one foot in front of the other, though his feet burn with the pain of the cold and his big toe aches from where he cut it on a rock. He grits his teeth and grasps her icy hand. As long as they are descending they will reach the bottom, he reasons. Her chipper mood is replaced with a sombre silence. No phones, no food, no blankets. They've outdone themselves this time. The ground levels out, and he's promising himself that he won't let himself be swept up by her impulses again, that in future he'll be more responsible, when a lone torchlight approaches them. They stop walking and stand still, waiting, listening to the footsteps that crunch against the stones that have replaced the mossy grasses. She pulls her hand away from his.

'Hello?' The voice sounds fractured, distorted by the Welsh elongation of the vowels. Conversation is inevitable. Ryan starts walking again, faster, and the shape of a man and a dog emerge. The stranger is illuminated from the forehead down, the bridge of the nose exaggerated against the storm of his eyebrows and beard.

'We may be lost – can you help us?' Ryan's voice sounds feeble to his ears; they are foolish foreigners wandering in unannounced and unprepared and the *may* rings false.

'Where are you headed?' asks the man. The sheepdog

comes into full view, wet fur and head down, tail curled between its legs.

'Dol Idris car park,' answers Ada.

'You're miles away, it's round the other side. From the top it's less than an hour, but from here, two hours at least. You must have walked in the wrong direction. My name's Huw, and you are?'

'I'm Susan and this is Ben.' Her decision to lie seems odd when this man is only helping them. It's not as if they know anybody here.

Ryan clears his throat, deliberating between pride and survival. He'd like to insist that they are fine and not lost at all, but their circumstances betray them. Huw speaks again.

'You can come with me, if you want to. The road's blocked to Dolgellau, flooded, but I can take you as far as Penmaenpool.'

'That's very kind, Huw, thank you. As you can see we're completely unprepared,' Ada says, stepping towards him. In the torchlight she sweeps her arm towards Ryan.

In the back of the car the stench of wet dog is overwhelming. Ryan shuffles his feet around, trying to find a flat resting place; welly boots and rubber mats brush against his bare skin. His toes are numb and he wonders how long it takes for hypothermia to set in. Beside him Ada is talking too loudly and he wants to ask her to be quiet. It's been a long time since he was in the back of a car; he'd forgotten how nauseating the bends are from this vantage, how bumpy the roads.

'You down for long?' Huw asks from the front. 'Brave to come out in shorts,' he says. A guffaw erupts from his beard.

'I told him,' Ada says, 'but he wouldn't listen. He's stubborn like that.'

'City boy, I guess,' Huw says. Another bubble of laughter bursts from the front.

Behind Ryan's head the hot breath of the sheepdog tickles

his ear. Its gravelly tongue brushes his neck. Only with Ada could he find himself in this situation, careening down tiny rock-strewn roads in the darkness. He tunes out their conversation.

She places a hand upon his knee and he pushes it away; this act of familiarity feels inappropriate in a stranger's car. The car slows and the headlights illuminate a river ahead, flowing at right angles to their road. Huw tuts loudly and shakes his head.

'There's no getting across here, not unless you want to swim it.' He turns now. 'You'd be okay, in your shorts . . .' – an impish grin – 'but you young lady, well, you'd catch your death of cold.'

She smiles to show her dimples. How simply she transforms herself at will; it's hard to reconcile her sweetness now with her urgent determination of earlier, sinewed arms hoisting him into position beneath her, the strong grip of her hands against his wrists.

Huw turns the car around and they head back in the direction they've come from. There's no option, he informs them, but to seek shelter in Abergwynant and retrieve their car in the morning, if the rain abates, that is. He can drop them at a hotel that can probably put them up for the night if they'd like. They would, they agree. Ryan thinks of his warm clothes and the large en-suite bathroom at their B & B.

Above the entrance to the hotel a tin sign swings in the wind. Ridge View Hotel, it informs him, though there's no view tonight. A single bare light bulb hangs inside the porch, illuminating the cobwebs above.

'Thank you, you saved us.' Ada leans over and kisses Huw on the cheek. Muttering thanks, Ryan forces himself to stroke the dog's head as he clambers out of the back seat.

'There's only one room left,' the receptionist informs them from behind the wooden desk at the bottom of the stairs. Ryan pulls out his wallet. She fiddles with her roll-up with one hand while tapping the keyboard with another. He saw the car park on the way in, empty except for an upended wheelie bin.

'Yep – you're lucky, there was a cancellation.' Luck is a subjective thing, Ryan considers as she leads them upstairs. The threadbare carpets shrink back from tobacco-stained walls. The building is larger than it looks – there must be twenty rooms at least. They do not pass another person or hear any sound of other guests. At the end of the hallway on the left there is a doorway; curled pencil-sharpenings of red paint fall as he turns the key.

'You from England?' the receptionist asks.

'For our sins,' he replies.

'Shout if you need anything,' she says, disappearing back down the hallway.

He sits on a bed and peels off his flip-flops, rubbing his toes between his hands. The bedroom is cold and there's mildew on the window frames. A single radiator on the far wall gurgles, emitting a feeble attempt at heat that can only be felt by touching it. The twin beds are separated by a dressing table with chairs on either side. The floorboards between them are freezing and littered with protruding screws. He opens a door.

'Shit.'

'What?' She looks up from the armchair where she is emptying her pockets.

'Where's the shower?'

'She said it's down the hallway.'

'You're kidding . . .'

'It's not the Ritz, you know.' She walks over to him and hugs him from behind. 'It doesn't matter, does it? At least we're here together.' Usually he appreciates her optimism.

'How long does it take for hypothermia to set in?' His teeth are chattering.

'You're such a hypochondriac.' She laughs and throws him a threadbare towel.

*

The lights in the hallway have gone off and he can't find the switch to turn them back on. He reaches for his phone torch, remembering too late that it is in the car miles away. The communal bathroom's redeeming feature is that it smells of chlorine, permeating through the holes in the ceiling; he grits his teeth as the lukewarm shower burns his feet. By the time he returns to the room she has dragged the two beds together and the dressing table and chairs are pushed against the far wall. She lies with her back to the door. He turns the lights out and slides in between the covers, wrapping his arms around her. She pushes back against him. He was craving sleep but his body takes over. She has this way of persuading him without a word being said. The beds rock against the thin walls as he moves inside her.. Afterwards he holds her against him, their bodies moulded into one. He breathes in the faint smell of her sweat and closes his eyes.

The next morning, sitting in the dining room, she reads the local papers. It took him half an hour to dry their clothes with a hairdryer. Breakfast is surprisingly delicious; bacon crisp against his tongue, buttery potatoes laced with red onions. A pot of coffee sits between them.

'Oy.' He nudges her foot under the table. 'Can you pass me one?' He gestures to the papers. The rain has stopped and he's looking forward to a long hot bath back at the B & B.

'I've got an idea,' she whispers suddenly. 'What do you think?' She slides an article in front of him; he looks at the headline: *Sheepdog walks 240 miles home.*

'You want a dog?' he asks, raising his eyebrows. 'I'm not sure we're ready for the commitment.' She kicks his foot.

'Not that one – look, below.' *Old farmhouse for sale, 4 acres, rural setting.*

'You're crazy.' He laughs and fidgets with the jam jar.

'I'm serious – look, it's cheap!' He peers at the details.

'There's a reason for that: you're paying for a pile of stones. We could go to the beach, get them for free.'

She sighs. 'You're no fun.' Standing, he pushes back his chair, kisses her ear. He catches a glimpse of the receptionist hovering outside the door, watching.

'Come on, let's see if the road's open again, catch a lift.'

For the second time in twelve hours he's being driven by a stranger, sitting in the back of a van with Ada up front charming the postman, who has agreed to drop them back at their car, assuming that they're happy to drive his delivery route.

'It'll be good to get a tour of the local area,' she exclaimed enthusiastically. It seems inevitable that the route would pass by the abandoned cottage from the paper. Ada bubbles with excitement, clutching the newspaper in her lap. The postman is telling her about the fat lady who lives on the right, whose husband left her for the local landlady, and the man who lives in the closest cottage, who used to own half the land in the area but lost it all when he gambled it away.

'Not long now,' the postman offers, turning slightly. He shrugs. 'Not as keen as the missus, then? Don't blame you – wouldn't touch it myself.' Ryan doesn't answer. He's been transplanted into the middle of someone else's fantasy and this trip to Wales is starting to feel like a very bad idea. The van stops a few metres back from an iron gate.

'It's one of the downsides to this location, the gates. Nine in total,' the postman announces. 'This land used to have multiple owners, so they divided it with gates and walls to separate the cattle. Now it all belongs to one farmer, but the gates remain.' He tuts loudly and gestures to the surrounding fields. 'The walls are crumbling so the gates are pointless, cattle and people roam as they please but God forbid a driver forgets to close the gates behind them. Fastest way to piss off the neighbours. Pain in the arse, if you ask me.'

'People are sticklers for rules,' Ada sighs. 'Darling, can you open the first gate, please?' She leans back and squeezes his hand.

The door is ripped from his fingers. The rain may have abated and the sun broken through, but relentless winds roll across the fields. As he struggles with the rusty lock, he catches his finger in between the frame and the gate. 'Fuck.' Back in the car, dishevelled, he abandons any pretence at civility. At the second gate she jumps from the van to open it. Finally, the ninth gate is opened and closed. The postman pulls the van over to the side of the road.

'I'll wait for you here,' the postman informs them. 'The road's too bumpy to drive down; it'd be the first thing needing doing, should you buy it.' Ryan's about to insist it's not necessary to delay the man further for a whim, but Ada is out already, walking between the potholes, arms open wide and face turned upwards.

'She's refreshing – you're lucky.' The postman winks.

His flip-flops have seen better days and the shorts that have only just dried out toughen up in the cold air. They should have gone to Greece, or Bermuda. What were they thinking? He hurries to catch up with her. The road is steep and tree lined with forestry land pushing in from both sides. In the distance he glimpses her golden hair, which she has released from its ponytail. The main road is out of sight when he sees the cottage, tucked into a clearing in the forest. Admittedly it's more intact than the photo led him to believe, a shape of a house at least. He's aware of his pulse racing. Ada runs towards him. As she pulls him towards the cottage he feels a knot unravel in his chest. She leads him to the front door.

'It's perfect, isn't it?' He had intended to feign interest to pacify her, but as he takes it in, the crumbling granite walls and the fireplace open to the sky, he can't ignore the enthusiasm skipping in his throat. His mouth is dry. It's like nothing he's ever considered. He's used to designing new homes, passive houses that leave a minimal imprint, frames that can be erected within days. Watertight, airtight, full of glass and light.

'It'd take us months to rebuild.' Instantly he regrets saying it. She claps her hands and embraces him. 'Hypothetically,' he adds.

'I knew you'd come around when you saw it,' she is saying, and he's trying to find the right words to let her down, but even as he flounders he knows that he won't find them because this pile of boulders in the middle of Welsh farmland feels as if it has been waiting for him. They round the corner of the cottage and emerge into the clearing beyond, where sheep scatter among the trees. They walk up the slope, his thighs screaming from the efforts of yesterday, up to the skyline and to where the ground levels and grasses flatten.

She passes him the map the postman has lent her. The Mawddach Estuary glitters in the midday sun below them and Barmouth sparkles beyond. In the distance the mountains of Snowdonia stretch out in mist-soaked peaks and the Llŷn Peninsula juts out defiantly at the edge of the horizon, at right angles to Bardsey Island, which rises anxiously from the sea. Turning 180 degrees, he sees the cottage down below them, nestled beneath the ridge of Tyddyn Shieffre. He sees the forestry land encroaching on the cottage and the brambles that spread like fingers latching onto the ruined windows and door. For as far as the eye can see there's no sign of a single person. He closes his eyes and opens them, willing something to shift and cast doubt, but the sun splinters above their heads and though there's every reason to turn and walk away, when she wraps her arm around his waist he knows that this must belong to them. A shiver runs through him. It is not theirs to take, but they have made a habit of taking what does not belong.

'Our own private vista.' Ada smiles and he knows that she has won; his judgement blurred. They walk back up the broken driveway slowly. As the van comes into sight, they see the postman pacing beside it.

'I thought you weren't coming back,' he says, opening his door and throwing himself into his seat heavily. 'I've a job to do, you know.'

'I'm sorry,' Ada says, 'we got distracted by the view.' Ryan clambers into the back of the van, his thoughts filled with the cottage that has already changed everything. London seems farther away than ever as the engine starts and they pull off, the postman muttering 'tourists' under his breath. Has it really been only four months since this whole thing started? He has a sense of hurtling towards something even as he knows he should be turning away.

Rules of an open marriage #2:

Our arrangement is a secret between us

London, December 2015

Emily coils her hair into a chignon and clips it high on the back of her head, smoothing a stray hair behind her ear. Standing back, she tilts her head. Too old: she's forty-three, not eighty-two. Unclipping it, she lets her hair fall over her shoulders. She prefers herself like this, more natural. She applies grey eye shadow to her eyelids and dabs highlighter onto her cheekbones. She pinches her lips hard and smiles to see them flush with colour. The best makeup in the world doesn't compensate for this good old-fashioned trick, learned when she was eight.

Turning sideways, she examines her profile. She wishes her breasts were larger, but nothing is perfect. She refuses to fall down the slippery slope in pursuit of perfection that so many of her peers have. She knows too well how it starts with a simple nip and tuck. It's inevitable that a few months later her nose would be too pointy and her lips too swollen. Before she'd noticed, she'd be walking around looking like an inflatable doll on steroids. She's going au naturel and to hell with anyone who complains about it. Perfection is relative, anyway.

Her legs ache from her bike ride, but this is how she'll preserve herself, with exercise and healthy food. She's glad that she had boys and does not have to deal with the neurosis and stresses of teenage girls. She's not sure she could handle the self-doubt and the diets. There's enough to worry about without adding to the list. She remembers her disappointment when she was twelve and she got her period; the wondrous anticipation of becoming a woman clashed disappointingly with the reality, the mess and inconvenience, and the depressing realisation that she was stuck with this for the next forty years at least. There were other things too: the realisation at fifteen that her breasts were not going to get any larger, that she would never have a cleavage to display without stuffing her bra; that there was nothing silky about legs and armpits and pubic hair. Then, soon after, the discovery that this thing called sex that they'd talked about as sacred was a perfunctory and clumsy affair, ultimately unsatisfying. And then, at university and finally an adult, a dawning comprehension that at this point, fully grown and equipped with freedom, she was not at liberty to pursue her increasing sexual libido with whom she pleased, as there were now expectations – such as commitment and monogamy – attached to the transactions. And then of course there was Charlotte, who could have changed everything, but didn't after all.

Her phone beeps and she thinks uncomfortably of the message she received earlier from her student, Leo. It's not like anything untoward has happened and he's a great writer, but she does regret giving him her number. Her husband comes into the bathroom behind her.

'You look gorgeous,' he says, brushing his lips against her neck. 'Don't be long, we're running late.'

'One minute and I'll be down,' she says, doing up her necklace and giving herself a final once-over in the mirror. In the bedroom she gets her handbag and checks for the essentials – car keys, lipstick, envelope with tickets to give him later, her surprise. She'll give it to him after the ceremony, once they're

alone. It's been so long since they've been away together with‑
out the boys. Every time she thinks of getting on that plane a
frisson of excitement runs through her.

Venice, three glorious days of wandering the alleyways
and meandering canals. It would have been better to go for
longer, but the boys have revision sessions for exams coming
up. Her husband works so hard anyway, wouldn't be able to
take any more time off. It'll be good for them to have some
time alone – she's missed him these last few weeks, though it's
been worth it. The award he's nominated for is well deserved,
a huge accolade for someone just into their forties. Carrying
her bag in one hand, high heels in the other, she pads across
the oak floor to the hallway.

Leaning over the glass balustrade she calls down, 'Coming.'
Down the hallway flanked with framed photographs, she
knocks on Sam's door. 'We're off, darling.' A pause and then a
scuffle before he opens the door, hair dishevelled.

'Have fun, don't be late,' he says. He winks and she cuffs
him playfully. It happened so quickly, this morphing into a
man. His body has filled out, his jaw widened. She notices girls
looking at him on the street. He's striking with his auburn hair
and bright blue eyes.

'Are you studying?' she asks. He rolls his eyes.

'It's the weekend, Mum.' She doesn't need to worry anyway:
he's naturally bright and has been eager to learn from the day
he started school. Tom, on the other hand . . .

'Call me if there are any problems,' she says, placing a kiss
on his cheek. 'Tom will be back around eleven; we'll be back
by midnight.'

'I'm not a kid you know, Mum, I'll be fine.' Behind him his
computer monitor is blinking.

Downstairs the car is waiting, engine humming. She checks
the back doors are locked. Closing the blinds on the bifold

doors in the kitchen, she notices something on the glass, a dark line, smeared. Following it down she sees the bird, splayed on the ground outside, highlighted by the motion sensor. Another one down. She doesn't have time to move it. The problem with so much glass is that the house is virtually invisible to the birds. She saw a blue tit mid-flight last week, heading straight towards her at the sink. She'd cried at the inevitability of it; there was nothing she could do but wait for the crack of its beak against the glass.

There's really no need for window coverings; they're not overlooked, are entirely isolated from their neighbours and surrounded by trees. Still, the traditionalist in her insisted on having them in the kitchen, at least. She doesn't like to think that while she's immersed in chopping an onion, eyes watering, someone could be outside looking in. The car smells of aftershave and a pink cupcake-shaped deodorising air freshener that swings from the rear-view mirror. She leans over and removes it, putting it in the glove box. 'I hate these things,' she says. 'Why would anybody think you'd want to make your car smell like a candyfloss factory?'

He smiles and puts his hand on her leg. 'No tights in December?'

She pushes his hand away. 'They always have the temperature turned up at these events. I hope they open some windows this time.' She looks out of the window at the grey pavements, street lights casting golden patterns on the wet concrete. He laughs and ruffles her hair with his left hand, then drapes his arm across the back of the chair. She's silent as they wait for the traffic lights to turn green. 'I'd still like to buy an old building one day, you know, with history.'

'Some people would kill to have our house,' he says, braking hard as a woman with a pushchair steps out from the pavement in front of them. 'Jesus, some people don't deserve to be parents.'

She sighs.

They pull into the driveway of the house that he's designed, where the ceremony is being held. Handbrake on, he turns to her.

'We're our own living history, isn't that enough?'

'You're enough.' She reaches over and puts her hand on his cheek to soften the mistruth. She thinks of the last time she saw Leo in the library, their legs touching. She didn't pull away.

It's strange going to an awards ceremony in a house. Everything is in its place: sofas in the lounge, beds in the upstairs rooms. As if the owner has popped out for some milk and in their absence the house has been infiltrated by a brigade of architects and project planners standing round drinking wine in their designer kitchen and inspecting the seamless joins between the floating counters, and the way the light falls right through the house to the basement, thanks to the installation of glass landings.

She recognises most of the people here from dinner parties, a pretentious bunch. Her husband was different from the start though, excited about architecture but not pompous.

'We're not going to change the world', he tells her, 'only little bits of it.'

'Emily, how lovely to see you.' Georgia, Phil's wife, is gliding towards her and Emily forces a smile. They've been meeting on dinner-party loops for years now. Emily can't stand her.

'Did you hear about poor old Martha? Poor dear, she's beside herself. I mean, being left for the nanny? What a cliché!'

It was inevitable to anyone who'd spent five minutes in her husband Greg's company. There's a feeding frenzy every time a marriage collapses round here. Georgia swans back to Phil, who raises his head and nods at Emily. He's marginally more tolerable than Georgia and Emily doesn't know how he can stand being married to her. Enduring her for one evening every couple of months is all Emily can handle.

'Poor Martha indeed,' her husband whispers. She hadn't realised he was listening. 'Her husband's a fool.' He leans in and speaks into her ear. 'He's blown it this time.'

'You knew and didn't tell me?' Emily feigns a hurt expression.

'Idle gossip is beneath you.' He kisses her nose.

It's the third marriage to collapse this year from their group. Emily knows it's unsympathetic, but she's tired of all the drama, the late nights providing cups of tea and tissues. 'You might feel differently if you actually cared about any of these people,' he said the last time she had clambered into bed at 3 a.m. after setting up the guest room again. It's true. She feels selfish, but it's so boring. Anna, her only perpetually single friend (now ex single friend) had accused her of being 'smug married'. What does that even mean? There's nothing smug about her marriage. It's not luck that it is working. She doesn't take him for granted. They have their fights, like anyone. She knows it's their arrangement that saves them from the tedium that fells so many of their peers, though she doesn't say this. Their rules. She could write a book about them. She should write a book about them.

'It doesn't just stay good,' she'd told Anna, 'it takes work. And compromise.' She'd thought of the last man, the thrill of it. She likes the rawness of unknowing that fades with famil-iarity. Less sacrifice than most marriages, she wanted to tell Anna, though she didn't.

A woman approaches them purposefully and her husband steps forward. He shakes her hand. 'This is Emily, my wife.' To Emily, 'This is Adeline, a consultant on my project. We've met before, virtually.'

Emily steps forward and offers her hand. 'Lovely to meet you, Adeline – congratulations.' Adeline dips her head and leans forward. She's ridiculously pretty, with her wide-open eyes and dimples when she smiles.

'Thanks. I find it all a bit embarrassing, really, the pomp and glory. But you've got to show face sometimes,' she says. Emily warms to her. This evening could be more fun than she'd anticipated.

'How refreshing, to find someone sincere,' she whispers to her husband when the consultant has been ushered away for introductions.

'Yes, she's an interesting character. Rather unorthodox, but she gets results. You know how I like to be in control, though,' he says. Emily watches Adeline as she accepts a glass of wine from the waiter. There's a confident grace to her movements, despite her claims of embarrassment. Her laughter is deep and surprising and several people turn. A man in jeans, a polo neck and suit jacket moves to the front of the room and taps his glass.

'Max,' Emily's husband whispers.

'The biggest challenge to any architect is to sit the house comfortably in the landscape,' Max says. 'What Mr Bradshaw has done here is nothing short of genius. Situated on the outskirts of London, this house needed to integrate its urban setting with the rural countryside it flanks. Not only was access difficult, but privacy was key.'

Beside her he dips his head and whispers, 'That's an under-statement, it was a bloody nightmare.' She remembers the day he came home furious at a rejection from the planning office to allow a temporary road surface to be laid. He'd sat and drunk himself into a stupor in his office and after she'd finally persuaded him to go to bed, he'd clung to her, childlike, until he fell asleep.

He reaches for her hand and squeezes it. 'I couldn't have done it without you. Thanks.' She squeezes his hand in response.

'Some people say that building a house is the last remaining act of careful making that we in the West still undertake.' There are small murmurs of agreement around the room, glasses clinking. 'That is nowhere more apparent than in this house, where style and quality are paired beautifully with authentic rural details, where crystal chandeliers reflect off polycarbonate partitions that slide on agricultural tracks, where water troughs feature as dazzling water displays . . .' He waves his hand to the garden.

He leans closer again – 'Those were hers' – he gestures to Adeline, who is across the room looking out of a window.

'I like it,' Emily says. 'Introducing affordable innovation . . .'

'Spot the writer,' he says. Emily digs her elbow into his ribs. Released from formalities, the atmosphere lightens and people talk louder. In a corner music is turned on. Ludovico Einaudi fills the room and she recognises the haunting, discordant tones of *Nightbook*, one of her favourite albums.

'Did you know that Einaudi's inspiration was Satie?' Adeline is beside her now, whispering in her ear.

'No, I didn't, but that makes sense, it's the same minimalist approach.'

'I love it, it's so haunting,' Adeline says.

'My thoughts exactly,' Emily says. 'It's great by the way, all these finishing touches,' she says, pointing to the ceiling where bare bulbs hang at different heights. 'Just shows that you don't have to be extravagant to be stylish.'

'Yes. There was some resistance at first to some of the ideas.' Adeline takes two glasses of wine from the waitress and passes one to Emily. 'Mainly from your husband actually, but he has extravagant taste.' She winks. Confused, Emily fidgets with her bag. Does she really come across as an extravagance?

'Oh,' Adeline laughs, seeing her confusion, 'not you, though you're lovely of course . . .' She wedges her glass of wine between her chest and her right wrist while tucking her hair behind her ears with her left hand. 'I've seen your house – he showed me, on a call once. He was trying to shape my palette for this project. I think he was a little offended I didn't take up more of his ideas.'

'Oh.' Emily smiles and relaxes. 'Well, he does pride himself on his taste, as you know.' Speaking a little quieter she adds, 'But it is rather expensive. There's a tendency to overcompensate for an impoverished youth.'

'And why not? Come and look at the upstairs – the bedrooms are glorious.'

Emily glances at her husband who is in deep conversation with Max. She puts her untouched glass of wine on a side table and takes the stairs two at a time behind Adeline, who scales them at high speed. Emily can see the muscles in the backs of her legs as she climbs.

'It's beautiful,' Emily is saying as she is rushed through the rooms: hardwood floors furnished with vintage rugs; a freestanding bathtub in the master bedroom.

'You haven't seen the crowning glory. Come on.' Emily follows her up a fairy-tale staircase that floats out from the wall. Two floors below the party continues, glass landings distributing flickering candlelight below. Then they're at the top, a half floor, really, a solid glass floor below them and a glass ceiling above. Adeline closes a door at the top of the staircase and the sounds from downstairs are muted into a quiet hum.

Emily finds herself pulled onto a sofa. 'Look.' Controlled by something invisible, the ceiling opens; the star-stamped sky floods in and the room breathes out. It's stopped raining. They stare at the silent sky.

'It's astonishing,' Emily says, turning. 'Was this your idea?'

'I wanted something special, a surprise,' Adeline replies. Emily whistles softly.

'Well, it's certainly that.' She turns to Adeline. 'I'm keen to buy somewhere old, do it up. Not just your standard restoration, but with a twist. Maybe you can advise us. When we're ready.'

'Yes, I think we'd work well together.' Adeline says. She flicks her hair out of her eyes. 'Plus I think we could win your husband over with some surprising innovations, open his eyes a bit.'

'I'm sure we could,' Emily says, and she's confident they would.

They sit leaning back on the sofa and Emily is aware of their legs touching, skin against skin. She eases away slightly; she wouldn't want Adeline to think that—

'You have bare legs, too,' Adeline says, the palm of her hand cool against Emily's thigh.

'Tights make me feel claustrophobic,' Emily replies, her voice strangled. She swallows.

'Same here,' Adeline says, putting her foot on the coffee table in front of them so that her dress slips higher up her thigh. 'Anyway, these events are always overheated.' Emily glances at her sideways and stifles a laugh.

'I couldn't agree more. Look, I should go back down, my husband . . .'

'I am sure he's surrounded by a sycophantic crowd right now – you know how they are. He's probably loving it; stay a little longer?' Adeline mimics a pout and Emily relaxes back into the cushions. 'So what do you do for a living, Emily?'

'I lecture in creative writing at UCL.'

'Impressive.'

'It pays the bills.'

'I'm always fascinated by writers, their ability to invent entire worlds.' Adeline laughs. 'It's a skill, right?'

Emily smiles. 'Or a burden. I've spent my whole life want-ing to make my money from writing and not succeeding.'

'Success is relative,' Adeline squeezes Emily's knee, 'and generally determination wins out, in my experience.' From downstairs the hum becomes louder, a wave of laughter. Adeline rolls her eyes.

'You're right. I hate these things,' Emily says.

'So what else, apart from the obvious ...' Adeline grasps Emily's left hand and twists the wedding ring round. It's too loose; a miracle it hasn't fallen off, really. She should have it adjusted.

'Lecturer, wife, bearer of children,' Emily says, distracted by Adeline's fingers against her wrist. She wonders if Adeline can feel her hot pulse beating against her cool fingers.

'So what sort of thing do you write?' Adeline asks, tilting her body towards her.

'Bleak and depressing fiction. It's therapy for my darkness.' Emily forces a laugh, her mind racing. She thinks of her husband downstairs, imagines him glancing at his watch and scanning the room for her. There's nothing in their arrangement that forbids this, but it's been a long time since ...

'You seem solid,' Adeline is saying. 'You and your husband, I mean. He's clearly besotted.' Emily thinks of the last time they made love. She wonders if besotted can also be comfortable.

'We've been together a long time,' she replies. 'Twenty-two years, in fact.'

'You don't look old enough to have been married for that long,' Adeline says, and Emily is glad that the room is dark, hiding her blushes. For the second time in the conversation Emily thinks of the arrangement that she has made with her husband, and feels an urge to tell this stranger the truth: she wants to let her know that it might be okay to take things further. No, she can't, it's one of the rules that their open marriage remains a secret. Adeline is out of bounds anyway, as they both know her. Although how do you define 'know'? The rules are there for freedom. It's just ... it's been so long since she met a woman like this, with no façade. Adeline's hand is back on

25

Emily's leg, her thumb moving in small circles across the soft inner flesh of her thigh, and something flickers inside Emily. The infinitesimal brush of skin against skin.

'Emily?' Adeline's voice brings her back. 'Do you . . .?'

'Emily?' Emily jumps at the sound of her husband's voice through the door and Adeline slips her hand back onto her own leg.

'Got bored downstairs, did you?' Adeline calls out, standing and smoothing her dress down.

'Sorry to interrupt but it's Nick's mum on the phone – we need to collect Tom.' He opens the door. Emily leaps from the sofa.

'What happened?'

'He's drunk. They sneaked in booze, apparently, but I'll go, you stay.'

'Of course not, this is your night, I'll go,' Emily says.

Adeline leads the way downstairs and Emily follows, willing the colour in her face to fade. Everything is bright and overexposed.

'Call me,' Adeline presses a card into Emily's hand. 'I'd love to go out.'

Emily smiles. 'Me too.'

At the door her husband kisses her forehead. 'Are you sure you don't mind going?'

'I'm sure. Get a cab home, okay?'

As she pulls out of the driveway, she sees him close the door. She realises she didn't ask Adeline anything about herself.

In the car Tom throws up three times. Emily is furious.

'What were you thinking? You're only sixteen.'

'I'm sorry.'

'I've never been so embarrassed. What must his parents think?' She'd cringed as Nick's dad reassured her that it was okay.

'I said sorry.' He winds the window down and hangs his head out.

At home, Sam is smug. 'Oh dear, little brother. Talk about shit hitting the fan.'

'Sam, that's unnecessary. I think he's learned his lesson.'

The tickets to Venice will have to wait until the morning. With the boys in bed, she walks into the garden with a large glass of wine, the air cold against her bare legs. What happened back there? She hasn't felt that since Charlotte. Her phone beeps and she checks it. *I need to see you, I need to know. Leo.* She ignores it. She doesn't know what she'd say anyway. She can't deny there's tension between them and she's unused to exercising restraint. But he's her student; it's different. Lying down on one of the sunloungers that no one's sat on since the summer, she lets her dress ride up her legs. She thinks of Adeline's thumb circling against her skin, and of Leo. As her fingers bring her what she longs for, she lets them fill her head. She doesn't notice that it's 2 a.m. and that her husband is still not home.

Rules of an open marriage #3:

What's done remains in the past

Emily met Charlotte at university. There was nothing outwardly remarkable about her quiet appearance and frugal use of words. They'd been paired up for an exercise and she emerged to Emily like one of those watercolour pictures for toddlers, the wet paintbrush revealing a rainbow-coloured picture from a blank white page. Once love is there it's impossible to imagine it absent. Charlotte and she were inseparable for the rest of their degrees. They shared everything: secrets, gossip, details of their lovers. The Charlotte from her classes became an outline. When they graduated they'd planned to move to London together and live out their dreams of becoming writers. The last night of university they'd drunk too much and fallen into Charlotte's bed laughing about the boyfriend that Emily had just ditched, their giggles ending abruptly as their lips brushed. There was nothing awkward; they discovered each other eagerly and without embarrassment. It was the start of something new.

But one week before the lease on their flat started, Charlotte had sent a letter.

Emily, you will think me callous and I do not expect you to forgive me, but I will not be moving in with you. I met someone. We have a future, unlike you and I. I will forever remember the times we have shared, but this was a transitory stage from which I am emerging. I fear that you may be trapped in this phase for some time, bouncing from one drama to the next. We are better off apart, now that our lives are starting properly, and I wish you all the very best with your future. Emily lost £500 on the deposit and was not invited to the wedding, which was held shortly after, when Charlotte fell pregnant.

Emily drowned her sorrows and made herself available to every man who made advances, of which there were many. Charlotte was a glitch and to be forgotten, for everyone knew that such experiences were as common and as formative as the exploration of oneself. She felt foolish for having attributed it greater value than it deserved. She tucked the experience away in her discarded memories and willed herself to forget.

That, as Emily remembers it, was the start of a grown-up life. Gaining paid employment as a writer proved difficult: hundreds of copywriting jobs applied for led to nothing; competitions she entered her fiction into were black holes. Emily joined the civil service; at least it paid her. She held people at a distance and when she met her husband, who was everything she was not – focused and ambitious and in control, she'd signed up gladly for the life that he promised. She loved him more than she expected to, which was not at all.

Two years ago she got a call from Charlotte's mother. It came from nowhere and knocked her sideways. Charlotte was ill and dying. She'd asked that Emily go and visit her in the hospice. *Would you do it, please?* her mother asked. *For Charlotte?* No, Emily would not.

Rules of an open marriage #4:

No financial agreements must be entered into with anyone else

Wales, May 2016

Ryan picks up the black ballpoint pen and twists it in his hands. He and Ada are here with their solicitors and it feels very real. Is it really only five months since the awards ceremony? Every detail of the evening is etched in his memory. Beginnings always are. Emily had been in a foul mood. In the car she'd torn the air freshener into pieces, then she'd complained about the heat. At the ceremony she'd brightened up when she met Ada and he'd felt bad that Ada's time was monopolised. He was relieved when Nick's mum called to tell them about Tom, and glad that Emily insisted on going to collect him. After Emily left, Ada persuaded him upstairs to admire their handiwork. Ada was barefoot and everything was fluid, loosened by champagne.

'I like your wife,' she'd said, politely.

'As do I,' he replied.

'I like you more, though,' she'd whispered, lacing her little finger through his. He'd hesitated.

'This isn't what I do,' he'd told her.

She'd smiled and said, 'You're sweet.' Ten minutes later he

was fucking her in the en-suite bathroom up against the wall, her bare feet wrapped around his hips.

He'd gone home afterwards to Emily and slipped between the covers. Ada had kept ringing him, but he managed to avoid contact until he stumbled across her in the guest room of his house after her night out with Emily in Dulwich. He'd been up all night holding back Emily's hair while she threw up, but when Ada asked him for a lift home he couldn't say no. It would have seemed rude, and sitting beside her in the car he was unable to resist her. He was a cliché of middle age, but he slept with her again, and then again. He stopped trying to resist her and gave in. He was hooked.

The purchase of the cottage is unforgivable. Bricks and stones lend the affair substance. He thinks of their wedding vows. A one-night stand is acceptable, but an ongoing affair quite another.

Until Ada he'd only been with one woman other than Emily, and even that was just to spite her after she stayed out with another man all night. He'd gone to the seediest hotel he could find and drunk shot after shot, and when the woman on the stool next to him came on to him he'd felt triumphant. He'd told Emily as soon as he was home, hoping that she'd realise at last how it felt to actually be on the receiving end of the arrangement that she'd insisted on, but she'd merely asked him if he'd used a condom and whether he felt better for having done it, to which he'd replied 'yes', although it was a lie.

He holds the biro in his hand and looks at Ada beside him. His solicitor clears his throat. He should put the pen down and walk away. Now would be the time. He'll tell Emily everything and perhaps she'll forgive him for so brazenly flouting their rules.

'Ready?' Ada says. He nods, and places the pen to the paper, signing his name to the mass of stones that they ambitiously refer to as a cottage, entering a financial agreement that the rules of his marriage forbid. His nerve does not waver. Is this how they all feel, the adulterers he knows, skipping from one woman to the next with no thought of consequence? He binds his name to the land.

Beside him Ada pauses, pen trembling slightly. He wonders if this is the moment that will snap the bond between them and set them free. But Ada crosses her legs primly and leans forward, the tip of her tongue sticking out between her front teeth, and signs her name firmly beside his. Outside in the rain again, she takes the keys.

'I'll drive – it's time for a celebration.'

It's funny how things turn out. Emily's insistence on financial independence had made it easy. She'd requested from the start that they run their finances separately, with one shared bank account for household expenses. He'd been hurt by this, feeling it a snub, but he agreed to it to keep her happy. So now, with money from his not insubstantial savings, he was able to invest in a cottage that Emily would never know existed. A dam has broken open. He can't stop the flooding and he doesn't want to. Everything is his for the taking. The breaking of Emily's rules brings him the greatest freedom of all.

They've installed a caravan on-site to stay in until the cottage is habitable. It's twenty years old and is not roadworthy, so they had it transported in. Inside its tinny walls the rain sounds like a machine gun. Tucked into a corner of the plot and buffered by trees on two sides, it rocks slightly in the wind. It reminds him of sailing in his youth, the gentle swell and fall of the waves where he and Emily used to go off the Dorset coast. Emily was a natural sailor with strong sea legs and a gift for predicting the wind.

'We should make a plan for the restoration,' Ada is saying as she cracks open the champagne that she has left chilling outside in a bucket of partially frozen ice. 'We need to make progress before winter sets in, make it watertight.' Ryan leans back on the bed that doubles up as a seating area and accepts a proffered glass.

'It's May; that's a tight schedule. Given we'll barely be here,' he says. Already Emily's been giving him a hard time, trying to make him feel guilty for so much time spent away these past few months. Ada climbs onto the bed beside him and wraps a leg over his. His T-shirt sleeve slips up and she kisses the owl tattoo on his upper arm.

'Why an owl?' she asks.

'A gift from my wife when we were young and reckless,' he replies.

'You, reckless?' she laughs. It bothers him that this amuses her. 'But seriously, why an owl?'

He shrugs. 'I was obsessed with them for a while. Look, don't you think it's a little ambitious to hope to be in before winter?'

'Ye of little faith.' She kisses his cheek. 'I'll do some research, ask around for recommendations. I know you're busy, but I can try and get up here more often if needs be. The only limitations are in your mind.' She's taken a sabbatical from work.

'It's hard work being a consultant,' he teases her.

'You're just jealous,' she replies. Sitting up, she reaches for her notebook, which she's wedged in between the edge of the bed and the window. 'Look, I made a list,' she says. She has incredible attention to detail. But he's not interested in lists. With only two days left before he goes home, he doesn't want to waste them on things they can liaise about by email. Pushing the notebook out of her hand, he grabs hold of her arm.

'Let's go and look at what we've bought ourselves.'

Champagne bottle in one hand, he tugs his wellies on with the other, over his waterproof trousers. They arrived fully equipped this time, a whole cupboard of their miniscule storage given to outdoor clothes.

'You're supposed to put them on under the trousers,' she laughs, bending down and pulling the trousers out from where he's tucked them into his socks. 'Otherwise the rain runs down the trousers and pools in your wellies.' Standing up, she grins. 'Honestly, call yourself an architect?'

'I'll make it watertight, you'll see,' he shouts, running the 200 metres to the cottage.

From this angle the cottage is obscured by the crumbling sheep barn. 'A guest house,' the agent had said optimistically. 'Firewood,' Ada had whispered. Up to the left he can see the sweep of the ridge, the promise of Barmouth beyond echoed in the distant sounds of the sea. There's something magical about horizons, the way they dominate what's right in front of you. 'A window is a horizon,' he's fond of telling clients, 'just a moveable one.' Hundreds of views he has found and framed for clients who come to him despairing: neighbours they overlook, the main road right beside them. The last client was beside himself. 'One tree and you managed to frame it perfectly – what luck. You'd never believe there's a wall right there,' he'd said, leaning out. There's no such thing as luck, just opportunity. He'd moved the window and reduced its size so that the wall next door was obscured by millimetres. It doesn't matter what's really there, but what you choose to see.

More slate tiles have slipped down the bank behind the cottage, the remains of the roof barely visible. At the entrance brambles block the door.

'They grow so fast,' Ada says, attacking them with the shears that she has left there. He heaves his weight against the jammed door and it opens reluctantly into a tiny hallway. On the left is a bathroom. There is a cracked iron bath in the corner that is littered with dead spiders and a chainless toilet waiting to be flushed of debris that has fallen from the walls. On the right is the main downstairs room. Something scuttles across the floor and an old piece of cardboard that's replacing a glass pane in the windows flaps freely in the breeze. To the left of the room is an old wood-burning stove, covered in soot. Its glass-fronted door is smoke-stained, concealing the contents. An old armchair that was grand once sits in front of the stove, its eagle-clawed feet now faded and charcoal-stained.

'They didn't mention a fire,' Ada says.

'Why would they?' Ryan replies. Ada is opening the stove now, rummaging inside. She pulls out a piece of old newspaper. 'Look, from 1975.'

In what was once the kitchen, a yellowed sink containing a solitary tin mug is the only sign of domesticity. He turns the tap on and escaped air hisses out like a last breath.

Behind him Ada wraps her arms around his waist.

'We'll make it perfect, we'll never want to leave,' Ada says. There's a flicker of fear inside him.

The staircase is brittle and missing steps, but a ladder takes them up into the eaves of the cottage where the floor is intact and solid despite tilting upwards at five degrees. They've agreed that they'll only focus on what needs replacing and fixing, preserving as much of the building and its history as possible.

'It'll be a workout to get into bed,' Ada paces up the room. 'Not that we'll need it, of course.'

There is only a tiny window in here and the wooden shutters open inwards. It's just big enough to squeeze a head and shoulders through, which is what Ryan does now. Nothing can be seen but the forest, pressing in on both sides; the ridge beyond is hidden in the treetops. It's better than he remembers, virtually a tree house.

'We wanted privacy and we got it,' Ada says, climbing back down the ladder. He follows and by the time he reaches the ground she is peeling off her waterproof trousers and the leggings beneath, fleece top followed by vest. She's not wearing a bra and her breasts swell against her ribcage.

'Where are you going, you nutter?' he calls as she walks out of the front door clad only in wellies. She heads straight for the ridge. Turning back, her long hair lashes her face and her long white limbs mottle quickly with blue.

'Come on – there's nobody to see,' she shouts. He follows her up through the bracken that whips red scratches into her legs, up onto the clearing, where the ground falls away below them and now she's dancing to an imaginary tune, asking him to join her. He grips her cold hands in his warm ones and presses her into him, moving to music that he can't hear. Minutes pass and then he is cold too, despite being clothed. Her skin is goosebumped and her fingers are pink and blue. He prises them from his shoulders.

'Ada, let's go in.' She doesn't answer and he's about to say it again when she looks at him. It's as if she sees straight through him, to his very core. 'Ada?' Now her focus shifts to something behind him, and he feels the horror of being discovered out here, in their private space. Her expression turns to that of recognition.

'There's someone there,' Ada says. They are miles from anywhere. He passes her his coat and scans the cottage and the field beyond, willing his eyes to penetrate the darkness of the forest.

'Where?' he says. She wraps herself in his coat, which dwarfs her. It is madness that they are here at all, not least because it is five degrees with the wind–chill factor and walkers die out in here in better weather. He looks behind them, but there is nothing but the cottage and the caravan and, behind, the mountain.

'He's gone,' she says, walking down the slope of the ridge, and he follows, still scanning for movement in the distance.

'Are you sure?' he asks, thinking of her strange expression

just before, 'What did he look like?'

'He looked, I don't know, tall, fair …' She stomps away from him and her white legs are vulnerable and thin between the hem of his coat and her wellies.

'Ada?' he calls, catching up. He is torn between trying to find the visitor and taking care of her. 'What's wrong?' he asks her.

'Nothing.'

The next morning sun pulses through the plastic windows of the caravan, waking him early. He throws his arm out across the bed; Ada is not there. He sits up, banging his head against one of the cupboard doors that has fallen open in the night. Rubbing his eyes, he peers through the chequered curtains. Sheep nibble grass just outside the door. Flinging one leg from under the quilt, he flinches. The sun is shining, but the temperature plummets at night. Back under the covers, he pulls on his long johns and socks, his thermal vest and hoodie.

From a sitting position in bed he can open the door. When he steps out, a rabbit sprints from underneath the caravan and off into the woods. Squinting into the distance, he scans the area. No sign of Ada. He doesn't know if she's taken the car – the road is still impassable, so the car is left at the top where the tarmac turns to rubble, tucked out of sight. He walks up the ridge slowly. Jesus, his head hurts. If they're to get the cottage built they'll have to drink less, or at least he will. No matter how much they drink, Ada doesn't seem to suffer. They can match each other glass for glass and he'll wake straw-headed and nauseous while Ada will have been up for hours and gone for a run. He can't recall whether her trainers were at the door.

At the top he sits heavily on the grass. Boats trawl the mouth of the estuary lazily, leaving stretch marks in the sea. It's Sunday and he's going home tomorrow. Reaching into his pocket, he switches his phone on. It's one of Ada's ideas not to check their phones when they're together. 'It ruins the magic,' she says. In principle he agrees, though he worries about missing something important. He angles the screen away from the light and checks his calendar. Like his mother's birthday. Reception is poor and as he calls the ringing cuts in and out.

'Mum? It's me, Ryan. Happy birthday. What? Yes. It's today. Did you forget? Well, at seventy-three you can be forgiven . . . What? I'm away for work, I told you. Back tomorrow. Okay. That'd be lovely. Our favourite place . . .' Out of nowhere Ada appears; she must have come up behind him. She's in her running gear, iPod strapped to her upper arm. She sits beside him and stretches her legs out.

'I'm going to go now, okay, but I'll see you soon. Have a good day,' he says, hanging up and putting his phone back into his pocket. No word from Emily or texts from the boys in reply to his wishing them well in their revision. Gone are the years when they missed him. Emily knows that he has met someone else. *Let it run its course,* she said. As if it's a battery-powered train. Would he have ended the affair if she'd asked him to?

'I don't believe in ownership', she told him from the start, 'we are capable of loving one another intellectually without needing exclusivity. It's not because I don't care. I've committed my life to you, isn't that proof enough?' It would have been nice to see a hint of possession though, at times. Once during a fit of rage he'd accused her of not loving him enough. 'I love you plenty,' she'd replied as he stormed out of the door. Plenty was not enough, he knows that now. But plenty was all she could give.

'Who was that?' Ada leans into his shoulder.

'No questions, remember?' he says, lying back on the grass. No questions about their other lives. No questions about the past, or the future.

'Fine, be like that.' She walks down the ridge.

'Ada, I'm kidding. It was my mother. It's her birthday,' he calls. She doesn't respond, 'Ada?'

Back at the caravan her movements are abrupt. She twists the cap on the thermal shower hard and the plastic comes away in her hand.

'What's got into you?' he asks, as she tries to reattach the shower hose, which has detached itself from the pouch of water. 'Here, let me do that.' She flinches.

'We had a no-phone rule and you broke it,' she says. It's an absurd statement.

'Right, when we're together. But you weren't here when I got up, so that didn't count. Come on . . .' He leans over and tries to take the hose from her again. This time she lets him. 'Can't a man wish his mother a happy birthday?'

She shrugs. 'It was just a shock, seeing you like that, hearing you speak to someone else. It reminded me of – well, everything else outside of this.' She bends to undo her trainers. 'I'm sorry. I thought you were talking to her. To Emily.'

'Well, I wasn't. But even if I was, you shouldn't jump to conclusions, if I was speaking to my wife there'd be good reason for it,' he says, placing emphasis on *wife*. 'What if there was an emergency?' He lifts the shower and places it in its cradle on the back of the caravan. 'There, it's ready now.' She stands under the shower naked and scrubs her skin with shower gel as the water drizzles down. She uses the loofah and it leaves grazes on her skin. He snatches it out of her hand.

'It feels like our time is together is so short, that's all,' she says.

He's agreed to make a plan. After lunch they draw up an inventory of all there is to be done. The cottage belongs to the landscape and to its past and they are just guardians.

In the library in Dolgellau they have done some research. It was a hushed and awkward visit with the pins from their visitor passes puncturing their coats. The stern librarian directed them to the darkest, smallest corner. There wasn't much information available but they did discover that the cottage belonged to a farm labourer back in 1932. He built it with his own hands, scouring the oak timber from the forest and the earth cob from his land. He threshed the wheat-straw, heather and gorse to thatch the roof.

The skeletal roof timbers that crouch over the cottage can be saved, but the interior walls are lined with clay that is damp and crumbles against their fingertips like aged cheese. They'll replace it with lime. The grey stones of the walls are from a local quarry and these too can be reused. The original format of the cottage will remain unchanged, with the tiny lean-to kitchen and bathroom receiving the lightest of facelifts. The traditional old crog loft upstairs will be their bedroom. As a mezzanine level it occupies only half the foot plan of the cottage. Back in its day it would have slept a family of ten. The staircase needs replacing. Unusable in its current state, it is missing half of its steps and sags on one side. It is blackened and Ada is convinced it was damaged in a fire, though there's no record of one to be found in the library. She complains of the bitter taste of sulphur in her mouth. The cottage has been empty for years and the hollow walls have been swept daily by storms. If there was a fire, any residue would have long since been washed away.

The window at the front of the cottage provides adequate light for downstairs, and the window in the crog loft is large enough to illuminate the small sleeping area. The walls of the cottage are half a metre thick and should provide adequate insulation for the colder months.

'We'll keep it sparse, simple,' Ada is saying now as she crouches down inspecting the stone floor.

'I agree,' he says, 'no ankle-deep carpets or gilded mirrors here.'

'In fact,' Ada grins up at him, 'how about no mirrors at all?'

'You revolutionary,' he says, moving to the window, through which he's spotted a buzzard circling. He thinks of Emily at home, moving through the transparent kitchen. 'Can we at least stretch to a rug for the floor beside the fire?' Ada walks over and presses her face against his chest, her anger of earlier gone.

'I think a rug is obligatory, given the circumstances, don't you?'

By five o'clock the light has fallen below the ridge and in the darkened cottage it grows hard to see.

'We made good progress,' Ada says as she struggles with the door. 'We need to source some local builders.' Though they'd planned to tackle this themselves, they've compromised. Staying long-term in the caravan does not seem as romantic as it did at first. Nothing dries out. He hasn't admitted it to Ada, but the rocking in the wind makes him feel sick. His sea legs aren't what they once were. He holds her hand as they return to the caravan.

'Do you have time to take this on?' he asks.

'It's a little late to ask that, don't you think?'

'It's a bigger project than I'd thought,' he says.

'We're architects,' she says, letting go of his hand and clapping her hands together. 'We love challenges, remember?'

'Yes, but . . .'

'Too late to change our minds now. Everything will be fine, you'll see.' She loops her arm through his and smiles. 'I left something in the car, back in a minute.' He watches her through the window as she walks away across the field, then turns the corner up the pitted road that leads to where the car is parked, out of sight. He lies back and stares at the dark patches of mould on the ceiling. Five minutes pass, then ten. He sits up and now he can't see more than a couple of metres beyond the window, it's grown so dark. What's taking her so long? He pulls on his wellies and his coat and shuffles across the bed to the door, bracing himself against the wind. It's picked up and the door protests as he opens it. He closes it behind him carefully, wary of the rusting hinges. He fishes the torch out from his pocket and shines it, picking his way carefully over the field that is laced with hidden holes waiting to trip unsuspecting feet. The road is not much better and as he turns the corner he is pleased to see the car still there. He turns his torch off. The lights are on inside the car and he sees the top of Ada's head, bent down. He's at the window before she sees him.

'Are you trying to give me a heart attack?' she says as she opens the door. 'I thought you were a ghost.' She slips something out of the glove box.

'I was worried when you didn't come back,' he says. 'What took you so long?'

'I forgot something I needed,' she says. 'I've only been gone five minutes. Christ, you scared me. Well, it's good you came, I don't have a torch.'

He's on the edge of sleep when she turns to him.

'I wish we didn't have to leave,' she says. He draws her in towards him, his body against her back.

'We'll be back soon enough,' he replies. Sleep steals her while he lies awake listening to the owls call across the forest and the creaking of the caravan. He wonders what she was doing back there in the car, and not for the first time he considers how little he knows of this woman who lies beside him.

Rules of an open marriage #5:

Be realistic: individual people have different needs

Years before

'The thing is, humans aren't biologically programmed to commit,' Emily said, lying sideways across the bed with her feet up on the wall. Below her legs Ryan shifted position and turned to face her. His shock of dark hair fell across his eyes. She swept his hair from his face and pressed her finger to his lips. 'Hear me out.'

'I don't think I want to,' he mumbled. 'Can't we just go for dinner instead? I'm starving. We're supposed to be celebrating.' She examined the engagement ring that he'd put on her finger just moments before.

'I just think we need to be clear about what we're both expecting.'

'Is it too late to back out?' He groaned and she thumped him over the head with a pillow.

'Idiot.'

'I only want you,' he said, sitting up and leaning back on his elbows. 'That's why I asked you to marry me.'

She shook her head. 'You think that you only want me, but once the novelty has worn off your impulses will take over and you'll be faced with a choice: to endure your life in a perpetually repressed condition or to betray me. I'm saying you don't have to make that choice. You can have both.'

'Unlike you, Miss Libido, I don't need multiple partners.' It's a long-standing joke between them, her past versus his.

'Thirty-six and counting,' she'd replied when he asked her how many men she'd been with.

'To my one,' he'd said, shocked.

'I love you,' she told him, 'but this is important: we need to walk into marriage with our eyes wide open.'

'Okay,' he sighed, swinging his legs out from under hers and climbing out of bed. He bent down and kissed her on the lips. 'Anything to keep you happy.'

They married in a register office with two strangers as witnesses, pulled from the street. He wanted a wedding party and guests, but she insisted that it be private. In light of his mother's disapproval it was probably best. It was more intimate this way. As they went through their wedding vows, their witnesses exchanged glances. The list of rules relating to their open marriage was long.

'There are so many of them,' Ryan had said in horror when she showed him, 'isn't this a bit over the top?' When they emerged as husband and wife into bright sunshine, the witnesses scuttled off onto the crowded pavement without congratulating them.

'Some people,' Emily giggled, standing on her tiptoes and kissing him. 'It's our life.'

Rules of an open marriage #6:

We will help each other to better understand ourselves

London, January 2016

'Thank fuck that's over.' Ryan swings the bags into the boot and slams it shut. He sits beside her on the passenger side. Emily's turn to drive.

'It wasn't that bad,' she says. The same conversation, year after year.

'I don't see how it could be worse.' He winds his window down as she pulls away from the kerb. 'Your psychotic sister and her brooding boyfriend, two family arguments in fifteen hours. Your father couldn't even be bothered to come out and say goodbye.' He reclines his chair, flicks on the radio. She sees her sister waving from outside her ex-council flat, Matthew standing behind her.

'I think it's better sober,' Emily says. 'Gives you more perspective.'

'The idea of tolerating New Year with your family sober is a bleak prospect indeed. It's so miserable here,' he says as they drive through the estate.

'It's fine,' she says. 'Anyway it's not like it would be any better spending New Year with your mother,' she says.

'That's low.' He flicks through the radio stations. She

hates it when he does that. 'Southfields is ruined by tower blocks,' he says.

'Not everyone is an award-winning architect, darling. When did you become such a snob, anyway?'

'Next year I'd like to spend it with Sam and Tom,' he announces, settling on Classic FM. Emily laughs.

'I'm sure they'd love that, New Year with their ageing dad, shimmying around on the dance floor.'

'Less of the old, please,' he says. The tension cracks between them. 'Anyway, clubbing is so last century. Now it's moody lounge bars and vaping, dissecting the parodies of celebrity culture and berating our politicians.' She joins the South Circular. Sober on New Year's Day: it's a revelation.

'Maybe I'll give up booze,' she says.

Ryan groans. 'Please don't. It'll be so boring.'

'Are you saying I need alcohol to blind you with my dazzling wit?'

'You need it so I can blind you with mine.'

'True,' she says. He slaps her thigh.

'I'll start tomorrow. I'm out tonight,' she says.

'And here start the excuses ... Where are you going?'

'I'm out with Adeline, remember?' She's been looking forward to tonight; they've been trying to arrange an evening since they met at the awards ceremony, but Christmas scuppered their plans.

'Adeline?' he says, sitting up straighter. 'Why?'

'Why what?'

'Why are you having dinner with her?'

'Can you shut your window please?' She can't hear a thing above the traffic. This early on New Year's Day and it's already heaving. He winds it up.

'Why are you having dinner with her?' he repeats.

'I like her, why else? She seems fun, which is more than I can say for most of the company we keep.' Ryan sighs loudly.

'I need the window open,' he says, 'I need fresh air.' It's pathetic; at forty-something he should know his limits.

'Christ, Ryan, why didn't you stop at the first shot?'

'It was the only way I could bond with Matthew. You should be grateful I make the effort to connect with your brother-in-law.'

'He's not – they're not married, remember?'

'Oh yes, I forgot about Sarah's phobia of commitment. Completely illogical, if you ask me,' Ryan says. 'What is it with you and your family?'

Emily thinks of her father and his affairs. Her mother completely defined by his indiscretions and his secrets. His lies. She spent her life hoping that he would change and he did not. Each time her mother found out about another lover, her faith in the world collapsed. Only late in life did her mother seem happy, her father resigned, as if old age had done for him what restraint could not. Arthritis and aggregated years reducing his opportunities in concentric circles until the circumference of his world became his home and his wife, at last, the centre. Her mother died not long after. All that waiting – for what? Emily and Sarah hated their father as children for what he did. But later Emily began to understand the fault was not his alone. Her mother wanted something he couldn't give.

'Why did you stay with him?' Emily asked her once.

'It was the seventies – it was what people did,' her mother replied. 'Anyway, I loved him.' Emily decided then that if she ever committed to marriage it would be with her eyes wide open. No secrets, no false promises. The idea that sex and emotion were intertwined and dependent was ridiculous and dated.

'She's entitled to her views on marriage, dear husband. Not everyone wants to be the other half.'

'But she is though, that's my point, whether she likes it or not.'

'More cohabiting couples stay together than married couples, and more than a third of married couples cheat, did you know that?' She can feel his eyes on her and the space between them solidifies into a physical thing, demarcated by the gear stick and the coffee cups.

'You do realise that means that almost two thirds manage not to?' Ryan says. Emily scoffs.

'See? This is the language that surrounds monogamy. Manage. Endure. Like it's a test of resistance. And people who survive it think they deserve a medal. For what?' She glances sideways at Ryan, whose jaw is twitching.

'Well, I know all about cheating,' he says.

Emily accelerates around a truck and pulls aggressively back in front of it.

'Let's not do this again, really? It's a new year – can we just forget the old arguments?'

'Far too much is made of the New Year, in my opinion,' Ryan says.

'Why do you have to do this now?' she says.

'Do what? You started it,' he says.

'I think you'll find you did,' she says, 'when you . . . anyway, you know what, you do it all the time. Just because you're hung-over and feeling crap, you don't have to bring me down with you.'

'Do what?'

'Goad me.'

'I'm not.'

'I'm just sick of you referring to yourself as the damaged party. "I know all about cheating." What's that supposed to mean?'

'You know exactly what it means.'

'Do I?' Emily says. 'You should never have agreed to it if you weren't comfortable with it. It was in our vows.' A white Audi shoots out from a side road right in front of her and she removes her foot from the accelerator. That was close, just inches. Ryan hasn't noticed and his mood seems to be getting worse.

'I didn't agree with it,' he says. 'I told you when we got engaged that I didn't want the rules or the bloody arrangement.'

'I think I'd remember something like that, don't you?' she asks.

'Do you have go out tonight?' he asks, changing the subject. 'We could watch a movie and get takeaway, start the New Year cuddled up . . .'

'I've been looking forward to tonight,' Emily says. 'We can do that any other night when I don't have plans.' Irritation pulses at her temple and she brakes hard as a bus pulls out in front of her. 'And for the record, for the millionth time, the very definition of cheating is to act dishonestly and there's nothing dishonest about what I do because I'm open about it, and we agreed upon it from the beginning. Did you know that only forty-three out of two hundred and thirty-eight societies across the world are monogamous?' Emily says. 'There's a reason for that.'

'It'll come to a bitter end,' Ryan says, staring out of the window morbidly.

'God, you're a pillar of light.'

'Go on,' Ryan says, 'I'm waiting . . . England is outdated in its views on monogamous relationships compared to Italy and France.'

'It's true,' Emily says, shifting gear, 'though I don't endorse the execution of affairs as secrets. True liberation is where we don't have to apologise for being human.'

'Some humans don't need external validation,' Ryan says.

'It's not about validation,' Emily says. She looks sideways at him. He looks so glum that she has an urge to shake him. Sometimes she wonders if he might leave and sometimes she thinks she wants him to. She can't imagine life without him, but . . .

'But what?'

'What?' She must have said it aloud. 'Nothing.'

He won't leave her; he will honour his wedding vows no matter what he might say in between. She reaches across the divide between them and puts her hand in his lap.

'I do love you,' she says.

'I know,' he replies.

He opens the window again.

'Where are you off to tonight?' he asks.

'Dulwich Village.' Petrol fumes catch in her throat and wind blows her hair in her face.

'What?'

'Tonight. Dinner at the Italian followed by drinks at the Fox.'

'I can't hear you . . .'

'Followed by rampant sordid sex with strangers in the park.' She can't help herself sometimes.

Maybe next year they can do something different for New Year. She's always overtired in January, swamped with essays to mark, drained by the chaos of social engagements, gift buying and family politics. It was a low jab of hers earlier, not his fault that his father disappeared years ago and that his mother is slipping slowly but surely into old age. Cocooned in her care home, she knows that Ryan feels guilty that his mother is there. But the thought of her mother-in-law living with them had been untenable to them both. She'd be unbearable to live with. Plus she hates Emily, so the decision was a non-starter. When they first got engaged they drove six hours to tell his mother and on Emily's way back from the bathroom his mother had grabbed her arm and said, 'He always picks girls like you – girls who can't be tamed.' There were blue bruises on Emily's wrist for days. Over two decades of marriage later, his mother still hasn't changed her mind about her. Emily simply isn't good enough for her son.

*

Back home Sam and Tom are hung-over, though they won't admit it. Slow movements and glassy eyes betray them. They've done a good job tidying up behind them and the house shows no sign of the party that rocked it until the early hours. In the bathroom bin Emily finds a used condom. Though both the boys are legally entitled to have sex, the thought of it makes her nauseous. Ryan mocks her selective Victorian values. He's right: she should be pleased to see a condom – proof of sensibility, at least. The boys have ensconced themselves in front of the TV in the lounge and are watching back-to-back *Star Wars*.

In the shower she shaves her legs and armpits, washes her hair. She thinks of the way that Ada laid a hand on her leg at the awards ceremony. It could have been accidental, but it didn't feel like that at the time. After some deliberation, she waxes her bikini line. It's been too long since she had a girls' night out. Her younger self would have been horrified to be presented with the idea that she'd only go out once every couple of months. Age has brought cynicism and caution. She's been burned attempting to navigate the social labyrinth of parenthood, with egos and judgement around every corner. The playground in particular was a terrifying place. 'A breeding ground for alpha females,' Ryan had remarked years ago, 'and subservient men.' There is some truth in this; formerly independent men cowed by their wives, brought out as Rottweilers where needed. Turning instead to the contacts that her job as a writer and later lecturer provided, she'd been more sociable, though more recently acquired friendships feel shallow. More comfortable in the company of men than women, she divides them into two categories: those that she sleeps with and those that she doesn't. More than once she has been accused of being insensitive.

In the mirror she checks her teeth, her tongue, runs grey charcoal above her eyes. Her phone beeps and she checks; it's another text from Leo, the fifth of the day. *Can I see you this evening?* In a fit of frustration she replies. *I'm out with people my own age and you should be too.* She hits *Send.*

It's a short walk from West Dulwich to the restaurant and she's nervous, an unfamiliar restlessness in her limbs. She's aware of cold damp patches beneath her armpits. She hasn't seen Adeline since the ceremony and has no idea what to expect. She wonders if she mistook Adeline's friendliness for something else and cringes at her surge of excitement when she got her text.

The grandeur of the college looms on her right, quiet now for a few days more before the children return from their holidays and parties, Tom and Sam among their number. Her boots click against the pavement. Turning the collar of her jacket up against the biting chill, she crosses beside the park. Relics of Christmas are strung through the air, stars and tinsel decorating the sky. She crosses the road to the restaurant, drawing lungfuls of cold air as she composes herself. Assume it is nothing other than a friendly drink, she tells herself, it's safer.

A wall of heat hits her as she opens the door. The restaurant is packed. Peeling off her winter coat, she's glad she wore a thin shirtdress beneath. It clings to her collarbone as she surveys the room. In the corner Adeline beckons, standing as she approaches, and even though Emily's only met her once, she knew she'd smell like this, of orange and citrus.

Adeline's hug is strong. Emily likes that she doesn't do air kisses, avoids the awkwardness they bring. Seated, they survey the menu and order. The first glass of wine is crisp against her tongue, and she feels her cheeks flush.

'Good Christmas?' Emily asks.

'So so.' Adeline leans forward and lowers her voice. 'Always a drama or two, this time of year.'

'Same.' Emily refills their glasses and leans back into her

seat. 'God, it's good to get out.' Adeline nods in agreement, and peels off her cardigan, revealing bare arms.

'You're brave,' Emily smiles.

'I'm always too warm – God knows what I'll be like with the menopause,' Adeline laughs. On her shoulder there is a bruise, a central knot of deep purple with mottled yellow seeping out.

'So, tell me about you,' Emily says. 'Last time it was all about me. Go on, spill – hobbies, interests, husband?' Emily says, noticing for a second time the absence of a ring on Adeline's finger.

'I love cycling,' Adeline says, 'running too . . .'

'Me too,' Emily says too quickly, 'cycling, I mean.'

'Really? That's awesome, we should go together, have you ever done a sportive?'

'A what?'

'A sportive – an organised bike ride. You pay to go, they map the route, provide the snacks.'

'What kind of distances?' Emily asks, feeling out of her depth. She just cycles to let off steam.

'Anything from twenty miles to a hundred,' Adeline says, 'But we could start small,' she adds quickly.

'Is it that obvious, the panic on my face?' Emily asks, laughing.

'I'll find us one,' Adeline says, 'to get us started.' Emily likes the sound of it being the start of something.

'I'd love to,' she says, 'but you'll have to go slow, or wait for me to catch up.'

'Cheers to that,' Adeline says, and they clink their glasses and down the rest of the wine. 'Oh, and to your other question, no husband. You look surprised?'

'It's just, I don't know, I just assumed you were – most people our age have settled down . . .'

'And there in that very statement lies the problem,' Ada says.

'Settle. It sounds like paying a debt.' She winks and stands up. 'Drinks next door?

The two bottles of wine they've shared have gone straight to Emily's head and the virtue of not drinking yesterday has vanished.

'Sure, why not,' she replies, throwing her coat over her arm. 'Start the year as we mean to go on.'

She loves the Fox, with its old-world charm and tables and chairs that haven't been changed for decades. They find seats in a corner beneath a picture of a hunt, the fox making a run for the horizon, horses circling in the foreground in confusion.

'I hope it made its escape,' Adeline says, tilting her head back to look at the painting.

'I'll get the drinks,' Emily says. The bar is crowded and three layers of people deep. A text from Ryan says they are all in bed. He reminds her about Sam's tutor meeting about his exams tomorrow. Remember to take a cab home. A frowning emoticon follows. *Yes, Dad*, she replies, with a smiley face. Technology has made children of them all. She's craving a cigarette, though she hasn't smoked for years. Back at the table Adeline's mood has dampened.

'I'm a bad influence, sorry,' Emily pushes her drink across the table.

'I don't get hangovers; it's a mixed blessing,' Adeline says, downing half the glass in one gulp. Across the room a cheer erupts from a table of men. 'Imbeciles,' Adeline mutters. 'Don't you just hate them?' Then, 'Of course you don't, you've got a good one.'

'I guess so,' Emily says.

'You don't sound very sure.'

Emily feels the need to defend Ryan, though she's well aware it's ridiculous given that she's the one who started this conversation.

'No, he is, he's a good man.'

Adeline stares at her across the table and raises an eyebrow.

'It's just, we've been together a long time, it can start to feel, you know . . .'

'Fortunately for me I don't,' Adeline replies. 'I'm a serial short-termer – longest relationship I've had was four years. Usually by then you've revealed all the hidden faults and there's nothing more to find; it gets boring.' Emily laughs. She likes Adeline's honesty – it's refreshing. Most people she knows are so worried about presenting a perfect image to the world that even people who were probably interesting once are now dull. One of the men from the neighbouring table approaches.

'Can I buy you ladies a drink?' he asks. Emily's about to say no thanks, when Adeline cuts in.

'That'd be lovely, thank you.' They watch him walk towards the bar and feel the eyes of his friends watching them.

'I thought you hated men,' Emily says.

'They have their uses,' Adeline replies with a grin. 'I'm off to the bathroom.' Emily sits and tries to focus on the fox in the picture, but it swims slightly. She shuts her eyes and tries again.

'You okay?' A familiar voice beside her, close to her ear. Too close.

'Leo?' He looks older out of the university setting, less like a student. 'How did you know I was here?' she says.

'Ways and means,' he says, and winks. Did he follow her here? But he doesn't know where she lives. 'Buy you a drink?' he asks.

'No thanks.' She shakes her head, the room spinning slightly. 'Think I've had enough.' At that moment the man from the neighbouring table appears, brandishing another bottle of wine. 'Thanks,' Emily says, avoiding looking at Leo.

'Can we go outside and talk for a minute?' he asks, gently cupping her elbow. She shakes her head again.

'I don't think that's a good idea.'

'But it is a good idea to accept a drink from strangers?' He gestures to the table of men beside them, who are holding their glasses up in mimic of a 'cheers'.

'Probably not,' she says. 'I think you should go.'

He pulls his coat on. 'If you're sure.'

'Hello, who's this?' Adeline is back from the bathroom and holding out her hand to Leo.

'Adeline, this is Leo. Leo, Adeline.'

'Call me Ada,' Adeline says.

'Nice to meet you, Ada,' Leo says, hovering behind the chair next to Emily.

'Why don't you join us?' Adeline says, gesturing to the empty space at the table, and now Emily feels mean, because he's clearly made an effort to find her and sure, he can be a bit full on, but he's fundamentally a nice guy and she can't in all honesty claim that she is immune to his charms. Adeline gives her a knowing look.

One bottle turns into three and as they're putting on their coats, Adeline presses a pill into Emily's palm. 'For the journey home.' As Emily stumbles out into the street at closing time she knows that she's going to feel like death tomorrow. She is unsteady on her feet and Leo takes her arm. Adeline is on her other side, talking to the group of men who bought them the wine, and as they head past the park Emily feels a surge of joy at the freedom of it all.

'There's a lake in the park,' she whispers to Adeline.

'Can I stay at yours tonight?' Adeline asks, but Emily is ahead of her, running across the grass towards the water. She tugs off her shoes and dips her toe in and it feels good, so cold and fresh. The sky is clear and ghostly, split with silver magic light. Fireflies pirouette above her head though she knows they can't be real, not here, in England. She reaches her hand up to catch one. Leo is laughing.

'What are you doing?'

'Catching them,' she says. 'Don't you think it's sad how they die so fast?'

'What do? Catching what?' he asks.

Emily throws her coat down on the ground and as she lifts her dress over her head she feels Leo behind her, undoing the button that has lodged her dress around her shoulders; his fingertips brush her back.

'You should go home,' she tells him. 'Adeline?' Adeline is some distance away, barely discernible on a park bench, in conversation with the only man left from the group.

'It's freezing,' Leo tells her. 'You're crazy,' and then she's in, swallowed up by the water. 'You'll freeze,' he shouts, stripping off his clothes. He jumps in and she feels him pulling her to the edge.

'Spoilsport,' she says. He climbs out ahead of her and pulls her onto the grass. Adeline and the man are swigging something from a bottle. Leo wraps his coat around Emily's shoulder but she can't stop shaking, her teeth clattering loudly. She giggles, then hiccups.

'Follow me,' Leo says, and leads her into a small pagoda in a cluster of trees. 'Here.' He sits her down and places her bare feet between his hands, rubbing them. 'Are you trying to kill yourself?' She doesn't answer. 'Why didn't you reply to my text messages?' he asks. He moves his hands up her legs. The truth is, she can't remember them, or anything else since she took the pill. She feels the blood returning to her legs. 'Emily?'

'You know why,' she gambles, hoping this is the right answer.

'This'll warm you up,' Adeline appears from nowhere and hands her the bottle. The liquid sears her throat. There's no sign of the man from the group. Leo takes a swig too.

'What are we going to do with her?' Leo says to Adeline, his hands still on Emily's leg. 'She's freezing. I think she's hallucinating too.' Adeline whispers something in his ear and then crouches down. Emily's vaguely aware of Adeline placing her cardigan around her shoulders and holding her close. She breathes her in. Then Leo pulls her to her feet.

It's well past midnight by the time Emily's fumbling with the front-door key. She tries to focus on the keyhole, but it's like playing pin the tail on the donkey.

'Here, let me.' Adeline takes the key and then the door is open. 'Water, painkillers, bathroom, bed,' Adeline says, and Emily follows her meekly before remembering that this is her house and that Adeline doesn't know where things are. She steers her towards the guest room and trips over a chair in an attempt to turn on the lamp. The buzzing around her eyes has subsided and she's able to focus slightly, a pinprick of a circle at a time.

'This place is amazing,' Adeline says, 'even better than it looked on the call.' The walls twist and morph into curves. Emily puts a hand out to balance herself.

'Here's a T-shirt,' Emily mumbles, grabbing one from a drawer and throwing it onto the bed. She can't remember the walk home, or what happened before, in the pagoda. Where did Leo go?

'Adeline?'

'Ada, call me Ada.' She's already in the guest bed, covers pulled up.

'Adeline, what happened, how did I get home?' Emily says.

Adeline winks at her. 'Tell you some other time, go to bed.'

'Did anything . . .' A memory of skin against hers, the gasp of warmth.

'A secret between friends, don't worry.' Adeline giggles and crosses her arms behind her head. 'Can you turn the light out on your way out, please?'

*

The room spins every time Emily closes her eyes, and a well of nausea is blocking her chest.

'Ryan.' She shakes him. 'I feel sick.' He turns away from her, tucking the covers around his body. 'Please can you help me?' she says. He turns reluctantly back and follows her to the bathroom. It's going to be a long night.

The light through the windows is sharp and Emily throws a pillow over her face. She needs water, fast. Reaching out her arm, she finds the bed is empty. Ryan must be up already. What was she thinking, getting so paralytic? She wonders if Adeline is faring better. At least she has blinds in the guest room. She should have slept in there too. Ryan and his bloody principles of light.

'Mum?' Sam pokes his head round the door. 'Setting a good example, are we?'

'Sam, don't . . .' He opens the window and the wintry air hits her face.

'Did you forget we've got an appointment this morning, about my exams?' Something's vaguely familiar, a sketch of a conversation too long ago.

'Really, today? It's still the holidays,' she says. He throws her dressing gown onto the bed. 'Can't you ask Dad to take you?'

'He's not here. He was up early – his car's gone.' What else has she lost to the night?

'Did you meet Adeline?'

'Your new friend? I saw something resembling a human crawl across the landing earlier. She looked better than you do, though. I think Dad's given her a lift.'

Emily hauls herself into a sitting position. 'Right.'

Showered and watered, she feels marginally better. Tom grunts good morning at her after she says it three times.

'What are you up to today?' she asks him, though

engaging in conversation makes her head pound harder. 'Tom?' Earphones plugged in, he can't hear a word she's saying. 'Tom?' Always the more difficult of the two, he's been harder work recently than normal. Scarcely around, and when he is, he's sullen and angry. 'I give up,' she says loudly. Tom doesn't look up from his phone.

Sam drives them to the appointment at the college. Her mouth tastes as if she's been drinking from a sewer. She's brushed her teeth five times. She tries not to speak unless she has to and is aware of Sam's tutor casting sideways glances at her as she stares out of the window. She zones out of the conversation.

'Don't you care?' Sam asks, on their way back to the car park.

'Of course I care; I just didn't have anything to add. It sounds like you've got everything under control.'

'It's a big deal, you know, doing my A-levels, going off to uni.' He walks ahead, kicking stones with his feet. She speeds up, though her feet hurt, and loops her arm into his.

'I know love, I know.'

Ryan's still not home and it's mid-afternoon. She can't find the shoes that she wore last night. She lies down on the sofa to wait for him and runs through the events of last night in her head. She remembers the first round of drinks bought by the men at the table – they'd not let them join them and had been accused of being teases. Then Leo arrived, though he lives all the way in Battersea, she thinks. Another bottle was bought by the men, and they'd let them join them for a bit then. One of them had propositioned her. She hopes she was polite, though has no memory of what she said.

There's something about the walk home, a moment in the park. A recollection of water. And Leo. Adeline, and hands on skin. She was so cold. She needs to check with Adeline. The shoes were new, a Christmas gift.

'Hey, sweetie.' Ryan's back. He bends down and kisses her hair. 'How are you feeling?'

'Better,' she answers, swinging her legs over the side of the sofa and arching her feet. 'Where were you?' She glances at the clock; it's gone five and outside the day has faded.

'I dropped Ada home – she was in no state to take the bus.'

'You took your time.'

'Traffic was awful, you know how it is,' Ryan says.

'Did Adeline have fun last night?' Emily stands and pulls her cardigan closer.

'What do you think?' Ryan laughs and ruffles her hair. 'Of course she had fun with my party wife. How's the giving-up-alcohol going?'

She's searched her bag, under the bed, and the garden. She's retraced the walk to the village and found one shoe sitting on top of the wall by the park, waiting. No sign of the other. It explains the raw skin on her feet if she walked home barefoot. Briefly she considers a hair of the dog at the Fox. Anything to relieve the throbbing in her head. But she recognises a group of mums from the college in the window and decides against it.

Home again, she opens the bedside drawer and pulls out the tickets to Venice. Valentine's in Venice – she can't wait to get away. Ryan has always loved surprises and they so rarely get time away from the boys. The more tied down they are by their combined responsibilities, the more they are dragged apart. She hopes that 2016 will be a year that brings them together.

Rules of an open marriage #7:

Always be transparent about how you feel

She met David in her writing group. He was the first man she slept with after getting married. He dropped hints for months that he was keen, and Ryan was away a lot for work. Her days had been hijacked with toddler-group meetings and a never-ending list of chores. One evening she let her hair down. They met for tapas in a dimly lit restaurant and David's leg pressed against hers beneath their tiny table; their shoulders touched. As wine flowed and inhibitions dwindled, he pushed his finger against her lips to stop her talking and, leaning in, whispered in her ear. His breath was warm against her neck and for that moment she was not just a mother, not someone's wife. It had been such a long time since someone bothered to pay attention. Back at his apartment David was gentle and generous; to only worry about herself felt good. When she woke it was morning. She'd forgotten the boys' football practice, but Ryan had understood. She'd made it up to him later. But David had pestered her for weeks.

'What happened to good old-fashioned one-night stands?' she asked David in their final conversation.

She was young and lonely and her husband was never there. It was a fact, not an excuse. Her flings were a preservation of what they had. She would not become the nagging wife who needed more than her husband could provide. Never would she coerce her exhausted husband into sex. It wasn't as important to him. He didn't need it as much. She knew this from the beginning and they had addressed it. She accepted what Ryan offered and sought gratification elsewhere when she needed. To claim that sex and love were mutually dependent was a fable. Around her relationships floundered, striving for a romanticised and institutionalised ideology that didn't work. Tearing under the weight of it. 'It's just a physical release,' she told Ryan, 'nothing more.' It's what she told him, and mostly she believed it.

Rules of an open marriage #8:

Agree how much time we'll spend apart

London, June 2016

Ryan throws himself heavily into the driver's seat and slams the door. He doesn't look up at the front door, where he knows Emily to still be standing. They've argued again, her anger clinging to his skin. He's running late and will hit rush-hour traffic. He wanted to arrive in Wales before it got dark. If he'd left just ten minutes earlier he could have avoided opening the nine gates in the dark.

'When are you back?' she'd asked as he headed for the door.

'Monday,' he replied.

'Right.' She's so stressed these days, not helped by her job, which makes her miserable.

'Don't be like that,' he said. As he leaned over to kiss her on the cheek, she'd recoiled.

'Like what?' she said, knowing full well what he meant.

'That. That face.'

'How would you like my features arranged as you go off to see your mistress?' Her words are barbed wire these days, designed to slice.

'Emily . . .' He'd leaned forward again, but she ducked and he stumbled.

'It's too much,' she said. Every sentence delaying him further.
'What is?'

'All of it. You're not even trying to hide it.' He stared at his feet. 'I thought we had rules,' she said. 'You know we do. What happened to *no repeat performance?*'

'How do you know I'm not seeing different people?' he asked, aware as soon as the words were out what a ridiculous concept this was for someone like him.

'I know you wouldn't,' she said. 'It's not you.'

'How convenient! You committed me to a set of rules that you knew would only benefit you. How selfless.'

'You're off every two weeks – it's too much. I'd like you to stop seeing her.'

'What, just like that?' he said. She nodded.

'It's not what we agreed on.'

'Not what we agreed? Sod what we agreed,' he said. She looked at him like he'd shot her. 'For twenty-two years I've tolerated you off doing whatever you wanted whenever it suited you. Listened to you telling me things I didn't want to know, until finally you stopped telling me.'

'The rules are there for a reason,' she said.

'Why didn't you say something sooner?' he asked.

'I thought it would be over by now, would fizzle out,' she said.

'Did you ever feel guilty for the pain you caused me as I watched you gallivant around?' he asked.

'If you didn't like our arrangement you shouldn't have agreed to it in the first place,' she replied.

'That's unfair,' he replied. 'It was agree or lose you. A no-brainer.'

'It's more than a quick fuck, isn't it?' she said, refusing to meet his eye. He nodded. 'Trust you to fall for her.' She'd flung open the fridge then and poured a glass of wine, downing it in one gulp. 'Go then, be happy.'

'All of this was your doing in the first place,' he'd shouted. 'Your great idea. Fuck the fact that marriage has survived as an institution for centuries, sod the fact that you love me, or did.'

'Have you not listened to anything I've said about marriage?' she said

'Emily and her great ideas, rewriting the rules of love. What happened to loyalty and sacrifice?'

'It was to protect us from failure.'

'Did it never cross your mind that we could have made it work, that we could have been one of the couples who have a happy marriage?'

'Everyone thinks they're different at first, Ryan, it's the whole trap of the thing. People get married to prove that they're different, better. Then when it doesn't work out, they're broken and expecting everyone else to pick up the pieces.'

'Well, congratulations on proving that we're better than everyone else – you got what you wanted, didn't you?'

'I didn't want this,' she said, gesturing to his bag. 'Why would anyone want this? We haven't made love since Venice, for God's sake, it's been months.'

'So it's about sex, then? Really? I'm sure you'll find a willing candidate to satisfy you – you always do. I'm pretty sure you've been with others since Venice, anyway.' He remembered the night she crept in a couple of weeks ago, straight into the shower. The way she fell asleep as soon as her head hit the pillow. He's learned these things about her; her deep sleep after sex, when usually she struggles.

'There's a difference,' Emily hissed, 'between what I do – and what you're doing.'

'The only difference is love,' he said, and as soon as he said it he knew that it was true. He couldn't look at her, wouldn't.

Three months ago he'd have thrown his bag down and embraced her, delighted that she cared. Three months ago he'd have ended it with Ada for this. Now the thought is inconceivable. He'd turned away and picked up his bag from beside the door. He'd thought of the cottage and its crumbling stones and the task ahead. The mountain air that fills him with light. The joy etched in the forest. But Emily wasn't done.

'I was a fool to think you'd be capable of being a good husband, a good father. How could you be, given what happened to you?' She spat the words out and they hung in the air between them, ugly and mean. He slammed his fist down on the kitchen counter hard and felt the skin split on his knuckles.

'I've been nothing but a good husband to you and a good father. Everything I've done. There's nothing of me left. The bloody daily grind of it!'

'Well, I'm sorry it's such an obligation. At least you're being honest,' she said. 'At last.'

His chest shuddered under the pressure of restraint, and when he had looked up she was in control again, her eyes dry, her jaw a determined line.

'I'm simply asking you to go away less often. The boys miss you. They need us too, you know. They're in the middle of exams, for God's sake. Did it ever occur to you to put them first?'

'Are you really going to do this?' Ryan said. 'Use the boys as a guilt trip? '

'We're not exactly the best example of love,' Emily said. 'You get to go away once a month tops, from now on. Otherwise I'll tell the boys, and I'm sure you don't want that.' And there she was, his ice queen. She didn't want him around more for herself, couldn't even pretend to care. It was a power play. And he had thought for a moment that she wanted him, that she cared. He should have learned by now. He knows that once a month at the cottage is not enough to do all that needs to be done. They will never get it ready for winter. He yearns only to be there. But of alternatives, what? An ugly divorce, the disintegration of all that he has worked for? He had looked at her pale thin face then, seeing the anger coiled in her shoulders.

'Hey.' Sam had wandered into the room. How much did he hear? 'You off somewhere?' he had asked, taking in Ryan's bag, his coat.

'Just for the weekend, kiddo,' Ryan said, cuffing Sam on the shoulder.

'You work too hard,' Sam had replied, taking a biscuit from the tin and heading back towards the lounge.

'Deal,' Ryan whispered as Emily opened the door and ushered him out, refusing to meet his eye.

Driving calms him. There's reassurance in the rhythmic hum of the engine and the mechanical shifting of the gears. He gets stuck on the motorway behind an accident and the journey takes him eight hours. He passes the wreckage, contorted metal strewn across the road and a barricade around what used to be the driver's side. He wonders if the driver made it, whether someone somewhere is losing a father, a mother. Traffic is diverted when they close the lane and he drives for hours down country roads, hurtling into the darkness. The gates on the final stretch seem endless and he loses count, surprised when he reaches the end of the track to the cottage. It's due to be surfaced tomorrow, so for now he swings the car under the trees at the top and hauls his rucksack from the car. It's raining again and he's soaked through within minutes. The trees on either side are indistinguishable from the cloudy night, the starless sky. Shining his torch bought from a service station on the way, he navigates his way to the caravan.

The cottage is on his right now, the window reflecting his light. He catches a glimpse of himself, a middle-aged man with a backpack. A second light behind him in his reflection has him checking his back, but when he turns again there is nothing but the bristling branches of the forest. He remembers the person Ada saw a while ago and dismisses the thought.

The caravan door jams and he wrenches it open, the smell of damp hitting the back of his throat. When he puts his hand on the bed he can feel it too, seeping through the cotton. The sooner they can get out of here the better. Ada arrives tomorrow, but for now he needs to sleep. He strips off and locates the thermal pyjamas he left under the pillow. He finishes the tumbler of whisky he has poured and climbs between the covers. He longs to bring Sam and Tom here; it's been years since they spent time outdoors like this together. It's been so long since he held them. He had thought he'd be useless at being a father, but from the moment Sam was born he knew he could do it, make it work. Emily had found it harder. They'd pull through somehow, stronger because of it, he told himself at the time. Now he's not so sure. Perhaps they've been in gradual decline and he hasn't noticed.

He wakes up coughing before first light, his throat dry. Inhaling, he sits. He can't shake the sense of something stuck behind his windpipe. A spider, perhaps. Who knows what creatures have made this their home in his absence. Moss grows in the crevice of the door beside his head. The forest is awash with birdsong. A cuckoo calls. He is lethargic and disoriented, his movements slow.

He makes a coffee on the gas burner outside and sits at the camping table. Beside him sheep laze in the grass, unbothered by his presence. Above the brush of the trees a rumbling approaches. Standing, he shields his eyes from the sun to see a lorry trundling slowly down the broken road. Today it's getting fixed. He feels a twinge of sadness for the isolation of the cottage that will soon be lost. Pulling on his trainers, he walks to meet the man who heads towards him.

'Morning,' Ryan says.

'Morning. Is Ada here?'

'Not yet, but I'm Ryan, her better half.' She should be here by now – where is she? What if something happened, an accident or worse?

'Adam – pleased to meet you. Gorgeous spot you've got here. Been doing these roads for years now and never knew there was a house down here.'

'Thanks.'

'Nice to see you putting it back on the map. We'll get started, then.'

'What's the process for today?' Twenty years of designing houses and he doesn't know how a road gets tarmacked.

'Base layer of large-grade aggregate first, that's what this beast is for.' Adam gestures to the lorry. 'Heated wheels to mould it into place. Got men coming shortly with the roller, pack it in. Then top layer of smaller aggregate, smoothed out. Easy.'

'Do we stay off it for a few days until it sets?'

'Nah, hour or so's enough to let it settle. Long as you don't accelerate too hard on it, or spin your wheels.' Adam laughs. 'You don't look like the spinning-wheels type, though.'

'I'll let you get on with it then,' Ryan says, mildly offended. 'Shout if you need anything.'

Back at the caravan Ryan empties his rucksack onto the bed, searching for the list he's printed out that Ada sent. Days are broken into hours, even coffee breaks accounted for. *The only gaps are at the beginning and the end of the day, where the wild things are,* he'd teased her. He walks over and stands in the front of the cottage. Each time they return he holds his breath, as if it might have disappeared in his absence. It looks injured, its doors and windows boarded with ply and the roof sealed with bright blue tarpaulin. The act of repairing it has rendered it sad. Work's started on the underpinning to stabilise the foundations and steel ties arrive tomorrow to stop the lateral spread in the walls. A beam to reinforce the crog loft will mean that soon a new staircase can go in. Getting mains and electricity connected will happen last.

He walks and places his hand against the stone wall beside the window, then his cheek. He imagines that he can hear it breathing and creaking inside. It's impossible to hear anything through these walls. The lorry has started layering the gravel and the forest buzzes at the sound, birds erupting in flocks from the treetops. Down the valley he hears cattle calling. It's a day for the beach, for the sea. He inhales the salt-tipped air.

Ada should have been here hours ago. *I'll be there at first light,* she'd told him yesterday. It's unlike her to be late. He texts her. There's not much for him to do. He was right to hand the project management to her despite initial reservations. He'd never have found the time to plan this, or have *made the time,* as Ada is fond of saying. What could be keeping her? Last time he'd noticed a grazed bruise, just below her collarbone, mustard yellow and fading but still distinct. 'I'm clumsy,' she'd said when she noticed him looking.

'We're all about the present,' Ada insists, 'everything gets altered otherwise.' It would be nice to know her better though, to understand what makes her tick. It wouldn't be so bad if things changed a little, now that they're committed to the cottage, would it?

'Ryan?' Adam calls him over. He walks to the edge of the road, which is now black and steaming. The whole landscape looks more solid, as if it's been filled in.

'We found these,' Adam says, holding his hand out. Ryan looks at the faded silver bullets and takes them in his hands, feeling the warm weight of them against his skin.

'This area was used for target practice in the Second World War,' Adam says, 'Perhaps they're from then. I found them when we were prepping the ground and thought you might like them as a memento. After all, they belong to you.'

'Thanks,' Ryan says putting them in the pocket of his shorts. He feels them banging against his thigh as he walks up to his car. He wants to check the news on the radio, just in case.

Switching on the engine, he opens the windows and the doors. The dry, hot air escapes and up here above the valley a welcome breeze blows in from the sea. He reclines his chair and flicks the radio on. He closes his eyes. More reports on the impending Brexit referendum. He flicks to the travel station: jams on the M5, an accident on the M32. He thinks of the accident last night, haunted by a shoe he saw lying a few metres from the car.

He flicks the radio off, then on again, then off. One, two, three times. He sits on his hands, frustrated. What is wrong with him? The number doesn't make a difference to anything. He hasn't done this for years, not since he was a child. His mother had brought it up at their lunch last week, her belated birthday treat.

'You were such a funny child,' she'd said, studying him across the table. 'Always so superstitious – counting things, repeating them.' Her face, once beautiful, is now a rouge-dotted clown's; eyeliner a centimetre out, her lipstick slipping down her chin.

'Her eyesight's going,' the nurse told him, 'but she's proud and won't be helped.'

Her slackened skin stretches across her bones like dried glue.

'I was worried for a while, you know,' she'd said, reaching out a vein-tattooed hand and placing it on his, 'thought we'd messed you up good and proper.'

'No Ma,' he'd replied, lying, 'you did fine.' Nothing can be changed or undone. Not her fault that she married an arsehole who beat her. Who beat him.

'Best thing I did, getting rid of your father.' She patted his hand twice.

'No Ma, he left us, remember?' She shook her head slowly, adjusted her brooch.

'Always did like to contort the truth didn't you . . .'

'It's Ryan, Ma.' He likes to tell himself that her confusion is down to age, but he knows that it's not. She's been reinventing things since he was a boy, recalibrating a palatable truth.

'Of course, Ryan who has Emily. How is she, anyway?' He wouldn't enter into this on her birthday. He shrugged.

'She's fine.'

'Don't worry, dear, I can tell she's left you, always knew she would. You're better off without her anyway. Always did go for the wild ones that you couldn't catch.'

'She hasn't left me Ma, she's fine; at home with the boys.'

She'd leaned closer over the table. 'I can tell these things, you know,' she'd whispered, and tapped her nose.

He'd forced himself to smile.

It's too hot despite the breeze. If Ada were here they could go to the lake together, dive into the clear blue ice water that steals breath from the body. Back down the broken road the engines are silent. Closing the windows, he locks up the car and walks down the hillside, taking care to keep to the edge of the drying tarmac. Along the sides of the road shorn branches and brambles lie in piles, casualties of the day. Hearing a rustle, he pauses, peering through the leaves and branches; there is a deer, frozen mid-step. Its eyes meet his before it bounds away out of sight. What else is living just beyond them, watching? They'll come back tomorrow, the men tell him, to finish up. It's safe to drive on. Its neat edges and smooth surface sit incongruously against the rugged surroundings. He wishes they had left it well alone, this hidden spot that is now tempting to people from the road.

There's a fridge in the caravan and it's full of melting ice. They need the car to charge it, but until now they haven't been able to get it down here. He'll go to the village and buy some supplies and then return and try out the new road. He'll get the fridge cold and load it for the next couple of days. On the way out he rattles the old iron gate that lies rusting in the hedgerow and wonders if they could restore it. Strip it down and reseal it and paint it perhaps, it could be good as new. Seeing something by his foot, he bends down and picks it up; a small sign, made of stone. He rubs his finger across the moss and mud that obscures it. *Cyfannedd Fach*. They didn't know the cottage had a name. He puts it beside the gate and makes a note to pick it up later and clean it up. Perhaps they can put it on the front of the cottage when it's ready. He'll look up what it means.

The drive is glorious. He rolls the windows down and laments not bringing his convertible instead. Past the nearest neighbour some three miles away, past the abandoned farmers' cottages tucked into the base of Cadair Idris. Beside the Cregennan Lakes he slows, their perfect turquoise mirroring the sky. There's not a soul in sight. The remoteness of this place is unsettling sometimes. Not now though, with not a shadow in sight. On a whim he swings the car to the side of the road and parks. The lake he's chosen is the smallest, fifteen metres across at most. Scanning the craggy peaks around him, he pulls off his shorts and T-shirt.

The water is warmer near the surface and colder underneath. His toes are numb within seconds. It's deep, though he's no idea how far down it goes. Local myth has it that a giant lived here once and that these lakes were created by his footsteps. Now they're used only by local children and the occasional tourist. He plunges underwater, eyes closed. He swims down until his ears hurt and his lungs are close to bursting, then turns upwards, erupting from the surface. Sun dries the droplets on his shoulders and as soon as he feels its pulsing heat he plunges again, and again; unsure which is better, the thrill of the descent or the relief of emerging.

Exhausted, he clambers to shore and air dries before pulling his clothes back on and continuing his journey to the village.

A bell clangs, announcing his arrival, this tiny shop the only sign of life in this desolate town. He's reminded of the bleakness of British coastal towns. Faded paint and crumbling shutters, an absence of life even on the weekends. Grabbing a basket, he finds milk, wine, some instant pasta meals. So different from what he would be having back home, gastropub food and gourmet organic meals.

'How are you doing?' The woman behind the counter recognises him. 'Ryan, isn't it?'

'That's right.' He smiles. 'Beautiful day.'

'Aye, none too common round here, as I'm sure you know.' She puts his shopping into a bag. 'We don't charge for the bags yet.' She winks. 'Down for the weekend? I heard they're repairing your road?' News travels round here quicker than wildfire.

'Yep, looks good.' He smiles to mask his unease.

'Not for everyone, what you've chosen. How are you finding the cottage?'

'It's great, thanks,' Ryan says.

'How's your wife doing?' she asks.

'She's not here yet. Joining me later,' Ryan replies. It's easier to let people assume what they want to. She looks up quickly.

'Could have sworn she came in the other day . . .'

'Must have been her doppelganger.' Ryan grins.

'Well, isn't that the strangest thing, must be my eyesight

packing in.' Passing him the bag she takes his change, sorts it into the till. 'Well, give her my regards when she arrives. Tell her to drop by. I've got some of those Jammie Dodgers that she favours, set some aside.'

In the car he drives fast. Perhaps Ada is there by now, but surely she would have sent message if all was okay? Short of sending out a search party, there's nothing he can do. He thinks of the woman in the shop; it's funny, he's never known Ada to have a sweet tooth.

The new road holds firm as he winds down it and through the opening to the cottage. He keeps the speed up across the field to the caravan, which he can see is still empty. He parks on the edge of the field, facing downhill in case he needs to get momentum going through the mud if it rains. He takes out a beer that he's brought. It's still cold. The day is in its last throes and the sun will be setting soon. He walks up the ridge to watch Barmouth dwindle in the light.

He's halfway up the ridge, chair under his right arm and beer in his left, when he sees them coming across the field. Pausing, he waits for them to come closer.

'Excuse me, sorry for trespassing ...' A woman in hiking gear approaches him. She has tanned, leathered skin and carries walking poles. 'We're missing one of our group and wondered if you'd seen her: forties, slim, about five foot ten, long brown hair.'

''Fraid not,' Ryan says, irritated by this intrusion on his peace.

'We've walked from Harlech, round the coast; she was ahead, but now we think she might have taken a wrong turn.'

'Where are you headed?'

'Penmaenpool.'

'Sounds like a long walk ...'

'Twenty miles at least, yes. We meet up every summer, but this is the first time we've lost someone. If you see her could you let her know we're looking? Her name's Marlena.'

'Of course. Good luck.'

He sinks into his chair and tilts his head back, face bathed in rays. Harlech. He remembers it now from his youth. A family trip to the castle, a treat to break up their latest migration from one place to the next. It should have been glorious. They'd spent the day on the sand dunes, with his father racing ahead. His mother was in the middle as usual, trying to keep everyone happy. He'd found a large sea snail and insisted on carrying it in his pocket, determined to keep it as a pet. He'd kept quiet about it but at the end of the day his father found it escaping in the car.

'Put it back,' he'd said to Ryan quietly, and just like that the day changed.

'Peter, he can't just put it back,' his mother had said. 'The tide is out, the sea is miles away now.' He remembers wishing she would be quiet, knowing well by then the consequences of her interfering.

'I just wanted to keep it,' Ryan had said, already unfastening his seat belt.

'Put it back where you found it,' his father said. 'We'll wait.'

So Ryan, nine, maybe ten, unfastened his seat belt and scooping up the snail carefully, clambered from the car and started off down the steep slope to the edge of the dunes. The tide was out by then, the sea a silver line in the distance. He'd made it up the second dune before he heard his father coming up behind him, panting and out of breath. The palm of his hand knocked him sideways and his skin smarted. Sand sprayed into his eyes, and before he managed to sit up his father had taken the snail from him.

'Give it back,' Ryan had shouted, scrabbling to his feet, not caring who could hear. In the distance he saw his mother, her skirt hitched up to her thighs and barefoot, running towards him.

'Ryan ...'

'Give it back,' he shouted again, jumping at his father's hands. But he was too small, too slow. His mother was panicking in the distance. His father stormed back to the car, his mother calling, and Ryan when he got there was too late to stop his father's boot slamming down, crushing the snail against the concrete, its insides spilling out.

Opening his eyes, he sees the first lights of the evening against the bruised purple sky.

'Darling.' Out of nowhere her voice startles him and he leaps to his feet, knocking over his beer.

'Ada? Where the hell have you been?' She wraps her bare arms around his neck and inhales him.

'What kind of greeting is that?' She smiles and pushes her lips against his. He tastes the warm sweetness of her breath. She's wearing cut-off denim shorts and a white vest. Her legs are suntanned.

'I was worried; you were supposed to be here hours ago.'

'Bad traffic, late starting ... Anyway, there's no *supposed to* here, is there?' She puts her face against his shoulder. He turns away.

'The things that have been running through my head. Why didn't you call me?'

'I don't have hands-free, didn't want to waste time stopping. Doesn't the road look great?' He nods.

'Are you looking forward to your family holiday?' she asks, sitting on the ground in front of his chair and drinking in the view.

'Dreading it,' he replies.

'That bad?'

'Why do you want to know anyway? No questions, remember?'

'Sorry I asked,' she says sulkily. Come to think of it, how does she know about the holiday? He's pretty sure he didn't tell her about their holidays plans. Any talk of their outside lives chills the atmosphere.

'How do you know about it?' he asks.

'What?'

'The holiday?' Ada lies back on the ground and pushes her arms above her head. 'Emily told me.' She shuts her eyes.

'Emily?'

'Your wife, remember?'

'Don't play games, it's not funny . . .'

'I'm not. I saw her.' Ryan sits up straight in the chair he has just sunk into. 'What do you mean you saw her?' Ada rolls onto her side so the right-hand side of her body is flanked by the vista of the hills behind her.

'We bumped into each other and had a coffee. It's no big deal.' No big deal. Of course he knew they got along, but he'd presumed all contact between them had stopped. After their night out in Dulwich Village he just presumed they'd lost touch.

'How many times have you seen her?' he asks.

Ada concentrates on a piece of grass she has plucked from the ground, rolling it between her fingers. 'I don't know, a few.'

'A few?'

'Three, maybe four times. I like her. Haven't seen her for a while, though.'

'And you don't think that's strange, to be hanging out with the wife of your lover?'

'Not really. I mean, I like her. We have things in common. Just because she's your wife shouldn't mean she can't be my friend too.'

'I can think of one obvious reason. What things do you have in common?'

'We like cycling – you know we did a sportive together, right?' Ryan vaguely recalls Emily doing a ride but she didn't mention it was with Ada, did she? He'd remember if she had. 'And we like having fun,' Ada adds. He feels nauseous to think of Ada and Emily in cahoots behind his back.

'What else did she tell you?' he says. Ada sits slowly and rubs her eyes. She stands and moves behind him, bending to put her cheek against his.

'Just little things, like the way you have a thing for your earlobes being nibbled and the way you let out your breath through your teeth when you come . . .'

'I'm not kidding, this is some weird shit you've got going on.'

'She talked about the cottage, or rather – an investment you had made.'

'She did not,' Ryan says, feeling like he's going to throw up.

'She did.'

'You didn't tell her anything did you?' Ada moves from behind him and stands in front of his knees, blocking his view. 'Of course not, how could I? She doesn't know you're with me, silly.' It doesn't bear thinking about. He deliberately hasn't told Emily who the affair is with. But something about Ada niggles. How naturally her lies come. He chooses his words carefully.

'How did she find out?'

'Something she saw lying around, can't remember what. Seems like you were careless.'

'Will you be seeing her again?' he says, fumbling with the ring pull of his beer.

'Maybe. I don't know. I like her.' She bends down now and kisses him full on the lips, lingering after he pulls away, pushing her lips back onto his. 'Don't worry, it doesn't affect us – she doesn't have a clue. I am the master of subtlety.' She laughs, and he feels a flash of sympathy for Emily and a rush of relief, before unease settles inside him like silt.

*

83

It's only later, when Ada is sleeping that the question crosses his mind: why did Emily not mention that she knew about the cottage? She took issue with him breaking the rules, so why not this one? And how long has she been on at him to buy a ruin and do it up for themselves? Surely this is her Achilles heel. He thinks of the effort that Emily has made to hold them together. Holding her hand in Venice feels like years ago, not months. Why would she keep quiet if she knew about this cottage? What else does Ada know that he doesn't? When sleep comes eventually it is fitful and broken.

Rules of an open marriage #9:

Never bring a lover into our house

He first saw Ada on a conference call. She commented on the painting behind him. He'd been surprised that she'd recognised the artist, his taste being obscure and rather niche – but not only did she know the painting, but she had a print of it herself, at home. *My wife doesn't like it,* he'd said, and they'd shared a joke at Emily's expense. *These writer types,* Ada had said, *so wrapped up in their own imaginations that they can't recognise a good thing when it's right in front of them.*

Ada was smart and good at what she did; they'd been paired together and they got along well. Without her he wasn't sure the project would have succeeded. She challenged him every step of the way and though often he'd end their calls frustrated, a few hours later he could usually see her point of view. He started to look forward to their calls and the way they mapped the weeks. They started to talk about more than work: just little things, stuff that Emily didn't have time for in the evenings, her eyes glazing over. Ada remembered things too, details. Still, he didn't expect to fall for Ada the way he did. It didn't cross his mind that it could be something more, until the awards ceremony.

Rules of an open marriage #10:

Always spend quality time with each other

Venice, February 2016

Emily hates flying and it's not just the powerlessness of being midair, suspended in a metal cocoon. It's the whole stress of it: the picking of what to take and packing; the order that must be made from chaos. The parking that must be booked, the traffic that clogs the arteries of the M4; the tedious waiting and queuing at the airport, the close proximity of strangers; the sheer size of the man to her left who got the window seat, his huge leg pressing her small one. Beside her Ryan is reading a newspaper. They are sixteen minutes into the two-hour flight and already beneath her sweating palms she is bored.

Tom and Sam will be at her sister's in Southfields by now. Their resentment at not coming clouded dinner at the restaurant last night. The waitress, sensing the atmosphere, stayed away. The service was shoddy.

'Why do you get to go away?' Tom had said, pushing his uneaten bolognaise around his plate. 'While we get to camp at Aunty Sarah's?'

'You could try and be happy for us — it's not often Dad and I get time to ourselves,' she'd replied, looking to Ryan for back-up. 'Anyway, it's hardly camping when you get your own room.'

'Yeah, to share with fuzzy duck here,' Sam gestured to Tom. 'I don't get why you need to have time alone anyway,' he added, 'You get plenty of time together at home when we're at school and out.' She'd looked again to Ryan for some contribution, then kicked his foot underneath the table. He startled and looked at her quizzically.

'Stop complaining, it's only three nights and you'll have fun with Sarah and Matthew.'

'Funny definition of fun,' Tom replied. 'Three days with no friends around, watching rugby. It's all they do all weekend.'

'I hate their flat,' Sam said. 'It's too small and the council estate is rough.' They've raised such snobs. Sometimes she is ashamed. To think of where she came from. One day she'll take them back to visit the tiny two-up two-down that she grew up in, surrounded by hundreds of other identical homes; row upon row of houses punctuated only by a tiny patch of grass with swings. She hasn't been back since her mother died, not even to visit her grave.

'Sam, can you stop complaining? It's fine, their house is fine, the area's fine. Not everyone gets to live like we do,' Emily said.

'It's three days, kiddo. It's not going to kill you to be a little bored.' Finally Ryan deigned to speak.

'But you won't be bored, that's the point,' Emily said, glaring at Ryan. 'Sarah's planned loads of activities for you to give you a good time.'

'Like what?' asked Tom.

'Skate park, cinema. I don't know, I didn't demand an itinerary.'

'Well, you should have,' said Sam.

'That's enough, Sam. If you can't be happy for us, the least you can do is be quiet about it.'

'She doesn't even like teenagers.' This from Tom, his words falling into silence.

In bed afterwards she'd turned her back on Ryan and tucked the covers tightly around her. He's been so distracted lately. The least he could have done was support her and defend their right to time alone. This morning she awoke still angry, and now, on the plane, she is exhausted. She checks her watch. One hour to go. She'd like to get her book out, but that would mean asking Ryan to pass it. Instead she examines the flight-safety instruction card. Ridiculous, really: who would ever stop to get their hand luggage out if the plane was going down? And really, has a plane ever successfully landed on water apart from that one on the Hudson? She vaguely remembers reading something about a landing in Russia, but the chances of surviving are slight, at best. So what's the point of the bouncy slide? Perhaps it's just to create a sense of hope. But do airline companies even think like that? She'd like to order a vodka, but it's breakfast time and she can't bear the thought of being stared at. She breathes in deeply, then out. She used to bring her own booze onto the plane in a hip flask, but 9/11 has put an end to all that. She can't even drown her nerves these days.

Beyond the man beside her she can see a silvery dash of clouds through the tiny gap in his blind that he has all but closed. Why do people choose window seats if they're going to block the view? She sighs loudly but no one notices and she adjusts her position, uncrossing her legs. So much for a romantic break – at this rate they'll be lucky to exchange three words. What frustrates her the most is that he hasn't even noticed how angry she is. The plane drops suddenly. She grips the armrests and closes her eyes. Turbulence. In the early days Ryan would hold her hand for the whole flight. Now he doesn't look up from his paper, though he must know how scared she is. She is angry at herself for needing his reassurance. She's a grown woman, for

God's sake, not a child. What difference does a hand squeeze make anyway? It's not going to stop the engine conking out or a terrorist from hijacking the cockpit.

She wishes Adeline were here. They'd drink vodka, not caring who was watching, and giggle at the man beside her with his hairy thigh encroaching onto her seat and his bare feet in his flip-flops with toes that sprout out over the ends like potatoes, twisted and deformed. Who wears shorts and flip-flops in February? She's been so looking forward to this trip with Ryan, but the mere thought of attempting to make conversation with him exhausts her and she considers the possibility that the weekend was a mistake, for revisiting somewhere from their past that preserves such perfect memories can surely be nothing but a disappointment. They should have gone somewhere different, somewhere new, then it wouldn't have mattered, but here runs the risk of ruining their Venice permanently. Nostalgia is not immutable to alteration by the present. She glances at Ryan, still ensconced in his paper. He's been different recently, more distant. She'd hoped that this time alone would reconnect them, but her frustration hovers just below the surface and she knows how these things go. When she gets back she'll contact Adeline; she hasn't seen her since their night out and she's keen to present a better and less drunken version of herself. She's nervous about the things she can't remember and the missing journey home. She'd like Adeline's opinion on Leo, too.

Her ears ache and she swallows hard, yawns behind her hand. Paper finished, Ryan turns to her.

'What?' she says, her ears popping.

'Do you want some water?' He holds out the bottle. She shakes her head. 'I know you'd like something stronger.' He winks, pushing his hand over hers. 'Won't be long.'

*

The airport is heaving even now, off season, but on the water taxi she relaxes. She loves it here. They came for a weekend long ago. They'd spent most of it in bed, emerging aching and giddy in the evenings to sip wine on the terraces and wander hand in hand around the squares. Hard to believe how far they've come from then. Climbing onto shore, Ryan reaches for her hand.

It's silly to be surprised that it's changed after twenty years. The jostling streets squeeze her along narrow paths, and canals that in her memories flowed uninterrupted now clamour with water taxis and drivers campaigning for business. It's hard to see the water between the hulls and when she does find it, dipping her finger in, it's not the clear green that she remembers. In the privacy of their ground-floor hotel room the footfall of tourists clatters endlessly the other side of the wall. Venice is sinking and she can feel it, those two to four millimetres a year accumulating slowly but surely. In the time since she was last here it has dropped six centimetres further into the water, a depth the length of her index finger; the depth of the pile of documents that her superior, Professor Dean, dumped uncere- moniously onto her desk yesterday, asking her to explain. The 'evidence' that Leo has presented.

How she wishes she had scrawled her name and Ryan's into the wall of the canal beneath the stone lip where they sat years ago sipping Limonata, skin stained with sweat and sun, arms entwined. Their names, engraved in the rock that would one day be submerged. She's getting sentimental in her old age.

'Penny for them?' Ryan asks, stirring his mojito. They are back in their favourite spot, once a traditional trattoria, now a restaurant proclaiming fusion food. She'll tell him now, about Leo, and he'll understand. A misunderstanding, she'll say, and he'll nod and reassure her, distracting her thoughts from an inquiry, an investigation. He'll put Leo's claims in perspective, the tantrums of a student with a crush. Leo's energy would be better spent on Chaucer. She won't mention the night that she saw him when she was out with Adeline. There's no need to introduce doubt.

'It's just . . .' Emily says. Next to them a woman clatters the feet of her chair against the stones.

'Yes?' Ryan says, and she sees years of smiling and squinting embedded in the lines around his eyes.

'I need to tell you something,' she says.

'What is it?' He reaches for her hand and rubs his finger over her wedding ring. She hates it when he does that. In the distance a siren screeches through the glow of the evening. What if it's an attack, organised or lone, a sharp nugget of hate buried in the heart of a moment that just happens to be now?

His phone beeps loudly and Ryan withdraws his hand. She averts her eyes, refusing to be the wife who complains about him checking. He presses something and puts it back into his pocket.

'On silent now. What were you saying?' But the moment is lost to the waitress who delivers their starters and by the time they are alone again, Emily has decided not to mention it, not to ruin their trip away.

They end the evening at Casinò di Venezia, the elegance of the building suspended above the water, Juliet balconies beckoning customers in. Laughter trickles through open windows, the sound of the wealthy and the hopeful blending with the croupiers. Inside she feels out of place; a masked ball in one of the rooms has overflowed to the tables, a movie set into which she has walked unannounced. Ryan exudes confidence and she's glad to have his hand behind her left elbow, whispering into her ear: roulette, poker, blackjack. She enjoys roulette the most and it's here at the table they find themselves now, choosing their numbers. The croupier is half her age and ravishing in a fitted dress with a plunging neckline, soft creamy skin exposed and a hint of her nipples through the cloth as she bends to the table. Emily feels underdressed and struggles to keep her eyes away, but Ryan seems unimpressed, focusing instead on calculating odds and advising her not to choose the numbers she has already chosen. Emily watches him and considers how well he has aged with his dark, silver-flecked hair. Distinguished. She sees how other women perform their invisible dance around him, never touching. She feels an urge to own him here, in front of them. *He's mine*, she wants to say, for now at least.

They lose, though not much. They don't exceed their £50 allowance for an evening. It's always been this way, though they could afford ten times this now. 'Spending should never be proportional to your income, otherwise you'll never accumulate wealth,' Ryan has always insisted. He's right of course, about this and so many other things.

Back in their room he undresses her, each strap and button a deliberate display of care; his lips soft against her skin. His hands are gentle and assured. Afterwards, lying in bed in the dark, his left hand cups her breast as if it is part of his own body. His breath slows.

A dark shadow forms at the back of her thoughts and she awakes uneasy. The bright Venetian light of the morning that ricochets off the water can't burn it away.

They've only been back home a few days but already Venice feels like months ago. She finds herself daydreaming of moving there. A tiny apartment would do, just large enough for a desk and a bed, a bathroom. Perhaps overlooking the water. She longs for a life undictated by deadlines and appointments.

Back from her early bike ride and drinking her third cup of coffee of the morning, she frowns. She is lecturing on 'The Writer's Voice' tomorrow, and it has struck her that for too long she has fallen into a voice that does not fit. *Polishing your voice and making it unique is the most important thing about becoming a writer,* she types into her slideshow. *It's the only thing that defines you on the page. When you are practising the craft of writing, being comfortable with your voice is as important as being comfortable in the coat that you wear all winter; as important as choosing a partner. Be careful when your voice is not yet formed, that the wrong one does not lead you astray. Wait for it to come. It'll be worth it.*

She wonders if she would have been happier alone. She was never the maternal type. When she was pregnant it felt like her body had been taken over. But the stability Ryan offered her was solid: a future. He is a good man. She could have given him the commitment that he craved. But at what cost? A love story that slipped into the inevitable quagmire of deceit and, potentially, divorce? In spite of his complaints about their arrangement, they've managed to preserve a crispness to their marriage that others have lost. Virtually everyone they know is divorced. They've had no need to lie to one another, no need to cheat. Theirs is an open canvas that they've invented. Lately she wonders about his late evenings working and his nights away. More than normal, for sure. Work is dividing them and she longs for their time back, away from distractions. Away from this mess with Leo.

The telephone rings and she moves from her desk beside the window, trying to hear where the sound is coming from. The problem with cordless phones is they're always getting lost. Through the kitchen and into the lounge she finds it wedged behind a cushion. It's Professor Dean, asking her to come in as a matter of urgency. His voice is stripped of warmth. It's not convenient, she's so much to do, but his statement was not a question.

The boys are at college and Ryan is in Plymouth. Another new-build, overlooking the sea. He sends her photos of the boats in the harbour and the glass palace that he is building.

Gone are the days she would have joined him there, fantasising that it was theirs. Jamming her phone into her handbag, she locks up the house, takes her car from the garage. The traffic will be awful and she should take the Tube, but the thought of being crammed up against strangers is just too much. Too many times she's had to claw her way to the door of the Tube and escape the underground, ejecting herself into random London streets, gulping at air.

Crawling through the traffic she winds the window down and imagines she is on her way to lunch somewhere, or the theatre. Pedestrians wait to cross the road, droves of suits swarming to the cafés and the restaurants, seeking temporary respite from their shuttered offices. Behind her a taxi honks as she drives slowly past Tavistock Gardens. She glares at the driver in her rear-view mirror and loses him as she turns left into Tavistock Square. As she drives up Gower Street, University College comes into sight. She remembers her interview here seven years ago, in the height of summer. She'd walked the last few stops, desperate to escape the sweating Tube. Her shoes were new and rubbed, and the blisters on her feet had leaked serum and plasma into her tights, which later dried and crusted. By the time she got to the interview the pain of standing through her presentation was excruciating. She'd soaked her feet in the bath afterwards and even then she'd had to cut the denier from around her skin before ripping the last shreds from her feet. Still, she'd got the job, heading up their creative writing programme.

It's her dream job. She can't believe that she is being hauled over the coals now by a student. And all because she cared. Parked and half an hour early, she considers texting Ryan, but that's not fair. He's working and it was her choice to keep this from him. It would be selfish to spring it on him now, to catch him unawares. Reaching for her briefcase, she checks herself in the mirror, rubs her lipstick off with a tissue.

The corridors smell of disinfectant and are quiet, most students in lectures or in the library. She wishes she were there now, curled up in corner with a book with the hum of the water cooler in the background. She heads to Professor Dean's office. She is tempted to text Leo and vent her anger, but she knows this would be a mistake; everything from now on is just accumulating evidence. As she raises her hand to knock on the door, she is aware of her vulnerability; she knows what the papers inside suggest. It is her fault to have let this go as far as it has.

Eight hours later, as the sun sinks into a winter evening, Emily pours herself a glass of wine. She sits in her armchair, looking out onto the garden, the perpetual smog of the city smudging the horizon. She has considered going for a bike ride to ease the tension, but her cycling shoes are still wet from this morning. Wine will do instead, and with the second glass she considers asking Ryan to come home. He could be at the door within four hours if he left now. In their rooms the sound of the boys on their phones seeps down the stairs; their busy social lives put hers to shame. She should have made more effort with her friends, could have joined a drama group or a choir perhaps, met more people. Then she wouldn't need to be alone right now. She sends a text to Adeline. *Meet up soon?* She places the phone on the table where she can see it.

Glass three and everything is a little less sharp. She feels better. She won't call Ryan, it's not fair to disturb him, he'll be back in three days and she'll tell him over dinner. He'll be calm and will put things in perspective.

By the second bottle she has become maudlin. Some food may have been a good idea. Ryan isn't answering his mobile. She types in the phone number of his hotel room clumsily, repeatedly hitting the 6 instead of the 3. When the line finally starts to ring into his room 240 miles away, she holds her breath, knowing that as soon as she hears his voice the tears will start to flow. But he doesn't answer and she rings again. It's late to be out, gone 11 p.m., and she knows how he likes his sleep while he's away. She dials the switchboard of reception; perhaps she's got the wrong extension. No, they inform her, that is correct for room 121, but there is a mistake of a different kind. There is no record of a Ryan Bradshaw staying there at all.

When she hangs up the room is charged with all the things she wants to say but hasn't. Her phone beeps and she checks the message from Adeline. *Is everything okay? I had a bad feeling.* Emily replies. *Not really, tell you next time I see you.* How good it is to have someone understand you. She knew they had a connection. Emily feels cheerier despite the fact that the fridge is bare, the restaurants shut hours ago, and her stomach is threatening to eat itself. She stumbles to bed leaving the blinds open, forgetting to lock the doors.

Rules of an open marriage #11:

Don't take each other for granted

Wales, Saturday 16 July, 2016

This time they travel together in his MPV; he's no wish to travel in her leaky car through the Welsh rain. There's no chance for Ada to be late, leaving him waiting at the cottage. He picks her up in the morning where she is waiting by Streatham station, rucksack in hand. The journey takes four hours. The holidaymakers of the summer are not coming here and the roads are relatively clear.

'How was your holiday?' she asks.

'I'd rather not talk about it,' he says. With Tom's GCSEs and Sam's A-levels cutting their school year short, they'd seized the opportunity to take a family holiday before the masses. It was a disaster, not least because all he could think about was Ada.

'How were the boys' exams?'

'Fine, I think. They're just happy they're off for the summer now.' He pauses and there's an uncomfortable silence. It never feels right to talk about the boys with Ada.

To pass time they play I spy and compete with riddles.

'My turn.' Ada sits with one foot on her seat and the other resting on the dashboard. He'd like to ask her to move it, as it is partially blocking the wing mirror, not to mention the dusty marks it's leaving on the car.

'A man is in a locked room. There are no vents and no windows. There is nothing in the room except a bed, a piano and a calendar,' she says.

'Can he play the piano?' Ryan asks.

'What's that got to do with it?' she replies. 'Don't go off topic.'

'It could have everything to do with it,' Ryan replies, overtaking a lorry. 'His musical gift could be his salvation, salvaging his mind as his body diminishes. They do that all the time in films.'

'Do you have to do that?' she asks as he swings back into the central lane.

'Do what?'

'Drive in the middle. You shouldn't hog the middle lane, it's for overtaking.' He snatches a look at her sideways.

'Are you seriously giving me driving tips?' he asks.

'There's nothing wrong with my driving.' She grins. 'Anyway, how does he do it?'

'Do what? You haven't told me what I have to figure out yet.'

'The man is in the locked room, with no vents and no windows. How does he escape?'

'With only a bed, a calendar and a guitar. Was that it?'

'Not a guitar, a piano.'

'Crucial detail I presume?'

'Well, yes, actually they're quite different: piano, guitar, guitar, piano . . .'

'Okay, with a bed, a calendar and a piano.'

'Yes. Do you need a clue?'

'Give me a chance.'

'Okay.'

Ten minutes later he's still thinking.

'Come on, this should be easy,' she wheedles. 'I'm putting you on a timer now: you have sixty seconds. '

'I've got it,' he says.

'About time,' she says. 'So what is it?'

'He eats the dates from the calendar . . .'

'Good.' She ruffles his hair.

'And drinks the water from the springs in the bed . . .'

'Genius, I knew it,' she says, smiling. 'Lock me in a room with you any time.' He pulls off the motorway. 'And how does he get out of the room?'

'What?'

'How does he get out? He's locked in . . .' she says, sighing loudly.

'That wasn't part of the question,' Ryan says.

'Yes it was. In fact, it's probably the most important part of the riddle. All well and good to eat dates and drink spring water, but they're not going to last for ever, are they?' She swings herself around in the passenger seat to face him.

'Technically you don't know that. It doesn't actually say how long they'll last,' Ryan says, laughing at her frustration.

'It's common sense that they'll run out at some point. Everything does,' she replies.

'Okay, let me think. By the way, do we need to stop for lunch on the way?' Ryan asks.

'Nope – I've got it covered. Picnic, check. Dinner, check. Wine, camping pasta, everything we need,' she says. He makes a mental note to insist on a proper dinner tomorrow, something nice, out somewhere. All well and good to be frugal, but he's not exactly cash-strapped.

'Come on,' she says. 'How does he get out?'

'He eats dates, drinks spring water and using strings from the guitar he unpicks the lock.'

'There's no guitar, I told you,' she says, looking out of the window now. 'You're doing it on purpose.'

'Doing what?'

'Getting it wrong.'

'Why would I be deliberately getting it wrong – how does that make any sense?'

'THERE IS NO GUITAR! It's a piano.'

'I got it!'

'You did not.'

'Did too. Listen. He eats dates from the calendar, drinks water from the springs in the mattress and uses the key from the piano to unlock the door. Ta da!'

'Finally.' She turns to him. 'I know what I'd do if I were locked in a room with you, a bed, a calendar and a piano.' He reaches for her right hand with his left and entwines his fingers into hers.

'And what would that be?'

'I'd destroy the calendar so that time was irrelevant and we'd make sweet music on the bed.'

He scrunches up his nose. 'Listening to Leonard Cohen, no doubt. You're so cheesy. If I was with you I'd choose the guitar over the piano so I could use the strings to tie your hands to the bed.'

'I'm cheesy? Leonard's pure poetry.'

It's been a month since they were last together. Twenty minutes to the cottage now, another eight tortuous gates. This time they have almost a week; he's lied to Emily, knowing that this long would be pushing it. He doesn't think that she believed his excuse about needing to spend time with his mother, but it's a safe bet that she won't follow him up to Manchester to find out; his mother's loathing for Emily is reciprocated entirely.

They arrive by midday. The cottage and then the caravan come into sight, the cottage unrecognisable, clad in scaffolding and tarpaulin. The trees are resplendent in their leaves and the evergreen forest banks behind them, bending to the breeze.

'Welcome home,' Ada says to herself, climbing out of the car. He likes that she calls it home, this half-restored cottage and a rusting tin can on wheels. He feels the reassurance of returning, the sense of belonging. As a child his homes were transient spaces, an endless move one to the next, his father's debt chasing his heels. When he was old enough to make decisions for himself, he promised himself he would have a house of his own. It took him eight years to qualify as an architect. By the time he graduated he had a scar in the centre of his forehead where he had rubbed his finger in concentration. It started off small, a tiny graze, but as the scab formed he picked it. Every time it was about to heal he rubbed it and it would crack and split again. Eventually it gave up healing and resigned itself to remaining a small thumb-sized crater in the middle of his forehead. Finally though, he had a job creating homes for other people.

Next he moved on to his second goal: to create a family. At university he'd been too busy for girlfriends and his single-minded focus on studying was off-putting to the most ardent of admirers. He knew though that he wanted the family that he had never had. He met Emily in a café when he spilled his coffee on her notebook, and in the second where their hands clashed awkwardly over a pile of napkins, he knew that she was the one. She was the most beautiful woman he had ever seen, out of his league and he knew it. For the first time, though, he felt that he had something to offer, a promise of a lifestyle, a hope. He listened lots and talked little and realised that despite appearing to have it all, a part of her was lost. He made himself indispensable over the following months, and slowly but surely she started to need him too. Need, he realised, was a powerful thing. When he finally summoned the courage to kiss her, she kissed him back. He thought that this was all that he could ever hope for and he waited for her to realise who he really was, a dreaded call or a subdued meeting in a darkened bar. It didn't happen and his world altered irrevocably. He discovered the joys of intimacy, a world that he knew little about. Experienced and spontaneous, Emily was everything he was not. While his peers were getting hot under the covers, he was studying. When for a brief period he was invited to parties, he'd bury his head in a book in a corner and shut out the couples on the dance floor. The invitations dwindled quickly. No one ever approached him. But Emily seduced him slowly and delighted in nominating herself his tutor. He longed to experience the world through her eyes and when she accepted his proposal of marriage six months later, he could not believe his luck. Though her proposal of an open marriage made his blood curdle, eventually he agreed to it, worried that otherwise she'd walk away. He wouldn't get another chance like this and he didn't really believe that she would utilise the freedom anyway. His naivety played a hand. He was aware there was a discrepancy between his needs and hers, her libido exceeding his, but he would work at it – after all, marriage was about effort.

Everything was perfect in the early years. They all needed him back then: Emily through her postnatal depression. Sam and Tom with their tiny perfect bodies and warm giggly cuddles. He'd never been so happy. But the balance shifted as the boys got older. Emily emerged from the sleepless years more resilient, stronger. Resentful, he thought sometimes.

He never wanted anyone other than Emily. It's just straightforward sex, Emily had explained to him. Without ties. But for him it didn't add up. There has to be something deeper, he insisted. It's not a mechanical thing. Old-fashioned and repressed, she called him. He didn't have an answer.

'Sentimental,' Emily called him. He accused her of being sexist.

'For decades men have been derided for explaining their indiscretions as beyond their control, so why is it okay for a woman to do the same?' he'd asked her.

'It's not the same,' she'd replied, 'because twenty years ago it would have been unheard of for a woman to imply that her needs were as justified as a man's. I'm just pushing for the same freedom that men have claimed for years. Still, there was something about her logic that didn't sit right.

He loves it here at the cottage, his home life and work receding. Here the only task is to eat, sleep and fuck. In the afternoon they check on the workmen and head to the lakes. Soon the days will be shorter. They want to make the most of the light. The staircase is going in today and he can't wait to see it. Now, above all else, he longs for them to be inside the four walls; he's tired of the caravan that is disintegrating around them. Originally they'd thought to keep it there for guests. What guests would sleep surrounded by moss and rust? A foolish idea for a future they have not planned. It has bothered him lately, what lies around the corner.

They picnic by the closest lake. Ada crouches low and puts her fingers in the water. The water is sky blue despite the grey clouds that hang like puffed clouds over the tops of the hills.

'It's the granite in the water that makes it blue,' he's explaining, but she cuts him off with a finger to his lips.

'Shh, don't ruin the magic of it with science. Taste it.' She puts her finger in his mouth and it tastes of earth and iron.

'It's magic in its own way,' he insists, 'the granite absorbs the light from the sky and reflects it back through the water.' She sighs.

'No, you're wrong, the blue is the lake's memory of summer days, stolen from the sky. But the lake is cursed, because although it carries the colour of summer in the water, it can never feel the sun. It must be torture to see the sun but never feel it.' She tilts her head back to the sky and closes her eyes.

For her this is a land of sixteenth-century highwaymen and winged dragons, of trolls resting beneath the bridges and pterodactyls screeching through the sky.

After they eat she peels back her layers one by one in the clouded light and dives into the water. Her body enters without a sound. She swims underwater; the only sign of her is a ripple. Diving in after her, the water crushes his lungs. Forcing his way up to the surface, he breaks through, gasping. She is beside him now, her shoulders fragile against the rugged elbow of the mountain behind her. Back on dry land he passes her a towel and her phone falls onto the ground. He notices a missed call. He picks up her phone and drops it into her bag.

Back outside the caravan, the warmth of the car is welcome and they sit inside it longer than they need to. The radio station they were listening to is replaced by a static crackle. Ada slips a CD into the player and Leonard Cohen's gravelly tones fill the space.

'He's so depressing,' Ryan says.

'Listen to the words,' Ada says. 'He's one of the greatest philosophers of our time; one of the greatest romantics too.'

'Each to their own,' Ryan replies, removing his keys from the ignition. 'It's all love and death, it's so bleak.'

'That's all there is to life,' Ada says.

They prepare for evening. The temperature falls while they sit outside. The trick is to wrap up warm before the cold seeps in. Their thermal long johns and their vests live here permanently, tightly sealed inside a dry bag to prevent the damp seeping in. Ryan pulls on his goose-down jacket and his hat, then lights the wood-burning stove they bought last time they were here. Ada slices chicken breasts and peppers, rinsing her hands from the water container intermittently.

'What's the occasion?' he asks, his mouth watering as the

onions caramelise in the pan, their sweetness mingling with the woodsmoke.

'Surprise,' she passes him a glass of Viognier, and clinks hers against it. He wraps his arms around her and inhales the fresh smell of her skin. His desire cuts straight through his hunger. 'Thought we deserved a decent homecoming – it's been so long,' she says, returning to the frying pan and adding soya sauce.

They had planned to examine the cottage and the new stairs, but they're too tired and it's late. In bed their lovemaking is gentle. She wraps herself around him. Afterwards they lie on their backs listening to the rain return, slamming against the roof. The caravan rocks and Ryan pulls the covers over himself, up to his neck. Ada twists and turns, restless.

By daybreak he feels sick from the motion of the wind. He sits and peers out through the checked curtains that hang limply against the plastic windows. Condensation sticks the edges of them to the frame.

'Shall we move in to the cottage today, assuming the stairs are fit for purpose?' He shuffles to the edge of the bed and tugs back the lock on the door, kicking it open with his foot when it sticks. It's a gorgeous morning, the rain of yesterday gone and the sky washed clear of clouds.

'Why not?' Ada says, laughing and clambering over him to get out first, 'We have stairs, a roof, windows. There's no stopping us.'

Apart from the fact that the walls are not watertight. It seems, according to the builder who Ryan spoke to, that the windows are not sealed properly, and the downpour of yesterday has seeped through the joins, pooling in streams and running across the floors of the cottage. Ryan looks in dismay at the mud. The builder wasn't happy to be disturbed on a Sunday and refused to come out until tomorrow.

'It's okay, we can move in anyway,' Ada says, dragging her

dry bag across the floor, leaving soil marks. 'Anything is better than the rust hut.' As they swing the door of the caravan shut, it falls off its hinges.

'Thereby ensuring that we can never sleep here again,' Ryan says with satisfaction.

The new staircase is glorious, spiralling upwards. Dust motes spin in the air above it. The wrought-iron handrail winds up to the crog loft, anchoring the space above. They've saved five feet of floor space by putting in this design, space that will eventually be filled with a sofa and a rug.

'You first,' Ada says, her foot poised at the bottom step.

'Beat you there,' Ryan shouts, sprinting from the door and doing an impressive hurdle over the bottom of the bannister before crashing unceremoniously onto the floor beside the fire. He definitely felt something twist and is worried he heard a crunch.

'Shit.'

Ada crouches down beside him and removes his shoe.

'What were you thinking? Do you think you're an athlete? Does it hurt a lot?'

'On a scale of one to ten, it's a nine.'

She peels off his sock, which reveals an ankle that's already twice it's normal size, an angry bruise spreading up his leg and down towards his toes.

'Should I call an ambulance?' Ada says.

'No reception,' he says weakly. He lies down on the concrete floor. It's damp and cold. He twists his head and puts the side of his forehead against it.

'I'll get some ice,' Ada says, jumping up and disappearing out of the door. More of a problem that the walls aren't watertight if he is to spend the night on the floor, he thinks, focusing on a spider's web above his head. He closes his eyes and breathes deeply.

'Can you move your toes?' Ada asks, back with a bucket. Putting her hands underneath his armpits, she hoists him onto a chair and he is reminded again of the surprising strength of her. He focuses on his toes and with immense concentration manages to move the big one.

'Good, that's good. And your ankle?'

He can move it a fraction to the right, and not to the left. 'Okay if I want to walk in circles,' he jokes. She lifts his foot into the bucket with cold hands and within seconds the pain is gone, his ankle numb.

'Thank you.' He grasps the ends of her fingers with his. 'I'm such an idiot.'

'That you are.' She smiles, leaping to her feet. 'Because now I get to go upstairs first and you'll have to see it vicariously.' With that she bounds up the stairs two at a time. He hears her clattering above him, her footsteps on the floorboards creaking from one end above his head to the other, until they stop.

She's silent for a long time.

'Ada?' Nothing but the rustle of old paper and the sound of the trees. She must have opened the shutters. 'Ada?'

He's aware of a trickle of water running across the floor and pooling around the base of the bucket; on the far side of the room a tarpaulin flaps against the outside of the window. No, it's not quite ready here. It's cold too. They'll need to buy some firewood. He glances at his ankle, now the size of a small football. What timing. He tilts his head to the side and listens carefully. What is she doing? Something drops on the floor above and rolls noisily above his head.

'Ada? It's not funny – what are you doing?' He's about to haul himself onto his good leg and drag himself up the stairs if he has to, when she appears at the top of the stairs, face flushed.

'Look what I found,' she says, clutching a cardboard box to her chest. She walks down the stairs carefully, placing the box on his lap. 'I need to go and buy wood and some firelighters for this evening, but you can keep yourself busy while I'm gone,' she says.

'I'll come with you. I could do with a change of scene,' he says.

'Nonsense,' she says, dismissing him with a pat to his head, 'you can barely walk. I won't be long and then we'll get this place warmed up. I'll get the name of a doctor too, just in case.' She nods at his foot and then starts coughing, her eyes streaming. She runs to the kitchen and hunches over the sink, running the tap. Back in the lounge she downs a glass of water.

'What was that about?' he asks.

'The smoke. Caught me right at back of my throat,' she says. Ryan looks at the empty, disused fireplace.

'What smoke?' he asks.

'Please tell me you smelled it too?' she says, wiping her eyes with the back of her hand.

'I can't smell anything,' he replies, 'Are you sure you're okay? You look pale.'

She swings her satchel over her shoulder and pulls on her wellies.

'Strange,' she says, distractedly.

'The cottage is in the middle of nowhere, Ada, the fire's not been lit for years. If you smelled anything, perhaps they're burning wood in the forest . . .' She grimaces.

'Probably my imagination. Right, I'll be back as soon as I can.' He nods and lifts the top off the box on his lap.

'I'll be fine. Can you get some painkillers too?' He listens to her footsteps until they blend with the birdsong and are then replaced by the car revving. She accelerates and then she is gone.

The pain is replaced by a dull throb. Upstairs the shutter bangs against the wall. Ada must have left it open. No wonder it's cold. Ryan zips up his jumper and pulls the hood over his head, his wrist catching the box that she's left on his lap and knocking it to the floor. Above his head the rolling starts again. The crog loft is on a slope. It is inevitable that things will slide in his direction. He forces his hands to unclench from the arms of the chair and, wincing, stands on his good leg. The movement knocks the bucket over and his swollen foot is free. Pain shoots up it as it touches the floor. Melting ice scatters.

'Damn it.' He bends painfully to rescue the box, but he can already see that the cardboard is soggy at one end and the photos that have fallen out are sodden. Lifting them carefully, he places them on the table. He'll dry them later by the fire.

Another knock comes from upstairs and looking upwards, he sees something small moving across the top stair. It drops noisily onto the next before continuing its journey towards him. Roll, drop, clatter. Roll, drop, clatter. It ends its descent at his feet. He bends to pick it up. A marble. He wraps his hand around it. It's been a long time since he held a marble. It was his thing when he was a kid. He loved the smooth hard shape of them and played with them for hours. It drove his father mad, like everything else. The marble is the size of a small plum, and orange flecked with amber that reflects the light. It warms in his hand like an ember. He puts it into his pocket. It must have been dislodged from somewhere when Ada found the box.

He waits for Ada's return, but there's no sign of her and the shutter needs to be closed, as the temperature is dropping by the minute. Hopping on one leg, he moves to the bottom of the stairs and leans forward. He swings himself up step by step, dragging his damaged right foot behind him. At the top he pauses. He wants to remember this, his first time upstairs since the staircase went in. With its beams restored and exposed, the room seems larger. The lime-washed walls are bright and the sloping floor and leaning walls give the room a quirkiness that is slightly unsettling. At the end of the room the shutters are wide open, the green wooden doors blending into the trees outside. Hobbling forwards, he reaches the windowsill and grasps it, leaning out. He inhales deeply. The gulls screech warnings from the sea. A storm is coming. Does it never stop raining? He wants to linger but he needs to sit down, the nausea returning. Where is the nearest hospital, anyway? There are so many important things they haven't considered. On the way back to the stairs he catches the edge of Ada's bag and her washbag falls out. The zip is open and a pot of pills spins along the floor. He sidesteps over to where it's nestled against the wall and crouches down, grabbing it with one hand. Holding it up to the light, he turns it until he can see the label. Then he changes his mind and drops it quickly back into the bag. As he does so a tube of something catches his eye and before he stops himself he reads the label. Vaginal lubricant. He's never known Ada to use it with him. What if she's not as into him as she seems to be? What if it's an act? He pushes the thoughts away.

He hears the car pull up and decides that he won't say a word; the last thing that he wants to be seen as is needy. Of course she's into him. She wouldn't be here if she wasn't. Ada opens the door, laden with shopping bags.

'I'm so glad to see you,' he says as she kisses him on the cheek.

She's amazing. It's only mid-afternoon and she's unpacked all of their stuff from the caravan and filled the fridge and kitchen cupboards with food. Candles flicker on the table and the fire is lit, warm flames licking the cold hearth. Upstairs she has improvised a bed with the mattress from the rust hut. Already it seems less damp, more solid. He's full of painkillers and wine and his mouth waters as she works in the kitchen, making a paella. The smell of onions and saffron waft out of the tiny lean-to, and he hears her humming to herself. She's super-fucking-human and he's lucky to have her.

'I love you,' he tells after they have eaten and are sitting side by side watching the fire. He glances sideways at her profile and waits for her to speak, but the only sound is that of the wood slipping into the golden furnace.

'Did you hear what I said?' he asks, reaching for her hand. She allows him to hold it, her fingers cold and motionless against his.

'Why did you do that?' she asks. Her face is masked, with no trace of her laughter from just moments ago.

'Do what?' he says.

'That.'

'Can't I speak the truth if the moment takes me?'

'It hasn't been the defining virtue of our relationship so far . . .'

'What hasn't?'

'Truth,' she says, pulling her hand away and placing it on her lap.

'Speak for yourself. I've been honest.' The space between them grows thick.

'Thank you,' Ada says at length, drawing her shawl closer to her chest. 'For telling me.'

'That's it?'

'You didn't just expect me to say it back, did you? We're not in primary school.' It's his turn to move now, tilting his body away from hers, the movement restricted somewhat by his bandaged ankle, which rests on a side table.

'It's just that . . .' He speaks slowly.

'What?'

'Well, I thought that – with all this . . .' – he gestures to the room – 'I thought it had become something more than just, you know.'

'Stop talking in riddles. More than what?' He can't believe she'd be so cruel.

'More than just an affair,' he says quietly.

'I told you: no promises for the future, no past – did you forget?'

Seven months have passed and so much has happened, yet nothing has changed.

'I thought that with our decision to buy this, things would be different. We're committed ...' he says, aware that he is whining. He is embarrassed. Why couldn't he just have kept his mouth shut? What if he's ruined it?

'I am committed,' she says, softness squeezing between her words. 'But when you label something it breaks it. Like a bubble when it's touched.' She rises from her chair and stands in front of him, bending to kiss him on the lips. 'Let's not ruin it, please?'

Rules of an open marriage #12:

Have no secrets from one another

London, April 2016

It's falling apart. Emily sits in her office staring at the screen of her laptop. A mug of coffee is beside her and the house is quiet. She needs to write this report for Professor Dean, though she doesn't want to. She cringes when she thinks of their meeting yesterday, his knock on the door of her office. She's started to dread the days she is at work, feeling constantly on edge.

'So, in your own words, you need to tell us what happened.' Professor Dean's words reverberate in her head. She stares at the blank Word document in front of her. It wasn't enough that she'd already talked him through her interactions with Leo from the day that he started in her class.

'We need to understand the full extent of the relationship,' he'd said. 'In writing.'

Relationship. How easily he's made it something that it's not. Her finger hesitates over the keyboard. The danger of putting something into writing is that it cannot be unsaid. The permanence of the written word is open to corruption and misinterpretation. Were she to write that she cared for Leo, this could be misconstrued. *A maternal concern or something else?* they've already asked her. How to define all the facets of emotion, professional and moral obligation, into one clear sentence?

'It's not a story,' she'd insisted angrily, 'with a clear beginning, middle and end.'

'You of all people should know that a story does not need to be linear, nor do the characters' motives need to be succinct,' was Professor Dean's reply. 'We're not looking for a story, we're asking for the truth.' Then, when she'd pressed her palms against her eyes, her throat aching from the defiance of tears—

'We're not saying you've done anything wrong, Emily, your professional record is flawless. But we do need to hear your version of events. His allegations are serious – abuse of your position, seducing him, manipulation of his emotions.'

'Nothing happened,' she said again.

'These documents suggest otherwise,' he'd pointed to the sheaf of emails that lay in front of her.

'They don't prove anything.' She'd stood then and paced between the window and the door.

'Not conclusively, no . . . But it doesn't take a huge imagination to consider the possibility of something going on outside of this correspondence, to fill in the gaps.'

The gaps. She'd met Leo six months ago at her first lecture of the term. He'd waited for her after class, introduced himself. He loved her writing, had read her short-story collection. She was flattered; it had been so long since she'd written anything of worth. He was in his final year of his English degree and planned to start working on his own novel soon. He'd love to hear her thoughts, he said, on his outline. 'Hard to judge,' she'd said, when she didn't know his writing. But one term later she'd been convinced. He was talented. There was a starkness that reminded her of Carver. He was intense and focused, unlike the other students.

In the canteen at lunchtime one day, he'd invited her to join him at his table. He'd told her about his idea for a novel. It was going to be from the perspective of a woman. 'Brave,' she'd commented. 'Hard to do.' It was an ambitious idea, a woman and the disintegration of her marriage. 'Easier to write about things you have experience of,' she'd said. 'Have something to draw on, even if it's a metaphor.'

'I like a challenge,' he'd said, holding her eye until she turned away.

Later, she'd read his opening chapters and given him feedback.

'Why did you tell him personal details about your own marriage?' Professor Dean asked her. 'Didn't you think that was crossing a line?'

Leo was upset with her feedback, couldn't handle the criticism – 'It's the biggest hurdle of being a writer,' she'd told him, 'you need to get over it.' He'd missed a couple of her lectures, and when she bumped into him in the library, she'd explained that his writing was superb, but some elements of his marriage construct were clichéd. 'It's what I told you,' she said, 'about having experience.'

'Tell me then,' he'd said, 'what's it really like?' She'd been reluctant to span the gap between lecturer and student and she told him so. But he was persistent. It seems foolish now that she shared so much, but he was good at listening and once she started talking she couldn't stop. He didn't judge.

She needs a coffee. From the kitchen she can see snowdrops hunching in the corners of the garden. Spring is arriving, though the ground is still frozen in the mornings. Last week she came off her bike, didn't see the black ice until it was too late. She was lucky, thirty miles an hour downhill and she skidded on a bend, spinning into the opposite lane. She picked herself up shakily and looked up to see the driver of the car she narrowly avoided standing over her. Embarrassed, she refused the offer of a hand and stood, trying hard to pretend that the world was not ebbing around her. Her helmet was cracked and her left thigh is still purple from hip to knee, but it's nothing compared to what it could have been.

At night she wears leggings when she sleeps; she doesn't want to give Ryan cause for concern, or worse, another lecture on responsibility. He already thinks her reckless, biking too fast, braking too little. He's away much of the time, but when he's home she finds herself tiptoeing around him. How quickly their home has become a storage place for secrets. Better this than an argument though, the inevitable descent into blame. When he returned from Plymouth she asked him how his hotel was, the one he hadn't stayed at. 'Fine,' he'd answered, disappearing into his office. He still doesn't know about the issue with Leo. She is glad now that she didn't tell him while they were in Venice. The growing chasm between them has made a liar of her when she checks her email and takes calls from her boss. This is how a relationship erodes, layer by layer, like rust.

Back at her desk, she stares again at the blank screen. She needs to get her timelines right if she is to do this properly. First she read his chapters, then in the canteen she told him about her marriage. No, that's not right – perhaps it was over coffee at her house? She can't remember the decision to invite him over. No law against it. He admired their house as they sat in the kitchen, hands wrapped around steaming mugs. He'd asked her about the photographs of Sam and Tom. Only a few years younger than him, they looked childish. She'd lent him a pile of books to study first-person narrative and the art of building suspense. When she walked him to the door, he'd kissed her on the cheek. A civilised parting. She'll leave out that detail – no need to feed their theories with red herrings.

The doorbell rings and she jumps. She's not expecting

anyone, the boys are in college and Ryan is in his London office today, though he'll be home later. They're out for dinner tonight with Georgia. Padding down the hallway barefoot, she looks through the blinds to see who's there. Leo. Hair falling across his eyes, blocking the door. He rings the doorbell again. She shouldn't answer it, should walk away back down the hallway into her office and shut her door. But anger propels her forward. Leo looks taken aback.

'Emily? I—'

'You shouldn't be here, Leo, not after everything you've done.'

'We need to talk.'

'We've talked too much,' she says, one hand on the wall and her leg wedged in the gap between them. The door handle catches her bruised thigh and pain shoots through it.

'I can explain,' he says, moving forward.

'No, you can't,' she says. Her voice is bitter, sharpened.

'I didn't mean for it to escalate, I'm sorry. It's just—'

'I don't want to hear it, Leo, this is my fucking career you're playing with here. All I did was help you.'

'I know, I ...' He's crying and Emily peers beyond his shoulder. They can't be seen from the road, but she can't leave him crying on her doorstep. She opens the door and ushers him in, aware of how he towers above her. She puts the latch on the door and leads him to the kitchen. He follows. She passes him a tissue and a glass of water and seats herself at the far end of the table.

'They've asked me to write it down,' she says. 'They don't believe that nothing happened between us.'

'Depends on your definition of nothing, I suppose,' he says. And still he insists. Fury peppers her stomach and she walks to the kitchen counter and places it between them.

'Depends?' she says, her voice edging towards hysteria. 'I put myself on the line for you, Leo, and this is how you repay me?'

'I thought I meant something to you,' he says, 'like you did – do – to me.'

'You were my student and my friend, Leo. But this is not how friends behave.'

'Don't patronise me. I'm not a kid.'

'Well, that's how you're behaving.'

'How am I behaving like a kid?'

'Throwing a tantrum because I wouldn't let you get into my knickers? Very mature, Leo. Well fucking done for handling rejection so well. Full marks for manipulation.'

'I couldn't stop thinking of you after I saw you in Dulwich,' he says. The hours that she has forgotten rise up, dark and shapeless. She recalls speaking to him and saying goodbye and nothing more. The memory is lost. He pushes back his chair and walks towards her and she puts her hands up in front of her, palms turned towards him.

'One step closer and I'm calling the police.' She knows this is absurd. It would be professional suicide. For them to find her here with her accuser in her own house with no sign of forced entry. He walks closer until his chest is level with her hands.

'Look at me,' he says, taking her hands in his and pushing her palms against his chest where she can feel the warmth of his body through his shirt and his heart beating. She hates the tug of desire. She steps back, snapping the moment.

'You have to tell them that nothing happened. Please, for me and my family.'

He scoffs. 'Now you care so much about your family.'

'I have always cared about my family.'

'Even your husband who doesn't deserve you? Where is he is now, away again? You're the one who told me about the loneliness of marriage, the sacrifice, the baby machine you felt like . . .'

'Yes, for your book, to be authentic. You're not my shrink – I was helping you. Helping your character.'

'You knew how I felt about you; don't pretend you didn't know. You knew it from the start.' She knew. The lingering glances, the gentle concern, his leg pressed too closely to hers when they sat. The press of his shoulder, the join between them electric at the slightest brush. But it was wrong; he was her student.

'I didn't know,' she says now, all sentiment strained from her voice. 'And if I had, I would have stopped our meetings.' Leo leans with his hands upon the counter, shoulders slumped towards the floor. The muscles of his back are outlined through the checks of his shirt.

'All I want is for you to acknowledge what there was between us,' he says, 'that I didn't make it up. That I'm not going mad.'

'And how would that help you?' she says, more gently, He meets her eyes and his anger pulses between them.

'How can you ask me that?' he says.

He walks to the table and picks up his glass, takes it to the sink. He runs the tap on warm and washes the glass carefully with the sponge, then dries it with the tea towel that hangs from the oven. He holds the glass out to her.

'We wouldn't want there to be any evidence of inappropriate behaviour, would we?' he says. She takes it carefully, though she longs to hurl it across the room and see it shatter. He walks to the door.

'Goodbye, Emily.'

'Leo, wait . . .'

'Enough is enough.'

'What will you do about the allegations?'

'I'll do what you'll never do. I'll do the right thing.'

She locks the door behind him and turning, leans her back against it. The armpits of her shirt stick to her skin and though she showered this morning she can smell herself, sweat and the odour of desire. She runs the shower on cold and winces as she steps under the water. She scrubs every inch of her skin and does not allow herself to flinch as the sponge crosses the bruise on her thigh. She scrapes her hair back into a ponytail and does not look in the mirror as she dresses. Back at her desk she types furiously and without pause, 4,000 words of explanation and fact and no room for any gaps.

By the time Ryan gets home she has pulled herself together. They're going out, though it's the last thing that she feels like doing. She needs to speak to Adeline. She needs to know what happened that evening in Dulwich; for all she knows Leo could have something on her that could count against her. She sends her a message suggesting they meet up sometime soon.

The restaurant is crowded and they raise their voices to be heard. On her left sits Georgia, and opposite sits Phil. On her right is *poor scorned Martha* (as Georgia insists on calling her), and across from her is Ryan. In between Ryan and Phil is Rupert, whom Emily hasn't met before, though she suspects that he is here for Martha's benefit. They decided on tapas for this evening. Ordering is proving challenging.

'I can't eat anything with seafood, meat or oil,' Georgia is telling the waitress, who is waiting patiently.

'Well, that'll be tricky ma'am, with our menu, though you could go for the asparagus, we could switch the oil for butter and serve it with a salad?'

'I didn't come to a restaurant to graze on guinea-pig food, good Lord . . .' Georgia ensures that everybody is now paying attention. 'There must be something besides flesh and grease . . .' The waitress shuffles her feet, twisting her pen between her fingers.

'Georgia, how about the stuffed peppers dear, they might

be okay?' Phil speaks lightly but frown lines dig trenches into his forehead.

'How about I take everyone else's orders and then come back to you, give you some time to think?' the waitress says. Georgia sighs.

'If you must, dear, but please convey to your chef that they really should cater for a wider palate.'

Martha nudges Emily with her elbow and winks.

'I'll have the chorizo, the prawns and the butter beans, please,' Martha says to the waitress, who smiles gratefully. Across the table Rupert grins at her.

'A woman after my own heart,' he says. To the waitress, 'I'll have the same as this lovely lady, thank you.' Martha blushes. Apparently her confidence has taken a beating since her husband left her for the nanny, according to Georgia, who is the fount of knowledge on all things divorce. Emily's not so sure, though. Martha's lost weight, changed her style and looks happier than she has ever seen her. Divorce suits some people and Martha is one of them. Emily hopes that she doesn't go for Rupert, with his lecherous smile and plump, swollen lips.

'So, what do you think of the referendum?' Phil asks, diverting attention away from Georgia, who is still interrogating the waitress on all the options that are not on the menu.

'Bloody foolish of Cameron, if you ask me,' Ryan says, pouring a glass of wine.

'Arrogant, all right,' Rupert adds, smirking. 'Tory confidence. A safe gamble though, we'll never vote to leave.'

'I'm not so sure,' Ryan says, smiling at Emily across the table, 'Emily here thinks that it's risky, to dangle a carrot over such a monumental decision.'

Emily nods. 'Too much choice can be dangerous. It'd be suicide for the economy, not to mention the potential fallout across Europe.'

'Beautiful and smart,' Rupert says, clapping a chubby hand

on Ryan's shoulder, 'You are a lucky man.' Ryan glances apologetically at Emily.

'Did you see Sam Cam's dress when he was interviewed afterwards?' Georgia rejoins their conversation. 'Shocker, honestly. You think with all the stylists she must have they could have chosen something a little more flattering.'

'I doubt that her outfit was the first thing on her mind at the time, dear,' Phil swigs from his glass and asks Rupert to pass the bottle.

'Still, She's supposed to be representing the nation; she should take her responsibilities more seriously. We have a public image to maintain.' Georgia takes a tiny mirror from her bag and puts on more lipstick. 'Don't you agree, Emily?'

'Hardly representing the nation,' Phil mutters. There's another three, maybe four hours of their company. Emily wants to hang herself. They're so dull. She wouldn't be here if it weren't for Ryan's benefit and he didn't talk to her in the taxi but spent the whole time on his phone, scheduling next weeks' appointments. Emily turns to Georgia and puts on her sweetest smile.

'Not really, Georgia. I think that if your husband has just made potentially the biggest mistake of his life, the last thing you'd be thinking of would be which colour best suits your eyes.' Georgia straightens in her seat and, placing her elbows on the table, clasps Emily's hands.

'Sweetheart, I think you're being a little melodramatic, don't you?'

'No, I don't actually,' Emily says. Georgia leans in and lowers her voice.

'Is everything okay? You seem a little tetchy.'

'Everything is fine,' Emily says loudly, as the men start a conversation about golf. 'Or as fine as it can be when England is heading straight towards ruin.'

'That's a little extreme,' Phil says, attempting a smile. 'We'll no more leave the EU than Ryan would leave you. Isn't that right, Ryan?'

'Yes, no – I mean, sorry, what am I being asked here?' Ryan puts his phone back in his pocket.

'It's just my opinion,' Emily says, as she sees their food arriving. 'No one has to share it.' She feels her phone vibrate in her pocket and checks it under the table. She replies to Adeline. *Great, let's plan soon. Having a horrible night X.*

Dinner over and Rupert suggests a trip to his members' club. Emily has committed herself to enduring the evening to make sure that Martha does not leave with Rupert. They walk from the restaurant to the club and Emily lets her coat swing open, enjoying the fresh air. Ryan catches up with Emily, leaving the others behind.

'Is everything okay with you?' he asks.

'I'm just tired,' Emily says. Ryan stops on the pavement and pulls her towards him, his hand on her lower back.

'I know this is hard work for you, but try and have fun, please?' As he pulls her closer she feels him pause. She looks up and sees him looking over her shoulder.

'What?' she says. He shakes his head.

'I thought I saw someone,' he says. He rubs his eyes. 'Must be going senile.'

The club is underground and semi-lit, catering for its clientele, wrinkles and paunches blending into sand-coloured walls beneath soft lighting. Rupert gyrates on the dance floor and Emily grabs Martha's hand.

'Come on, let's do some shots.' At the bar they perch on stools and watch while the tequilas are poured. They lick their fingers and run salt around the edge of their thumb and forefinger.

'How are you really?' Emily asks.

'I'm great. So much happier. It got so tiring, waiting for Greg to leave me.'

'You knew all along?' Emily says. Martha tosses back a second tequila.

'People always know. Deep down. It was exhausting pretending to be normal. Hoping that I was wrong.' Turning on her stool, she faces Emily so that their knees touch. 'Are you okay? I mean, you and Ryan?'

'What do you mean?' Emily looks over her shoulder to where Rupert and Phil are now can-canning around the room.

'It's just, you seem ... I don't know, slightly on edge. Different.'

'We're fine,' Emily smiles. 'He's working hard and there's a lot going on with my work. But we're solid.' Slowly but surely she is losing him. There's someone else, she's sure.

Ryan lunges across the dance floor, placing a sweaty kiss on Emily's forehead.

'A dance with your old husband?'

'I'm happy watching,' Emily says, patting his arm. 'Go have fun.'

Three shots later and the room is spinning. The toilets are down a hallway lit by mirror balls. Emily misses the last stair on the staircase and twists her ankle. Bending down to rub it, she notices a man leaving the ladies' toilets, rubbing his nose.

'Phil?' she says, holding her ankle as he approaches.

'Emily, are you okay?' He offers a hand and she stands, levelling herself. Behind him a woman emerges from the ladies, smoothing her hair with her hand, looking a little worse for wear. As she draws beside them, she smiles knowingly at Phil, adjusting her glittery vest strap, which has slipped below the top of her gold bra. Emily catches Phil's eye and he pats her arm.

'Must be getting back. Georgia will be looking for me.'

Emily nods and watches him as he disappears down the hallway, catching up with the woman as they reach the stairs.

Emily adjusts her clothes and hits the flush button. She washes her hands in the sink and dries them with a scented towel from the basket. She pumps vanilla-scented cream from the dispenser and massages it into her hands. The door swings open, almost knocking her over.

'Adeline?' She is wearing a backless dress and high heels and more make-up than the last time they met. 'I barely recognised you. What are you doing here?' Emily says. Adeline leans forward and embraces Emily in a hug. Emily feels her eyes prick with tears.

'What's wrong?' Adeline says, pulling away. She presses her thumb against Emily's cheek and catches a tear.

'I'm just drunk and emotional. I'm not always like this, you know,' Emily says. 'God. You must think I'm an alcoholic.'

Adeline laughs. 'I'm not one to judge.'

'You look amazing,' Emily tells her. It's true. Since she last saw her Adeline seems to have grown in stature and it's not just the heels.

'I've been working out,' Adeline winks. 'You should join me. How about that bike ride we talked about?' Emily nods.

'That'd be great,' Emily says. 'I should get back upstairs or they'll be sending a search party.' She rolls her eyes. 'See you there?'

Things have gone from bad to worse on the dance floor and Georgia and Ryan are dancing, their shoes discarded at the bar. Phil sips a scotch at a table behind the DJ. Emily orders a mojito at the bar and sits beside him.

'It isn't what you think,' he says, staring fixedly at the table. Emily remembers the woman with the gold bra.

'It never is,' she replies, stirring ice with her finger. She scans the room and sees Adeline in conversation at the bar. Phil starts to say something else and Emily stands before he can continue.

'Back in a minute,' she says.

'Emily, I need your opinion on something.' Martha appears beside her with a smirk on her face. 'What do you think of Rupert?' Emily glances at the bar again, realising that it is Ryan that Adeline is in conversation with.

'He's a sleaze,' she says dismissively. Martha looks disappointed.

'Really? I thought he seemed fun. Emily, are you listening?' A thought has occurred to Emily: what if Adeline is telling Ryan what happened that night in Dulwich? What if Adeline knows something about the hours that Emily can't remember? 'What's up with you today?' Martha is saying. Emily looks at her.

'I'm sorry, but I think you can do far better than that lecherous toad. It's just my opinion, of course.' Emily walks away, leaving an open-mouthed Martha.

'Hey,' Emily says to Adeline at the bar. Ryan looks uncomfortable. 'Everything okay?' Emily asks.

'Yes, fine. Ada was just telling me about the rumour that this place is shutting down. Such a shame.'

'Really?'

'Yes,' Adeline says, 'they're reinventing it for a younger clientele. It's where the money is, apparently.' Emily examines Ryan's face for a hint of anything wrong, but his smile is back in place.

'Drink, darling?' Ryan asks Emily. She nods, putting her glass on the counter. 'Ada?'

'Yes, please.'

'Three Rusty Nails coming up.'

Georgia drags Ryan back to the dance floor.

'So what are you doing here?' Emily asks Adeline.

'I'm with him,' Adeline nods at a tall swarthy man currently embroiled in some kind of tango with a woman half his age, her bare thigh tucked between his legs. Emily laughs.

'Boyfriend?'

'In the loosest sense of the word,' Adeline replies. 'He's a fuck buddy really. It's good to see you, though. Seriously, let's get together soon, okay?' She reaches out and pushes Emily's hair behind her ear. 'You can tell me what those tears were about too.'

'Everything okay?' Ryan is back beside them. He gives Adeline a funny look. 'We should go,' he says to Emily. As Emily walks towards the exit, Georgia grabs Emily's elbow.

'Be careful,' she says, and nods towards Adeline, who is still standing at the bar. 'She's trouble.'

Emily laughs. 'You mean Adeline? Don't worry, she's the best company I've had all night.'

It's late and Emily is tired. She turns off her bedside lamp. Ryan turns towards her.

'Did you have a good time? You seemed a little off . . .'

'You didn't have to be so rude to Adeline,' Emily says. 'You were so abrupt.'

'It was late and we had to go, that's all.'

'It was my first interesting conversation of the evening and you had to ruin it,' Emily says.

'You're being ridiculous,' Ryan says. 'I wasn't rude.'

'We're so middle-aged. I hate our friends,' she replies.

'Speak for yourself – I'm happy. You used to be too.'

'It feels like a long time ago,' she says. She waits for him to reply, but there is only the sound of his breathing. She remembers a time when he would never have gone to sleep on an argument. She closes her eyes and falls asleep thinking of Adeline.

Rules of an open marriage #13:

Always put family first

Wales, Monday 18 July, 2016

Ryan's head hurts; his ankle too. The front door is open and sunlight streams in. Outside Ada is sunbathing. He's remembered that he needs to get sign-off on his most recent drawings for a property in Cornwall he's taken on. He may need to do some work while he's here. With fears of the market drying up in the wake of Brexit, he can't afford to be lethargic. He grabs a walking pole from beside the door. Turning right, he makes his way slowly up to the ridge.

In the distance the estuary shimmers. Leaning back on his elbow on the grass, he scans his inbox; nothing from the client, a smattering of mails from companies he should unsubscribe from, an email from Sam with a link to a car he's seen – optimistic as always. He's about to put his phone back in his pocket when he notices a missed call. Emily. It's unlike her to call while he's away. Since their holiday they've barely spoken. She is set in stony silence and anything they say will lead to an argument anyway. His phone rings.

'Emily, is everything okay? I was just about to – no, I was, I literally just ... Reception isn't ...' She's talking too fast and tripping over her words and he feels his chest tighten.

'What do you mean gone? Since when?' Tom has gone missing.

'I saw him yesterday evening but his bed hasn't been slept in.'

'You're sure?' he says.

'Of course I'm sure. Don't you dare ...' He listens with minimum interruption and hears her anger drain into despair. There was a time when they'd have been together for this, his hand on her back. He wonders fleetingly what she was doing to not notice the absence of her son, then realises that he doesn't really care.

'I'll come back,' he says eventually. 'He's my son too.' After she hangs up he rubs his forehead and pushes his fingertips into his eyes until he sees floating specks. Shit. Tom has always been tiptoeing on the edge of danger, while Sam is even and grounded. Tom's the one who smokes too much weed, drinks until he's sick. In his most soul-searching moments Ryan has wondered what impact their relationship has had on Tom. They've made sure the boys don't know about their arrangement, but Tom lives his life as if it's running out and there's something unnervingly familiar about his hedonism.

Back down by the cottage Ada has turned onto her back and put her towel over her face. Her breasts gleam white in the sun. He scans the field but no one's there. He clears his throat as he crosses the field awkwardly, dragging his bad ankle. She doesn't move and when he reaches her he realises she is sleeping, her lips parted slightly and a thin line of sweat pooling in her clavicle. A heatwave in Wales, a day for languishing.

'Ada,' he says, then louder, 'Ada?' She shifts slightly and he says her name again. She lifts one arm and pulls the towel back from her forehead, squinting against the sun.

'What?'

'Something's come up. I need to go home.' She sits upright and the sudden movement makes him jump, and now she pulls on her bikini top, pressing her flesh into the small triangles that are too small to contain her breasts. She stands, holding the towel in front of her torso with a modesty he can only assume is fake.

'You're kidding, right?' she says. 'We only just got here.'

'It's Tom: he's gone missing, hasn't been seen since last night. It's probably nothing but . . .' He limps after her as she makes her way back to the cottage, pausing at the door that she has slammed in his face.

'Ada?' Inside she has pulled on tracksuit bottoms and stands facing him with her arms crossed, wearing an expression he hasn't seen before.

'How old is he again?' she says.

'Sixteen.'

'And has he never gone AWOL before?'

'Not without . . . no.'

'Not without what? Yes or no?'

'Stop interrogating me, Emily's frantic. It's my son we're talking about here.'

'Really? Or is it Emily who needs you? Christ, Ryan. Is this how it's to be? She clicks her fingers and you go running?'

'That's not fair; he's never done this before. It's been hard on him.'

'What has? Pretty rich kid, posh private school, lives in a glass palace – must be really hard on him.' There's a bitter whine to her voice.

'I mean this, us – maybe he knows something's up between me and Emily. All these trips . . .' He sweeps his hand at the room pointlessly.

'So now it's my fault he's gone missing?' she says.

'Of course not, but he's just a kid with his own issues and the bottom line is, if I don't go back I wouldn't forgive myself if something happened. Surely you can understand that?'

'When I was a teenager I ran away from home all the time. It's a teenage right to be truant and absent – and you deal with it by

133

pandering to him? Next time he wants a bit of attention he'll do it again.'

Ryan sits down heavily. She's sapped all the power in the room. She sits beside him and puts a hand on his knee.

'Look, I know you're worried, but what can you do there that you can't do here? It's not as if you're going to scour London street by street. And Emily's there if he goes home anyway. It might not even be safe for you to drive back in the state you're in.' She leans closer and rubs his shoulder and he can smell sweat and sun on her skin. *No*, he wants to say, *my loyalty is there, to him.* He coaxes the words to his tongue but they won't come. He is afraid of losing her. He despises himself for his weakness. She reaches for a tumbler and opens the bottle of brandy she has brought, his favourite. He watches the copper fire splash into the glass, the way it glows against her fingers. She passes the glass to him and then, as he is about to take it she pauses, holding the liquid gold against the light.

'If you really have to do it, then you should go,' she says. 'I just don't want to see you rush off without thinking it through.'

He shakes his head. 'No, you're probably right – what could I do there anyway, really, I mean . . .' Perhaps if he says the words enough he will believe them.

'Maybe you should go,' she says, sipping from the glass herself, her top lip glistening, 'I don't want to be responsible for your guilt if you don't. I've been selfish. This is your son; you choose.' She flings her legs over the arm of her chair and nestles into the backrest, her breasts half exposed. 'You go, I'll stay. If he comes back soon then maybe we can salvage a day or two.'

Ryan stumbles up to the ridge to phone Emily with the help of a walking stick, though the pain in his ankle has gone, numbed by the brandy. She is furious, accusing him of being a lousy father, a penis-led prick. Tom's not back, she informs him, but he shouldn't waste his time worrying, she wouldn't want his real life to taint his pathetic fantasy.

*

Back inside the cottage he downs another drink to prevent the hangover from crawling into his head. While Ada showers he sits at the table and stares at the dark knots of wood. She emerges wrapped in a towel, her hair damp and tousled.

'On a mission to finish it?' She nods at the bottle.

He stares at her and thinks he doesn't know her, this woman who would put herself above a child. He thinks uncomfortably of Emily, doing the best that she could for the boys even though it wasn't intuitive. All the sacrifices he thought a duty, not a choice. He was wrong; his assumptions of obligation arrogant. There is always a choice, and Ada chooses Ada.

He should bite his tongue, but alcohol has loosened his temper and before he thinks it through he is accusing her of manipulating him, seeking control. It's a pointless conversation as he'll be going nowhere, stuck incapacitated in the middle of the Welsh mountains, and, as she says, it was his choice to be here and not there, the decision being left to him. Nor, she points out, did she force him to drink; in fact she'd prefer he hadn't polished off the best part of a bottle of expensive brandy that deserved to be savoured rather than scoffed. He retorts that it wasn't a choice at all when she made her feelings so blatantly clear, and she casts him a derisory look and asks him if he is really so used to being under the thumb that he can no longer think for himself. He doesn't have an answer, limping around the room, which feels small and claustrophobic.

Fear burrows into him. He's been up to the ridge several times to check his phone and Emily hasn't called. Tom could be lying at the bottom of a canal or stranded. He could be mugged or kidnapped or worse, dismembered. These thoughts gather substance and escape his lips and now Ada is accusing him of melodrama and saying that she didn't sign up for this, it wasn't part of the deal and it isn't what she wants. After that there is silence. He feels that he might choke on all the things they've said, and pushes his way outside to where the sky stretches like a blackout blind, punctured by stars.

'They're all dead', he tells Ada when he turns and finds her standing beside him in the field.

'Everything dies eventually,' she replies. He sees that she is crying and jubilation runs briefly through him. Then she is kissing him and, caught off guard, he kisses her back. He wants her to need him. She drops the towel that she is still wearing and unbuttons his trousers. On the ground she waits, her back bare against rough grass. Crouching down into the dry earth, his ankle shoots pain up his leg. He lowers himself onto his side and slides a hand up the inside of her thighs. She opens them to him. The tips of his fingers brush against her and her thighs tense against his fingers. He will not give her what she wants, not yet. He's given her too much already. He shuffles down until he is by her feet and, ignoring the throbbing in his ankle, he shifts his weight to his knees. He wants her to tell him that she needs him. He needs to hear it. He lowers himself down to her body, running his tongue along the soft skin of her inner thighs and feels her stiffen as his tongue finds what she wants. He pushes his palms against her thighs and she swells against him. He knows her body, at least. Her noises are small and foreign beneath the vast sky. Close, closer.

He stops, pulling away. She reaches for his shoulders to bring him back but he is faster and now standing, winning at something at least. He walks back towards the cottage, barely limping for the adrenaline pumping through his veins.

In the cottage it is bright and he snaps off the lights, leaving only the candle lit.

'What the fuck was that?' She comes in, face flushed and eyes shiny bright.

'Not in the mood after all,' he says, pouring himself the last inches of the brandy, washing the taste of her from his tongue.

'And that's it?' she says, slamming her hand down on the table and knocking the empty bottle onto its side.

'Yes,' he says, throwing logs onto the fire.

'You don't get to do that,' she says, walking over and taking his glass from him, pouring the contents down her throat.

'I think I do,' he says. She reaches out and slaps him hard. His cheek stings and his left eye waters. He puts a hand to his face.

'Two can play at your game,' she says. 'You don't get to make all the decisions.' She slaps the other cheek and he's not quick enough to stop her. He suspected this was inside her, waiting to come out. Six months ago their meetings were liberating. They savoured only the moment. Impermanence was exciting. But since they bought the cottage something has changed and he's struggling to name what it is. He wonders if the act of committing to the cottage has cost them their lightness. Ada is volatile and her frustrations thinly veiled. He worries about which word to place after another.

'Go on, then,' she says, standing inches from him. Her face is pale save a patch of colour on each cheekbone. At this moment he hates her. Emily would never taunt him in this way. She knows how he was abused by his father. How easy it would be for him to slip into his shadow. Ada lifts his left hand with her right one and presses her fingers against his palm, opening his hand out. She slips her hand to his wrist. 'You know you want to. Hit me.' He shakes his head. A lifetime of resistance. She's misjudged him. She says it again. He is turning away when she catches his shoulder with her arm and he is reminded again of the sheer strength of her. A dull ache travels through his upper back.

'Jesus, Ada, that's enough.' And now she's got to him and her triumph rises like a flag. Before he can walk away she's in front of him and blocking him and the only option is to push her aside or stand still. He drops his hands to his thighs and clenches his fists, feeling his nails biting into his skin. She pushes him against the table.

'You don't get to start something and not finish it,' she says, kneeling down and taking him in her hand, and even as she says it he knows that this is his greatest weakness, that he cannot walk away. Ada's mouth is on him and he feels her hot breath and his anger and tension unfurl even though it's not pleasure, even though she's too rough and he already resents this betrayal of his body. He hardens against his will, submitting to the painful thrust of her mouth. The rush towards sweet relief is nearly over and then she moves away and grabs his hands. She pulls him to the floor with her. She kneels and he stumbles forward so that his ankle buckles and his knees bruise against the flagstones. She reaches back and puts him inside her, her hands pulling his up her body, cupping her breasts, pulling him closer. He tries to pull away but she pushes back against him and there is nothing tender: this is brutal and primal, this thing that he mistook for love. He feels the skin on his knees tearing. He despises his weakness. She slides forward a fraction, losing her grip on his hands. The movement is minimal and she grabs his hands harder, digging her nails into his, trying to pull him back with her. It's all he needs and he softens, the momentum lost. She pushes back against him uselessly. He slips out of her and she turns, flushed. Still on his knees, he falls to his elbows and places his forehead against the floor where the chill of the evening seeps in.

'Christ, you're pathetic sometimes,' she says, and when she stands he knows that she has given up. He hears her running the tap in the kitchen and pouring a glass of water. He rises shakily to his feet and tests his ankle. In the candlelight he can see that his knees are bleeding. He pulls up his trousers and sits at the table, facing the wall. He feels violated. Is this what Emily's rules were to protect them from? He hears Ada go up to the crog loft and shortly after she comes back down, her shoes echoing against the wooden stairs. He feels the suck of the wind as she opens the front door and listens to the cottage sigh as it slams behind her.

Rules of an open marriage #14:

Never treat each other like second-class partners

London, May 2016

'Mum, can we go somewhere in the summer holidays?' Sam says, shovelling mouthfuls of cereal into his mouth with his left hand while texting with his right.

'I'm not sure, babe – it's pretty last minute, everywhere will be booked . . .'

'Our exams are finished by mid June and then we're free. Please? It can be an exam celebration.' Emily considers it. It'll be cheaper out of season and she hasn't been paying the boys much attention lately.

'I'll look into it,' Emily tells him. 'No promises.'

'I don't mind where we go; anywhere is better than staying here,' Sam says. Emily looks around the kitchen and out through the doors to the garden where their swimming pool is almost built in readiness for the summer.

'You don't have it so bad,' she says, slapping him on the shoulder. On the other side of the table Tom groans.

'It's because Amelie dumped him,' Tom says, with uncharacteristic concern. 'That's why he wants to go away.' Sam blushes and rolls his eyes. Tom grabs his bag. 'See you later.' Emily watches Tom leave.

'Are you okay?' she asks Sam. 'I liked Amelie – what happened?'

'That's not why I want to go away,' Sam says. 'It feels like we never spend time together any more.' Emily thinks uncomfortably of how preoccupied she's been.

'I'll do my best,' she tells Sam. 'What's with Tom leaving so early, anyway?'

'He's in love,' Sam tells her, and rolls his eyes. 'He walks partway to college with her in the mornings.'

'Really?' Emily says. She's lost track of the number of girls that Tom has dated briefly and then abandoned over the past couple of years.

'Yep.' Sam stands up and swings his bag over his shoulder. 'Gotta go, Mum. See you later.'

'Cereal, bowl, sink,' she calls out. He sighs and drops the empty bowl into the sink, where it cracks a glass.

'I'll talk to Dad about the holidays,' she tells him.

'Didn't realise you two even talk these days!' Sam says, opening the door. 'See you later.'

'I'll be home after you, remember?' she calls out, 'I've got my sportive today.'

In the bedroom she rummages through her drawer for her cycling clothes. She gets dressed quickly; Adeline will be here soon. She pulls on the padded shorts that make her waddle, and a long-sleeved top. Downstairs she runs through her checklist, helmet, yes, cleats, yes, hydration. She's glad to be busy. Empty hours have a way of leading her thoughts back to Ryan and she's doing her best to stop unravelling.

Last night he came home later than usual and went straight to the shower. She was in the kitchen preparing dinner when he came down.

'How was your day?' she'd asked him, focusing hard on the onion that kept slipping from her grasp. She tilted the tip of the knife and pressed down hard into the flesh, eyes watering.

'Busy – the usual, you know.'

'I know,' she'd said, running the tap to take the sting out of the onion. Her eyes still water regardless, but she does it every time just in case it will eventually work.

'Where were you this evening?' she asked him. He was sitting on the sofa with a newspaper on his lap. He opened it noisily and didn't look up as he answered her.

'With some of the lads from the office. You know, the bonding thing. Had a couple of pints in that pub on the corner.' He hates work politics.

'Who?' she said, chopping peppers.

'What is this, the third degree?' At this she'd stopped chopping and pressed her hands against the counter.

'I have a right to ask you who you were with. You are still my husband . . .' She hadn't smelled beer on his breath when he came in. He doesn't even like beer.

'Let's not do this now – I'm tired,' he'd said, striding to the door. She'd looked at the knife right there in front of her, sharpened just hours ago.

'Inconvenient is it, to talk about the elephant in the room?' she'd said. He'd paused then.

'What is it you want to know?' he'd asked, closing the kitchen door.

'Who is it?'

'Who is what?' he answered.

'Don't play games,' she said. He walked to the fridge and poured a glass of wine, then stood at the doors to the garden drinking it. She'd wanted then to tell him not to say it. To put her fingers in her ears.

'There is someone,' he said finally. 'I didn't mean for it to happen. Emily, look at me. I'm sorry.'

'You're breaking the rules. No repeat performance, remember?' It's all her bloody fault, if she hadn't insisted on their freedom perhaps they wouldn't be here now, like this.

'Pardon me for forgetting about our regulations.'

'Why don't you end it?' she asked.

'I don't want to.' She waited for him to continue. The silence stretched out like string.

'Right,' she said. 'Is there anything else you want to tell me?'

'Not that I'm aware of,' he answered. 'Is that it?'

She could have driven a spear into his heart. Torn his eyeballs out with salty hands. He walked towards the door. Her eyes flicked to the knife on the counter.

'You don't get to walk away,' she said.

'I think I do,' he replied.

'End it,' she told him.

'Are you going to make me?' he asked. She shook her head, willing herself not to cry. 'I've waited for you so many times,' he said. 'You can wait now.'

'I'm not sure I want to,' she said.

'Says the hypocrite.'

'It's different,' she said, 'and you know it. Are you willing to do this to the boys?'

'They don't need to know,' he replied.

'It's pretty fucking obvious. They're not idiots,' she said. He stared at the floor.

'No. But hopefully we can minimise any disruption to them.'

'Where were you last week?' she asked.

'Work, I told you.'

'I know it wasn't work, stop playing me for a fool. You came back wind-burned and glowing. Work doesn't do that to you.' Ryan pulled a chair out from the table and sat heavily.

'We went to Wales.'

'Where did you stay?'

'Does it matter?' he asked. *Yes*, she longed to say, *it does matter. I want to picture the room you fucked her in and the position of the bed. I want to know what you see when you opened your eyes in the morning and whether you think of me when you slip your fingers inside her. I want to know whether for a single tiny moment you feel regret. I want to know if she thinks it's funny, how much you eat after sex. How you breathe out between your teeth after you come.*

'No,' she'd replied. It'll pass: the novelty, the tackiness of the hotel rooms and the synthetic sheets; the affair will be transitory and without substance.

'Emily, I—'

'Who is she?' she asked. At that moment Sam walked in on his phone, oblivious to the conversation. They suffered through dinner, which felt stilted and awkward, and after, when the boys were in their rooms, she'd turned to him.

'Okay, you win. Let it run its course.' He simply nodded. She knows that to force his hand now will end badly for them all. She doesn't want to insist that he ends the affair, doesn't want to watch him pining for someone else. It's not without its risks, though, the card she's played. She's gambling on him getting bored and on loyalty winning. It's hard to quantify love. Georgia would have a field day if she found out.

Outside a horn toots. Adeline. Shit. Emily grabs her kitbag and wheels her bike outside, locking the door behind her.

'Hey,' Adeline climbs out of the car and opens the boot. 'Just put it in here, if you remove the front wheel it should fit. How've you been? Feels like ages since I saw you.'

'What, a whole three weeks?' Emily laughs.

'Everything okay at home?' Adeline asks.

'He's fucking someone. He told me,' Emily says. She looks sideways at Adeline, who is focused on the road.

'No shit. That sucks. Can't say I'm surprised though, you both seemed pretty uptight when I saw you at the club,' Adeline says.

'Were we?' Emily asks. Adeline nods and shifts gears.

'I sense these things,' she says. Emily looks out of the window.

'How do you feel about it?' Adeline says, as an afterthought.

'I suppose it was inevitable really,' Emily replies. 'What will be will be.' She doesn't want to talk about it, she's realised. 'How is your fuck buddy?'

'That's over. Turned out he was into some seriously kinky shit, even by my standards,' Adeline says. Emily stops her imagination wandering.

She navigates bus lanes and cycle paths aggressively to get them to Crystal Palace where the ride starts.

'Not scaring you, am I?' Adeline asks, nodding at Emily's hand on the grip rail. Emily removes it sheepishly and pushes it under her legs. 'We'll aim for the sixty-mile route. We can drop out sooner if you're struggling but I'm sure it'll be a breeze. Feeling confident?'

Emily nods. The truth is she's not, she's terrified, and as they park near the starting line she realises that cycling for fun is a world apart from this organised event. Hundreds of people in Lycra swarm the car park in various states of undress. People brazenly rub cream between their thighs and in the case of a woman nearby, on her nipples. She raises her eyebrows at Adeline, who looks like she could be in a photo shoot. Always at ease no matter what the situation. Emily envies her easy confidence.

'Chafing,' Adeline says.

'I feel sick,' Emily replies.

'It's good to push yourself out of your comfort zone,' Adeline says. 'Come on, you'll be fine.'

The first twenty miles are glorious, the sun is out and the roads are quiet. They cycle alongside each other, chatting. At the first snack station they eat enough calories for a week. But at twenty-five miles Adeline speeds up and Emily's energy is waning. She manages to keep her in sight and draws level at a crossroads.

'I need to rest for a few minutes,' she shouts to Adeline, but Adeline doesn't hear her and pulls out. Emily follows suit but is forced to pause halfway across as a car speeds through, and she doesn't get her clips out in time. She falls heavily on her right side, the bike trapped between her legs.

'Are you okay?' A man on a bike beside her dismounts and puts out a hand.

'Thank you,' she replies, mortified. There's a graze along her thigh and a bruise inside her knee. She doesn't see Adeline until the finish line, where she's waiting by the side, cheering her on.

'You did brilliantly,' Adeline says, hugging her.

The changing room is split into mini cubicles designed for one, but Adeline follows her in.

'We can chat this way,' she says, peeling off her jacket. Emily hangs up her towel in silence and sits on the bench, reaching down to remove her shoes gingerly. 'Are you okay?' Adeline asks. 'You're very quiet. Didn't you enjoy it?'

'Well, I didn't think I'd be doing it by myself,' Emily says, abandoning any pretence at being adult. Adeline flinches slightly, then sits down beside her.

'I'm sorry,' she says, 'I got carried away. I was making good time and thought I could beat my PB. I got distracted. It was selfish.' She leans forward to remove her shoes. 'Jesus, what happened to your leg?'

'I fell,' Emily says, tears springing to her eyes. What's wrong with her today? Adeline bends down to get a closer look, resting her arm in Emily's lap.

'Does it hurt?' she asks, touching the graze with her other hand. Her elbow is pushing into Emily's groin, not unpleasantly, and Emily wonders if she should say something. 'It'll bruise badly,' Adeline says. Emily shifts slightly back into the bench. The room feels too close, full of the smell of their sweat, and there's a fuzzy feeling in her head, like the one she used to get as a child when she'd watch someone concentrating on something without them knowing. She's holding her breath and is horrified to feel a familiar pulsing beneath Adeline's elbow. Adeline doesn't know, she can't know what she's doing, her movements are too small, too discreet to be intentional. But Emily does, and it feels wrong, but she's caught up in it now and before she can break the moment, she's come. It happened so fast. She stifles a gasp with her hand and Adeline kicks her shoes off and sits up, looking straight into Emily's eyes. 'Did I hurt you?' she asks, and Emily shakes her head. Adeline puts an arm around her shoulders. 'I am sorry about earlier – I'm a lousy friend. I'll make it up to you.' She finishes changing her clothes and waits for Emily by the door. 'Do you think you'll do it again? The sportive I mean,' she adds, when she sees Emily's face. Emily can't look her in the eye and is quiet on the drive home.

'Are you okay?' Adeline asks her when she's pulled into Emily's drive.

'I'm just tired,' Emily replies, opening her door.

'Emily if there's something I—'

'I'm fine Adeline, really. Just not used to cycling so far.' Adeline puts a hand on Emily's shoulder.

'If there's anything I can do.'

'You've done more than enough already,' Emily says, stepping out of the car. Instantly she feels lighter. She takes a deep breath. 'Take care.' She shuts the door. Adeline winds down the window.

'See you soon for lunch, then?'

'Sure,' Emily calls back over her shoulder as she unlocks the front door.

*

The house is empty, the ghosts of its occupants in every room; an empty mug and cereal bowl in the lounge, an empty crisp packet on the counter. There was a time when walking into this house was a warm glass cocoon. Now more often than not it's empty and all she can hear is her footsteps. She walks the kitchen floor to the fridge and pours herself a glass of wine. It must have been a mistake, what happened with Adeline. And anyway, she doesn't like women now. Not like that. Not any more. The phone rings and she ignores it, refilling her glass, which she has half downed. The phone rings out and Emily paces. Why now? Perhaps it's all a reaction to Ryan's fling, her anxiety playing tricks on her body. Everything's heightened, alert. The phone starts to ring again and Emily lifts the receiver from the stand, not recognising the number.

'Hello?' she answers.

'Emily.'

'Leo. You—' How did he get this number?

'I can't do it; I can't do the right thing.'

'I heard you transferred onto another course?'

'Yeah. It's not the same,' Leo says, his voice breaking.

'It will take time.'

'I don't want time. It's driving me crazy. Everything comes back to you. The corridor where we talked about Joyce and you telling me to see through the bleakness. The library where we sat. The car park, the place where I always watched you leaving.' She sits on the bottom of the stairs with her feet tucked below her cradling the glass of wine, the phone curved against her neck.

'Please, listen,' Leo says.

'How did you get my home phone number?'

'It's written on the handset. I saw it when I came round. Don't you want to be wanted?' he says. 'I want you more than I've ever wanted anything.' Emily rubs her hand across her forehead. 'Look, I've got a proposal for you,' Leo says. She should tell him to stop. She should put the phone down and block his number. She badly needs a shower. She moves the phone away from her face and places her finger above the red button. If only it were so easy to erase things. To forget.

'Arthur Schopenhauer, have you heard of him?' he asks. She puts the phone back to her ear.

'The nineteenth-century philosopher, you mean?'

'Yes. In *The World as Will and Representation* he argues that beneath the world of appearances lies the world of will, a fundamentally blind process of striving for survival and reproduction.' He takes a deep breath.

'You're not exactly—'

'Hear me out. The whole world is a manifestation of will, including the human body; genitals are objectified sexual impulse, the mouth is objectified hunger.'

'It's not doing it for me, Leo.' She laughs and then regrets it. She doesn't want him to think that she's laughing at him or worse, not listening.

'Schopenhauer believed that the most powerful manifestation of will is the impulse for sex.' She'd forgotten he was studying philosophy too. 'He said it's the will-to-life of the yet unconceived offspring that draws man and woman together in a delusion of lust and love.'

'That's romantic. A delusion.' She laughs again; she can't help herself. 'Are you reading this from a script?'

'Harsh,' he says, 'Hear me out. BUT he claimed that with the task accomplished, their shared delusion would be broken, gone, *kaput!*'

Now she sees where he is going with this.

'You're not proposing we—'

'I think it will cure me. You too.'

'Leo, I told you, I'm not—'

'What you say and what you show me are two different

things, that's part of the problem. I know you better than you think.'

She won't deny the truth in this; she's known it from the moment they met. When she's next to him the urge to touch him is so strong that she has to hold her own hands. They never run out of things to say and he properly listens when she talks.

'Look, it doesn't hold true. If it did, why do so many people stay together?' she says.

'We try to override our instinctual desires with intellect. Marriage is just an institution established for the greater good – its foundations are biblical. But it's outdated and restrictive; that's why so many people are unhappy and can't make it work. Please meet me. Just once. I think it will fix us.' She's never told him about her open marriage. It's one of the rules. She, at least, respects them.

'It's not that simple,' she says sadly, thinking of his allegations. To lend them substance would be disastrous.

'You're not my teacher any more,' he says. 'And I promise to withdraw my allegations if you just do this for me. If not for yourself.' The inkling of something is starting in her head. What better way to prove that she's into men? To blast any romantic notions of Adeline out of the water? She wouldn't be breaking any rules and what has she got to lose? Ryan has drifted, the boys are almost gone. Her career is on the brink of being dismantled, her reputation damaged irreparably. She closes her eyes against images of Adeline in the changing room, the curve of her breasts. The longing she'd had to touch her and her fierce shame after. Why shouldn't she have sex with a handsome young man if she has the opportunity? Isn't this the very freedom that her marriage affords her? She imagines Ryan with his ongoing lover and a rod of rage runs through her. A few moments and it would be over, done, and perhaps then she wouldn't be having an orgasm from the touch

149

of someone's elbow. Maybe there is some truth in Leo's theory, after all. How would they know if they didn't test it? But then she catches sight of herself in the hallway; a harrowed forty-three-year-old, skin starting to crumple around the edges. What is she thinking? He's jeopardised her job and stalked her, pestering her relentlessly. He's clearly unhinged; to take things further would be to play with fire.

'No Leo, we can't. Please don't call me again.' Replacing the phone on the handset she walks quickly upstairs and undresses and climbs into the shower. She runs the water so cold that her skin goes numb.

Rules of an open marriage #15:

Remain in control

Wales, early hours of Tuesday 19 July 2016

In the middle of the night Ryan wakes disorientated. Sitting up, he leans on one elbow and swallows hard. His throat is dry and sore. He reaches for his phone and it illuminates briefly before the battery dies and the room is again plunged into inky darkness. It's 3 a.m. Everything hurts; his head, his knees. Even his penis is aching. He is bruised.

Slowly the buzzing in his head subsides and the sounds of the forest return. An owl calls. He rubs the tattoo on his arm. He gave up trying to see them long ago. That's why Emily encouraged the tattoo. A reminder that not everything can be captured. Reaching into the pocket of his jeans beside the bed he fishes out two pills, cold and smooth. He lays them on his tongue. Reaching for the glass beside him his hand catches the edge of it, knocking it to the floor. Water trickles across the sloping floor and he hears it fall drop by drop onto the top step, then the next. The glass rocks on the floorboards. He swallows the pills dry and they scratch his throat.

Under his pillow is a torch and he reaches for it. Sliding his hand between the sheets and the pillowcase he waits for his fingers to touch its cold metal shell but they find only the rough cold stones of the wall behind his head. The moon glimmers through the open shutter. It's too cold to sleep with it open but he's glad now for the light that sketches the contents of the room: a chair, the glass on the floor beside him. Ada's empty side of the bed. He listens for any sound of her downstairs, but there's nothing. Surely she should have come back by now? It's been hours since she stormed out.

They should have put a lamp up here, but in their impatience they forgot. He swings his good leg over the side of the mattress and then his bad one, ignoring the throbbing pain as he stands. Hobbling to the window, he looks out into the darkness. Perhaps she is fetching something from the caravan. She wouldn't think twice about crossing the field at this time of night, path lit by torchlight.

Standing stiffly and propping one hand against the wall, he pees into an empty flower vase that he finds on a shelf. The hot stream splashes noisily against the glass and the smell of ammonia is reassuring. He's functioning, at least.

Lowering himself back onto the mattress, he adds Ada's pillow to his own and props himself up. His head is still pounding. Without meaning to, he falls asleep and when he wakes again she is still not there. He is reminded of the times as a child that he would wake in the night, banned by his father from leaving his room. The hours spent sitting motionless in bed propped on one elbow, muscles rigid with exhaustion and head riddled with fear, listening to his mother crying. He watches the open window. The sky above the tops of the trees brightens as the darkness dilutes. As the sun rises, the shadows in the room change and then comes the sharp, electric morning light that picks out each detail more sharply. He looks at the creases of the quilt upon his legs and the flat, smooth other side of the bed. He thinks then of Tom and his headache returns along with a dull ache at the back of his throat. He remembers snatches of last night and feels nauseous. He needs to charge his phone so he can call Emily. The charger is downstairs. Tom could be in trouble for all he knows; what is he doing here when his son could be dying? He wishes he'd gone home yesterday when he could, that this day had been started at home in London where he belongs. He wishes that yesterday had not happened, that the brutality of last night could be undone. That his time at the cottage was untainted. He's angry with himself for falling for Ada's tricks and her manipulation, but he can't displace this blame. He put Ada above his son and he can't undo it. Well, he can change it now, get in the car and drive away, be back by lunchtime. Leave Ada to her fun. She's a grown-up. He sees the game that she is playing, forcing him to choose between herself and his son. Tom and Sam win, every time from here on in.

Going down the stairs is slow, each stair a potential liability. He plugs his phone in and puts the kettle on, rubbing crusted blood from his cuticles where her nails dug in. She was rougher than he realised. Too exhausted to shower before bed, it had taken all of his strength to make his way upstairs. He throws cold water on his face and catches sight of himself in the bathroom mirror. Just the faintest hint of a bruise across his left cheekbone. If he didn't know where to look, he wouldn't see it. His shoulder throbs when he peels off his top and he inspects his back, but there's no visible damage. He should never have let it go as far as it did. He struggles to reconcile her in his head. He was drunk; she must have been too. If only he'd gone back to London.

He opens the door to the cottage and steps into a bank of mist that creeps in from the coast. It's cool on his skin and a welcome relief after the temperatures of yesterday. Outside, the car is still there, so wherever she has gone, she's on foot. Anyone else and Ryan would be worried to think of them out at night alone, but Ada belongs here, moving among the cool water and the brittle mountains without hesitation or doubt.

On his way to the ridge he sees her underwear, discarded and covered in dew. He blocks an image of him crouched between her knees; his need to punish her surpassing desire.

As the phone rings at his house in London, Ryan realises it's too early to call really, not yet 6 a.m. Emily picks up on the second ring, breathless. Before she can speak he does.

'I'm sorry, I'm coming home, I'll be there by lunchtime,' he tells her. She talks over him, telling him not to come. She got a call from his girlfriend Ella's parents in the middle of the night. They had tracked Ella and Tom down and interrupted a road trip. They'd found them checked into a hotel in Dover and halted their plans to cross the Channel the next morning. They brought him home.

'Dover?' Ryan cuts in. 'Where the hell were they headed?'

'God knows.' Emily says. 'Her parents checked her emails and Facebook account and found a message in her deleted items that gave them away. They said Tom had planned the whole thing.'

'Look I should come back,' Ryan says. 'What a mess.'

'I wouldn't bother,' Emily says, 'I'll deal with it.'

'But I—'

'Don't bother, I mean it.'

He makes a decision back at the cottage. Still no sign of Ada and it's been almost eight hours. Long enough to warrant a search. He finds his walking stick and a rucksack, throws in water and some fruit. Progress is slow and his ankle throbs. Sunrise sheds a milky glow across the sky, casting everything in hues of grey. As he passes the caravan the dejected door hangs off and the inside is clearly empty.

At the far side of the field behind the caravan is a gate that leads from their field into the woodland and it is here that he heads now. His head is clearing and clarity seeps in. When he's found her, he'll leave her. He's too old for these games. Yesterday was a glimpse of what lies ahead. It was reckless, dangerous even. Unforgivable to put her before his son. At the gate he leans briefly, one hand on the post, and looks back towards the cottage that grows smaller as the darkness shrinks back. There is a movement among the trees that catches his eye, but when he peers into the green darkness, it is still. He wonders how anything grows where no light can reach.

Descending into the valley below, he cups his hands around his mouth and calls out her name. It echoes down the valley and ricochets into the mouth of the lake quarry. Emerging through one of the disused access tunnels for diggers, he is confronted with the turquoise water that spreads the length and width of the quarry, flanked on all sides by forty-foot cliffs. Slate is heaped around the edges of the water casting silvery reflections on the surface of the water. There's no one here at this time of day, though he knows people use it for diving practice in the height of summer.

The cliffs loom over his head, the edges protruding above their foundations like diving boards. People regularly hurl themselves off the ledges at high speed into the water, though not everyone makes it. The path they need to clear to reach the water is wide and can't be seen from the top. In the time since they've had the cottage two people have died and local media is campaigning for warning signs to be displayed around the edges of the quarry. Ryan doesn't think it would make a difference; if anything, it might draw more risk-takers in. Some people are drawn to danger.

At the edge of the lake Ryan bends on his good knee and refills his bottle. The water is icy, from a spring. Glancing up, he sees a stag at the far side of the lake. It raises its head and watches him, its ears pricked, then bends and sips from the turquoise shore. Ryan replaces the cap on his bottle and stepping back slowly, sits down on a grassy bank. The sun is rising swiftly and the glint from the water dazzles him. He shelters his eyes and sees the stag turn away, back towards the disused tunnel. A doe and two fawns teeter towards him, and as they grow closer he sees that one of them is limping. The stag and doe rub faces as the injured fawn struggles and falls, its mother nudging it up again with her legs. He contemplates trying to capture the fawn to get it to a rescue centre, but he knows it's a ridiculous idea while he's barely able to walk himself. He'll do some research later; perhaps someone can come out to take a look at it.

Standing, he winces. His ankle has seized up and the heat of yesterday is in the sky. He makes his way down the south side of the escarpment below the quarry and pushes through dried bracken and fallen trees. There's no sign of Ada or anyone else. He should go back to the cottage and wait; it's possible she's already returned and if he were a gambling man he'd put money on Ada surviving far better out here than him. Making his way slowly back to the cottage, he remembers a story his mother used to tell him about the lady of the lake. A beautiful damsel who lived alone on a rock beside the water was spotted by a farmer who fell in love with her. Romance ensued and she gave up her solitary life to live with him in his village. She bore him three sons and at first all seemed well, but in time her behaviour became increasingly erratic. When she professed to have special powers of intuition, the farmer worried for her sanity. She did not take well to his cynicism and in time she returned to her lakeside, leaving the farmer and their children broken-hearted. Be careful who you choose, his mother told him.

He sees the police officers before they see him. Their car is parked outside the cottage, one officer standing leaning against it and the other sitting inside with an arm flung out of the window. Realisation slams into him. As he gets closer, the man in the car climbs out and the two men walk towards him. Fear pricks the back of his neck.

'A oes gennych eiliad ar gyfer rhai cwestiynau?' The older officer asks him, holding out his hand. Ryan shakes it.

'I don't speak Welsh.'

'Nid yw'n siarad Cymraeg' the older man says to the younger one, who now speaks.

'Do you have a moment for some questions?' he translates.

'Of course,' Ryan tells them. 'Please, come in.' The officers are hard to understand, their dialect strong.

Ryan leads the way, leaving his walking stick outside the front door, walking for the first time in two days without support. He is excruciatingly aware of Ada's underwear still outside in the grass, sodden in dew. He half expects to find her inside making breakfast, but as soon as he opens the door he knows she is not there.

'Please, sit.' He gestures to the armchairs and the officers do, removing their hats. 'I think I know what this is about,' he says.

'We have some troubling news,' says the younger officer. Ryan swallows hard. This is insane – she couldn't have. He should have leapt from the flagstone floor yesterday and to hell with his ankle, run after her into the open night and begged her to come back. What right did he have to send her spinning to her end? The pain in his chest is sharp and very real. He catches his breath and holds it. He puts his face in his hands.

'The body of a woman was found close to your house. By a local farmer,' the officer says.

'*Marw*,' adds the older man.

'Dead,' the other officer clarifies.

'Where was she?' Ryan asks, sitting up straight and pushing his hands under the cushion of the chair.

'Just over there,' the younger man says, gesturing to the forest beyond the fence.

'We think she was out walking. There was an accident. A leg broken in three places. Nobody would have heard if she had called. It's unusual for someone to go missing at this time of year. Weather is good, visibility high . . .' The officer trails off when he sees Ryan's face.

'Are you okay?' he asks. Ryan nods, standing and moving to the door. He needs air. The young officer walks to Ryan and puts a hand on his arm.

'We thought you should know, given your proximity to where she was found. There may be further inspections of the area. We wonder if you've seen or heard anything unusual?'

'When did you find her?' Ryan asks, pushing back the well of nausea in his throat. There are so many questions he doesn't want answered.

'Three days ago,' the older officer replies. Ryan turns, unsure that he heard right. Three days. THREE DAYS!

'There was no one here when we found the body, that's why we came . . .' Ryan pushes down on the door handle and stumbles out of the room into the sunshine. He lifts his face to the sky and thanks a god he does not believe in. The officers follow him out.

'I'm sorry,' Ryan says to them, 'I thought it was someone else.' The officers exchange looks.

'It was hard to identify her body – she'd been there for weeks,' the younger officer says, 'but we know now that her name was Marlena, thirty-six years old and on a hiking holiday with friends.' Ryan stifles the urge to laugh out loud. It was ridiculous to have assumed the worst. Ada is invincible. They look at him strangely and he sees himself through their eyes, grinning absurdly in the face of a death.

'Why don't you sit down and we can talk this through,' the younger officer says without smiling, leading the way back inside.

'It was a case of mistaken identity, sorry,' Ryan says, rearranging his face into a more sombre expression and sitting down. 'I thought it was Ada. My partner', he adds. 'We had an argument and she walked out.'

'And your Ada? How long has she been missing?' the young officer asks, frowning.

'Since yesterday,' Ryan says, 'but she'll come back; she always does. A hiking holiday you say?' Uneasily, he remembers that blistering hot day in June.

'If you did see or hear anything the coroner may want a statement from you,' the older officer says stonily. 'As you can imagine, her family are desperate for answers.'

'I remember,' says Ryan, 'I saw her friends when they were looking for her. I forgot about it until now.'

'Anything else you might have forgotten?' the officer asks, casting a look at his colleague and rolling his eyes. Ryan shakes his head.

'She didn't have a phone or an emergency flare on her. It's possible she died of dehydration,' the younger officer tells him. 'Though we've got to consider all possibilities.'

'Of course,' Ryan says, 'her poor family and friends.'

The younger officer speaks, animated. 'Yes, a shock to the community. Not often we hear of unexpected deaths round here. Most are on the coast – swimmers, climbers. People who don't know the area taking risks. But this was an ordinary hiker on a walking holiday.'

After they leave, Ryan sits for a long time staring at the unlit fire. He considers the bottle of wine he saw in the fridge this morning but decides against it. He wants to be sober for when Ada returns. He should feel worried at the thought of her enduring another night outside. He thinks of the walker and how many different sounds of life she must have heard in her wait for death.

Rules of an open marriage #16:

Have faith in intuition

London, May 2016

Monday and the week has started badly. The call from the college came just after lunchtime. Sam was playing cricket and they think he's broken his collarbone. The timing's terrible. He's got his first exams next week. So now Emily is on her way to St George's Hospital, window down and humid air clogging her lungs. She never wanted Sam to play any dangerous sports but Ryan insisted and so followed years of freezing on the sidelines of rugby fields and cricket pitches, stamping numb feet against frozen earth or baking in the sun. She took her little boy, whom she'd cossetted against the world in soft mittens and babygros, and thrust him into a pitch where parents gathered round like pit bulls. It felt counterintuitive to clean his wounds and ice his bruises and send him back the following week. It builds resilience, Ryan said, still proud of the crooked finger from his own youth.

A bus honks as she swerves to avoid a cyclist and she slams her fist down on her horn. Bloody buses, the dinosaurs of the London roads, still thinking they own it despite the growing web of cycle lanes that suggest otherwise. She used to love going on buses when the boys were small. It was the highlight of the day for them, back when she was not working and they were not in school. She's stuck in traffic beside a park and, nearby, children are playing on the swings, their mothers sitting on a blanket beside them in deep discussion. Everyone looks happy and relaxed. She never could adjust to the social structure that having children brings. She envies their slow movements and easy smiles, the way their children run to them for a snack or a tissue now and then. There is a whole chunk of life that she has missed out on that cannot be clawed back.

She remembers Ryan's disappointment in the early days when he'd return from work to find her sitting in a dishevelled lounge, lights down and the boys with their noses pressed to the telly. *You should go out with them*, he'd say, *do child-friendly things*. *They're happy with this*, she'd insist, one eye on the clock, waiting for it to hit 5 p.m. so that she could have a glass of wine. *It's all they know*, was his standard reply, the look on his face far worse than any reprimand. That first walk to the bus stop was a milestone. She remembers the joy of leaving the house, the freedom. There was no stopping once they'd started. They travelled the entirety of London by bus. Never-ending day trips of packed lunches and parks. *Bus* was Sam's first word long before he managed Mum or Dad. But once again Ryan didn't approve, insisting the boys would be better off at toddler groups and Monkey Music mornings. 'You don't understand what it's like,' she told him.

She crawls into Tooting Broadway, another area where Ryan wanted to live that she wouldn't consider, now unaffordable. The transient and fickle housing market has no loyalty to anything but money. She'd like to move out to the country where the air has room to move and the sky stretches infinitely, where the rain when it comes is wet and cold and doesn't stick like glue to clammy skin.

She daydreams about a writing cabin by the sea, the only

distractions the calling birds and the singing waves. She has enough to buy somewhere modest, just. She's made enquiries. But it would be every penny she has saved. Ryan's never bought into her dream of having a second property. *Why commit to one location when you can travel freely?* he says. Maybe now is the time to do it, while he is distracted.

Back home the proof of his betrayal is on the table. She opened the letter addressed to him this morning. She's never opened his post before. She'd expected it to be some sort of clue – a bill from a hotel, or a receipt. When she lifted the seal carefully, steamed from the kettle, she'd slid out the paper inside. It was a letter from a Welsh estate agent, particulars for a property in Wales. Nothing more than a bundle of stones really, though it promised so much more. A holiday retreat, a weekend idyll. A home away from home. *A chance to make your mark*, the description stated. She thought of the times she's implored him to consider a holiday home away from the city. The times she's dreamed of throwing their stuff into the car on a Friday and taking off somewhere else. The thrill of escape. It hurts more than his affair. She slid the letter back into the envelope and pressed the seal with clean, careful fingertips until it looked unopened. He'd never know and perhaps she'd never tell him. Perhaps it wouldn't matter in the end anyway. She considers telling Adeline about this latest indiscretion when they meet for lunch tomorrow. She didn't seem that interested in Ryan's affair last time they met, so perhaps she won't. She feels slightly sick at the thought of seeing Adeline again after their last encounter.

The car park is heaving, cars crawling in ant-like rotation waiting for a spot; the ticket inspector is spotless in his blue suit and weaves between windscreens peering through his reflection to inspect dashboards. Emily sighs and taps her fingers against the steering wheel, trapped now between an MPV and a Beetle, unable to go forwards or backwards. *It's not serious,* they'd said when they rang her, *people break their collarbones all the time — it's just painful and takes time to heal.* *There's no bone breaking through the skin,* they'd told her, *surgery won't be necessary; no damage to the nerves in his arm.* *He'll still be able to sit his exams.* Her phone rings and she answers it; it's Ryan.

'I haven't seen him yet . . . not serious, no . . . no rush, I'm here . . . Sure, see you at home.' She puts her phone back in her bag and jumps as the car behind her swerves angrily around her and into the spot she's had her eye on. Finally parked, she navigates the ticket machine, which is accepting only coins. She doesn't have any and the emergency button for assistance doesn't work, transmitting a piercing crackle that hurts her ears. She leaves a note on the dashboard and follows signs for A & E. Distracted, she finds herself in a waiting room in the oncology department. She turns to leave but stops. At the end of the row next to a small table piled high with magazines is a water cooler. She is so thirsty. Beside her an elderly man stands shakily and inches across the room where he fills a plastic cup. Painstakingly he carries it back across the room to where Emily is standing and passes it to an elderly woman who accepts it without thanks. As he turns and starts to head back across the room towards the cooler, Emily goes over.

'I'll get it for you,' she says gently, placing a hand upon his arm.

'There's no need, dear,' he says softly.

'I know,' Emily says. 'Please, let me.' He tilts his head and nodding agreement, shuffles back to his seat beside the old lady. When Emily brings him the water he looks at her with watery eyes rimmed pink.

'That's very kind of you. Are you here alone?'

'I'm lost, actually.'

'Aren't we all?' He leans forward and Emily mirrors his movement, ignoring the eyes of the nurses at the reception desk.

'I'll just ask reception which way to go,' she says. 'I'll be fine,' and she pats his arm with familiarity.

'We all think we're fine until we're not.' He strokes the back of the hand of the woman beside him who in turn looks up at Emily, smiling weakly. 'Mildred here, fine for eighty-two years and then wham, out of the blue it came, and knocked her sideways.'

'I'm sorry,' Emily whispers, 'I hope you recover soon.' Mildred has started weeping, silent tears that she makes no effort to brush away. *We are all reduced in the end,* Emily thinks, *one way or another.* Back in the main corridor the Tube rumbles beneath her feet and through the linoleum floor. The signs for A & E are highlighted in neon yellow and she wonders how on earth she missed them the first time round. She spots Sam straightaway, with his sweaty windswept hair, right arm in a sling. He's pale, his hair even brighter than usual. He leans into her hug and she strokes the back of his neck with her hand.

In the car he rests his head against the window and groans.

'I'm such an idiot,' he says, 'I should have jumped out of the way of the ball. It was going too fast.' Emily laughs.

'You're only human. We all make mistakes.'

At home she settles Sam on the sofa and goes into the garden with her mug of tea. Though it's only May, the promise of summer hangs in the air, oppressive and thick. The pool, which is now fit for use, beckons tantalisingly. Five minutes later and she's in, braced against the water as it envelops her. Shoulders down quickly. She remembers the drill. As a child she loved the trips to the seaside: the suck and pull of the tide against her sinking toes; the salty taste on her fingers and the promise of fish and chips after, the scent of vinegar lingering in her hair long after the gulls had eaten the last of her scraps. And now as she feels the drag of her body against the water and her heart quickens, she is decided: she will buy that cabin of her dreams. The boys will love it and she'll use it more now that they are older. They can even take their girlfriends there. Finally she'll have somewhere to make her mark, her own small dent. She swims until her feet are numb and her fingers blue.

Halfway up the ladder and reaching for her towel, she sees Ryan heading towards her, beer in hand.

'How was it?' he asks, nodding to the pool behind her.

'Good,' she answers, pulling her towel around her quickly, feeling exposed.

'I can't believe I haven't tried it yet,' he says.

'Well, you know . . .'

'I know, if I were here more then I would . . .' She shoots him a look and he throws his free hand in the air. 'I have a lot on at the moment, come on . . . How's the patient doing?'

At that moment Sam appears at the glass doors, and Ryan kisses Emily's cheek; 'For the sake of appearances,' he whispers. Emily recoils through icy skin. She loathes these false displays of public affection. Conversations are essential and bearable; around the boys they manage a sense of joviality. When she told him she'd booked the holiday he couldn't even feign excitement. The sensation of his lips against her skin irritates her as if there are barbed thorns beneath her skin, their pointed tips pushing determinedly against her dermis from the inside.

'Mum, what's for dinner?' Sam asks. Glad of the distraction, she walks barefoot back to the house. She hasn't seen Tom come home, and putting down the saucepan, Emily goes upstairs to his room. The door is shut and she hears a giggle, then a laugh. Not Tom's. She braces herself, then turns the handle and pushes the door open.

'What happened to knocking before you enter?' Tom says. Emily's eyes adjust to the dimness of the room and makes out Tom sitting up in bed with no T-shirt on.

'Do you have to live in darkness?' Emily says, walking to the window and opening the blinds. She turns back towards the bed. The quilt beside Tom unfurls itself into the shape of a girl. In the bright light from the window Emily sees her blush, her dark hair hiding her eyes.

'Mum, this is Ella; Ella, this is Mum.'

'What happened to our rule about not closing doors when girls come round?' she asks Tom. He stares at her in fury.

'I'm sorry Mrs Bradshaw, it's my fault. I suggested it.' Ella sits up straighter and pulls the quilt up to her chin. She looks so young.

'We'll talk about it later, Tom. Get dressed,' Emily says. 'You should probably get yourself home, Ella.' She always thought she'd be the liberal mum, the envy of her son's friends with their conservative, stifling parents, but this is pushing it. Tom's sixteen but Ella looks younger. Jesus Christ, she could get in trouble.

In the kitchen she washes her hands and feigns a lightness that she doesn't feel. She's made carbonara, Sam's favourite, and he seems in good spirits if slightly high, the co-codamol doing its job. She hears the front door shut. Ryan raises his eyebrows at Tom's absence and she ignores him.

'Are you here tomorrow?' she asks Ryan. 'In the day, I mean?' He nods. 'Good, I have a lunch appointment but Sam needs keeping an eye on,' she says. 'I've said he can stay at home and revise and just go in for his exams next week.'

After dinner she goes back up to Tom's bedroom. This time she knocks. He's on his computer and refuses to meet her eyes.

'We should talk about what happened,' Emily says.

'I'm not a kid, Mum,' he says.

'How old is Ella?'

'Sixteen. What does it matter?'

'Of course it matters. I can't have this happening here, on my watch, do you understand?'

'Is that all you care about, it being on your watch? How it will affect you?' Tom says.

'Are you using contraception?' she asks. Tom drops his head into his hands.

'We're not idiots.'

'Am I really such a selfish person, Tom?' she asks. He doesn't answer. She gives up.

Downstairs she opens her laptop. She sets filters on property websites, selecting her criteria – budget, location, sea view. There was one she fell in love with years ago. An old fisherman's cottage in Dorset perched upon a rock, sea crashing below. 'Think of the floods,' Ryan had said. 'Think of the storms,' she'd replied, a flutter of excitement in her chest. Damn his opinions and her capacity to listen, empathy her greatest strength and flaw with its willingness to bend. Two bedrooms would be nice but one would be fine – the boys can sleep on the floor. She goes for function over design and soon has a shortlist of three for further consideration, all within a five-mile radius of each other, chain-free and looking for quick sales. Thumbing through her diary, she's surprised how little is in there and remembers the days where she longed for some space between the lines. She could go down to Dorset at the weekend; the boys will be busy and Ryan's away again. A road trip would be fun. She'll book herself into a B & B for Saturday night and set off at dawn. She can already feel the coastal breeze against her skin.

The next morning she wakes to the sun on her face. Ryan has opened the window and birdsong filters in. He never usually opens the window at night; the caterwauling of urban foxes breaks through his sleep. He hates the cold in the winter and the pollen in the springtime that fluffs in his chest and throat. The arguments they've had about the window. He is still asleep

beside her. He used to be a poor sleeper, his dreams punctuated by nightmares and his eyes snapping open at the slightest
sound. Lately though, he sleeps deep and still. Turning back
to the window, she closes her eyes and drifts in and out of
consciousness.

She wakes again to the alarm clock screeching in her ear.
Fumbling on her bedside table she knocks the clock to the
ground where the back falls off, the batteries rolling across the
floor. Showering quickly, she dresses for the day. She doesn't
want to look like she put too much thought into her outfit,
so she settles on simple jeans and white shirt. Only she knows
about the lacy underwear beneath and she considers briefly
removing it for something plainer before chastising herself for
even considering that it matters. No one will be seeing it, that's
for sure. The jeans hang a little looser than they did before.
She scrunches her hair up into a knot and pushes her feet into
her Converse. On her way out of the room she shakes Ryan
awake. Tom's door is closed and when she pushes it open his
room is dark and smells of incense. She flicks open the blinds
and opens the window wide and he stirs somewhere beneath
his pile of covers.

'Quick, you'll be late for school and you can't afford to do
that now.' He'll be lucky to pass his GCSEs at this rate. He
mutters incoherently and she pulls his covers back; his hands
bolt out and grab them, pulling them back up.

'Leave me alone, I'm ill.'

'Ill? Weed hangover more like.'

'Mum . . .'

'Get up, Tom,' Emily says. As she closes his door behind her
she hears him pulling himself heavily out of bed. Down in the
kitchen Sam is already at the table eating cereal.

'How are you feeling, love?' she asks.

'Sore but okay.' Always a trooper, more straightforward
than Tom by half.

'Make sure you take your meds, okay?'

'Do you think I can swim?' Sam says. She looks at him.

'Are you serious?' He nods.

'What do you think?' she asks, putting water into the coffee machine. Why is it every time she wants a coffee the beans are out, the water is empty and the dregs compartment needs emptying? Walking to the fridge, she holds a glass under the ice-maker. A slow hissing sound escapes. Out of water too.

'Morning.' Ryan walks in wearing his dressing gown, towel around his neck.

'That's just cruel,' Sam says as Ryan slides open the doors and disappears towards the pool.

'You'll be back in before you know it,' Emily says, kissing Sam's cheek. The rhythmic splashing of Ryan's swimming starts up.

'Mum, can you give me a lift?' Tom emerges.

'Jesus, you look rough,' Sam says. Tom grabs a fistful of cereal and jams it into his mouth. 'That's mine.' Sam grabs the cereal box with his good arm and waves it in the air.

'Mum?' Tom implores. Emily checks the time, she's meeting Adeline at midday – why are there always delays when she has plans? She's seeing their lunch as an opportunity to rebalance things, clear the air. They leave Sam in front of the Xbox and Ryan in the shower. Tom sits in grumpy silence beside her and when she pulls over he climbs out without kissing her goodbye.

'Later,' she calls to his receding back.

On the way home she picks up some fresh bread and cheese for Sam's lunch. Pulling out of the parking bay, she notices smoke coming from the bonnet. Shit. Halfway home the power steering goes and just as she pulls into their drive the engine conks out. Rolling to a silent halt, she pulls the handbrake on. Just what she needs.

An hour later and the recovery men are on their way. She'll have to take the bus to Peckham, where she and Adeline have agreed to meet. In his office Ryan lets off a sheen of good health; his skin glows and the room smells of mint shower gel.

'You off?' he asks.

She nods. 'Remember to make Sam take his medication.'

'He's a big boy, Em.' She glares at him. 'Okay,' he says, 'got it.'

The bus is half empty, a blessing because the heat rises in waves off the pavement and folds its way through the bus, stifling her. She climbs to the top deck and systematically opens all the windows, the air cooling as they gather speed. She checks her lipstick in her mirror and twists the bracelet she is wearing. Pulling out a book, she shifts back in her chair and jams her knees against the back of the seat in front.

The café is easy to find, squeezed in between a bookshop and a dry cleaner. The tables outside on the pavement are empty and Emily walks hesitatingly inside, phone in one hand. An elderly man nurses a cappuccino in a corner and a harassed woman with toddler in tow sits near the back, patiently trying to eat her croissant with one hand while preventing the toddler from pulling her hair with the other. A faded painting of an olive grove hangs on the wall. Emily checks her watch. She's perfectly on time. Back outside she chooses a table for two and orders a macchiato. Not that she needs any more caffeine charging through her blood. She sits on her hands to steady them. The minutes tick by slowly and she starts to worry. What if she's forgotten or changed her mind? She should have texted to remind her. She reaches in her bag and pulls out her book again. Her eyes graze the pages as her hands turn them, but she can't concentrate for the palpitating in her chest. Since the sportive she's been overthinking things. Adeline's texts have seemed distant, distracted. She'll give it half an hour and then she'll leave.

It's her fault she's in this position, friendless and desperate. All the years she's given up to Ryan's friends. The dinner parties she's endured all blending into one long ghastly show of self-promotion. She berates her foolishness for going through the motions despite her better judgement. The last real friend she had was Charlotte and she didn't even go to her funeral. Since then she's had a handful of fleeting acquaintances no more memorable than the man she buys her newspaper from in the morning. Even her sister is fixed permanently at arm's length. There's something wrong with her, something that people can spot. An impermeable knot in her centre. Even Ryan has veered away. Not veered, been pushed. She drops the book on the table and puts her head in her hands. She's such an idiot. All those years of convincing herself she was the ideal wife, playing the part. The perfect hostess, long-suffering dinner-circuit companion, selfless multitasking mother of two, patient and often solitary wife. Never once complaining about his trips away, their time apart.

The fleeting jumble of one-night stands, pleasurable for minutes but reduced to something shallow and dirty the moment she went home. Ryan always knew when she'd been with someone else, even when she stopped telling him, at his request. 'You're assuaging yourself of your guilt,' he told her, 'it's selfish.' So she wrapped herself in a cloak of secrets. She told herself that their marriage was better off for it, for her not needing him. Lies, she realises now, her independence a fabrication of her own invention; the other men a bid for attention; adoration for a moment better than none at all. How much braver it would have been to admit the truth, that she was scared he couldn't love her in the way she needed.

Now he doesn't need her and she has nothing to offer. Of course he will leave her for the other woman; it's foolish to wait in hope. She feels the loosening of his ties to her, to them. Only a matter of time before he goes and does not return. All the things that cannot be undone.

'Emily?' Raising her face from her hands, she sees Adeline in front of her, a look of concern on her face.

'Adeline.' Emily stands and leans forward, kissing Adeline on each cheek awkwardly. She should have hugged her instead. Why does Adeline have this ability to unnerve her, to throw her off balance?

'Sorry I'm late,' Adeline says. 'Timekeeping really isn't my thing.' Emily gestures to the chair opposite and dismisses her apology.

'It's not a hardship to sit and read,' she says, waving her hand to get the attention of the waitress.

'How are you finding it?' Adeline asks, nodding at *The Days of Abandonment* as Emily returns it to her bag.

'Heartbreaking, raw – have you read it?'

'Didn't appeal,' Adeline says. 'I like escapism.' Emily smiles.

'Nothing escapist about this story,' she says. Adeline orders a coffee and puts her sunglasses on.

'Glorious weather, don't you think?'

'Bit hot,' Emily answers. 'How've you been?'

'I can't believe we haven't seen each other since the ride,' Adeline says. 'Crazy, isn't it?' Emily is flung straight back there into the changing room, the heat of it. Leaning forward, Adeline lowers her voice. 'How've you been? You look different.'

'Everything's fine, I guess. And you?'

'From the beginning, please, every sordid detail.' Adeline grins and leans back in her chair, twirling a hair band around her fingers. Emily hesitates, unsure what she means.

'Come on, spill. What's going on with that student? I wanted to ask you before but I forgot.'

'What?'

'The hot one, from Dulwich Village.' What does Adeline remember that she doesn't?

'Nothing, really. He's just got a crush on—'

'Oh come on, I saw the chemistry between you.' Emily blushes and feels sixteen again. She sees herself reflected in Adeline's sunglasses. There's a hint of a smile in Adeline's tone. Emily feels mortified. First Leo and then the changing room, Adeline must think she is one hormonal mess. She clearly recognises Emily as a fraud, an imposter as both a wife and as a friend.

'Nothing's happened with Leo, but he wants it to.' Adeline reaches out her hand and places it on Emily's arm.

'And you don't?'

'It's complicated.'

'It didn't look like nothing, that night in Dulwich,' Adeline says. Emily changes the subject.

'Ryan's buying a place with his lover. In Wales,' Emily says. Adeline's face arranges itself in shock and she digs her fingers into Emily's wrist.

'What a shit,' Adeline says, at a loss for words. 'How do you know?'

'I saw something about a cottage, on the table. I shouldn't have looked. I wouldn't usually, but ... it's hard. I think Sam and Tom know something's up. Tom's stoned all the time and Sam seems needier than usual.'

'They're more resilient than you think, I mean, my God, if a shrink analysed my childhood I'd be in an institution,' Adeline says.

'The thing is,' Emily says, 'I was wondering whether you would have any idea ... who it might be, I mean.'

'You mean he hasn't told you?' Adeline says. She moves her hand back to her lap and shakes her head, rummaging in her bag for her phone, which has started ringing. 'I wouldn't have a clue, I don't know him that well; he was just a colleague, you know.'

'I wondered if you'd heard anything when you worked together . . . rumours, that sort of thing. I know he respects you,' Emily says. Adeline's phone beeps and she frowns and puts it on silent.

'He was always so professional, so focused,' she says. 'But these things happen all the time without reason. How's your sex life?' Emily blushes. 'Don't be coy.' Usual café talk for Emily is school runs and coffee, occasional small-scale gossip. 'Well, we don't have to if you don't want to,' Adeline says, 'I just thought . . .' She laughs disarmingly. 'I always go straight for the jugular, sorry.'

'It's okay,' Emily says.

'Okay?'

'Comfortable. Nice.' Emily cringes inside.

'Passionate!' Adeline laughs.

'You know what it's like . . .' Emily says, and instantly regrets it.

'I'm not sure I do,' Adeline says. 'People assume that all marriages are created equal, but they're not. What "comfortable" means for you might be a tempest for someone else.' In spite of herself, Emily laughs. A tempest indeed.

'We've always had different needs,' Emily continues. 'That's why it's so surprising, his affair I mean. The sex was always more important to me than it was to him.'

'It'll probably fizzle out. These things usually do,' Adeline says, dipping her finger in the cream from the rim of her cup.

'Spoken from experience?' Emily raises an eyebrow.

'Everything fizzles out for me eventually,' Adeline says, and Emily feels inexplicably sad. 'Look, should we scrap the coffee and go and get a real drink instead?' Emily nods and pulls her wallet out with a shaky hand, dropping a note onto the table.

In the darkened bar the awkwardness dissipates and Emily sinks into a leather sofa. Adeline sits opposite on the other side of the table and Emily has to strain to hear her.

'What are you going to do?' Adeline asks. Emily scans the room, a handful of people scattered in corners. Nobody she recognises.

'Wait it out, I think. Nothing else I can do, really. Unless I leave him.'

'Is that an option?'

'No. I owe him this.'

'Owe him?' Adeline pushes her chair back and walks around the table. She sits next to Emily on the sofa where her bare knee brushes against Emily's jeans.

'It's a hard institution, marriage, so I've heard,' Adeline says. 'Don't beat yourself up.'

'I just wish I knew who it was,' Emily says.

'Why?' Adeline asks. 'Does it matter?'

'What do you mean?'

'Does it matter who it is? Surely the issue is the act itself?'

'Maybe you're right . . .'

'I mean, you don't seem exactly spotless yourself.'

'What's that supposed to mean?'

'You know, with Leo,' Adeline says. Emily decides to come clean.

'Look, the truth is I can't remember a thing about that night after leaving the pub, apart from swimming and being really cold. So I really don't know what happened with Leo. I'm worried I—'

'I warned you not to go with him, but you wouldn't listen and off you went into the pavilion, leaving me waiting on the bench with whatsisname,' Adeline says. Emily reminds herself that it's dark in here and that no one can see.

'That's not what happened,' Emily says uncertainly. 'You saved me from hypothermia, remember?'

'That's an interesting way of putting it.' Adeline laughs and the people at the next table turn around. 'It was freezing, though,' she adds, 'so you got that part right. Do you really not remember? I came over to help but it was clear that you wanted some time alone with him, so I made myself scarce until you re-emerged, quite warmed up.' Her smile is wicked. 'You regaled me with a detailed account of the whole experience on the walk home, the roughness of the wood against your back, the release after all the months of resistance.'

'Resistance?' Jesus Christ. Emily wants to dispute this as nonsense. Adeline could have got it wrong – they were all off their heads – but how would she know about the waiting?

'You know – you trying to do the right thing for so long and then . . .' With Emily unable to respond, Adeline continues. 'Nothing illegal about it, though, he's a grown man. That's what you kept saying.'

She shouldn't have come here, shouldn't have met with Adeline, should have stayed at home wrapped in her secrets.

'He was a student, wasn't he?' Adeline says. Emily is beyond hearing, her breathing threatening to implode her chest. She thinks of Leo referring to that night. The song and dance she may have unwittingly performed. All the texts and emails that he's sent since. Her insistent denial.

'I think you got the wrong end of the stick,' Emily says in a small, quiet voice quite unlike her own.

'Don't worry, I'm not judging you. I didn't breathe a word of it to Ryan when he gave me a lift home the next morning. Your secret's safe with me.'

There's a flash of lightning outside the bar and a crack of thunder whips the road. Within seconds the bar fills with pedestrians seeking solace from the rain that has come from a cloudless sky and now lashes against the windows. The room fills with body heat and laughter.

'Crikey, it's Armageddon,' Adeline says, standing and reaching for her wallet. 'Another drink?' They drink and it dilutes what's been acknowledged. If she drinks enough perhaps these hours can be lost too.

'Look, I wanted to ask you something,' Adeline says. 'Why don't you call me Ada like everyone else? I don't mind.'

'I like Adeline,' Emily says, shaking her head. 'I don't want to be like everyone else.' Adeline leans over and brushes her fingers against Emily's cheek.

It's close to 8 p.m. by the time they stumble out onto the pavement, and Emily's discomfort has diminished in direct correlation to the increasing quantity of alcohol that she's consumed. They've tilted the world back on its axis. The rain has stopped and steam rises from the pavements, forming transient clouds. Adeline links arms with Emily, insisting that they stop for one more drink before heading home, despite the fact that it's clearly a bad idea.

The boutique bar she picks is small and intimate, tucked up an alleyway between a closed dry cleaners and a newsagent.

'Come on,' Adeline says, slipping her arm out of Emily's and grabbing her hand.

'Where are the toilets?' Emily whispers.

'I'll show you,' Adeline says. She leads her up some narrow stairs at the back of the bar and into a darkened corridor lined with William Morris wallpaper. Flecks of gold reflect the dim lights. 'This was quite something back in the day,' Adeline tells her, pushing open a double door, 'Some people say it was a brothel.' Emily stumbles into a room the size of her bedroom, off which several doors lead. In the corner is an armchair and a dresser, and along the far side of the room a long narrow shelf runs beneath a mirrored wall, lined with perfumes and potions.

'Very fancy,' Emily smiles. 'It's a Tardis. How do you know this place?' She peers at herself in the mirror. It could be the lighting, but she doesn't look too bad, considering.

'I'm doing some work here,' Adeline says. Emily goes into the nearest cubicle, from which she can hear Adeline humming to herself. She is tying her hair back in the mirror when Emily re-emerges. She washes her hands and dries them with a paper towel, then uncaps one of the lotions and pours it into her palm. It feels expensive and silky smooth. Emily rubs some into her neck and turns to find Adeline beside her, head bent close to hers.

'Smells lush,' she says, winking. 'Come on, there's something else I want to show you.' Turning left out of the bathroom, Adeline leads the way up yet more stairs to the top floor. Emily had presumed that there would be apartments up here, but there's no sign of residents or segregation, just another long narrow corridor of doors.

'Are we going to get in trouble?' Emily says, giggling.

'I do hope so,' Adeline says, testing one of the door handles, then inserting a key, a triumphant smile on her face. Inside the room there is an old-fashioned double bed and a sink in one corner. Adeline walks to the sash window and tugs it roughly. Emily hears the street noise flooding in. Emily peers out into the street below. She turns to find Adeline locking the door and laughs nervously.

'Are you kidnapping me?' Adeline walks across the room to Emily and takes her hands in hers. And now Emily is sure that Adeline knew exactly what she was doing in the changing room.

'I just thought you deserved to have some fun for a change, it's not fair that Ryan gets to have it all . . .'

'Adeline, I don't—'

'Shhh.' Adeline's lips are on hers and Emily kisses her back. She feels Adeline's tongue touching hers, delicate and probing. She feels the thrill of anticipation. She pulls away.

'I'm not . . . I mean, I don't,' she says. It's been more than twenty years since she was with Charlotte. The only time she's been with a woman. She can't do this. The years of inexperience are a hurdle she's not equipped to jump.

'Don't do what?' Adeline says, putting a hand around Emily's wrist and pulling her closer.

'This, with women.'

'Even better,' Adeline says, pulling her towards the bed.

'What if someone comes up?' Emily says. 'We shouldn't be here.'

'So many excuses, so little time,' Adeline pats the bed and Emily sits beside her. Adeline pushes Emily back and lies beside her, pushing her hair back from her face. Adeline runs her finger down Emily's neck. Emily wishes she hadn't had so much to drink. It's not that she doesn't feel desire but – Adeline slips her hand into the top of Emily's shirt and beneath her bra, and despite her reservations Emily's nipples harden. She thinks of Charlotte all those years ago. Adeline reaches with her spare hand for Emily's, and places it underneath her own top, against her stomach. Emily feels insecure. She is acutely aware of her own body: the scars from her caesareans; her breasts, which, though small, are no longer firm.

Adeline is unbuttoning her shirt and now her lips are on Emily's breasts, her tongue tracing their outline. Emily flexes her fingers against Adeline's stomach and moves her hand up, finding her breasts. She's forgotten how beautiful a woman is to touch. She pushes her back onto the bed and pulls up her shirt, feeling Adeline's nipples harden against her tongue. Her skin tastes sweet, like honey. Her lips circle Adeline's breasts and explore their fullness, so different from her own. Adeline breathes faster and she pushes Emily onto her back. She reaches for Emily's hand and holding it, slips it down inside the top of her shorts, which she has undone. It's a language that doesn't require words. Adeline wriggles out of her shorts and tugs down Emily's jeans, finding the side of her underwear and pushing it aside. She slips a finger inside Emily, then two.

Emily tenses up, her hand still against Adeline's underwear. Adeline grabs her hand.

'Like this,' she guides her and then Emily's fingers are inside Adeline and though Emily wants to do this and she can feel Adeline wet against her fingers, she can't find the rhythm, can't feel it either. She pulls back, trying to push away Adeline's hand from her body, pulling her fingers away from Adeline.

'I can't,' she says to Adeline, feeling shame flood to her face, 'I'm sorry'.

'You can,' Adeline says, and kisses her gently on her lips, her fingers still inside Emily. 'I know you can. We can try something different if you'd like,' she says, moving down Emily's body and kissing the inside of her thigh.

'Not here, not like this,' Emily says, twisting her body away. Adeline's fingers are pushing deeper now, and Emily feels panic rising. 'Stop it,' she tells Adeline, reaching down for her wrist and pushing it away with her foot. Adeline catches Emily's ankle with her other hand and Emily freezes, aware of her vulnerability and the fact that she is dry now and the friction of Adeline's fingers is starting to rub. Adeline laughs and lets go of her ankle, withdrawing her fingers slowly, rubbing her thumb over Emily's clitoris as she does so.

'I'm sorry,' Emily says, dressing in shaky silence while Adeline watches her. She wishes that they had just had their drink in the bar downstairs as planned and both gone home.

'You wanted me, I could feel it,' Adeline says, pulling on her shorts. 'I think you're scared.' The lamplight from outside the windows catches the definition in her legs, casting dark lines along her hamstrings, and shadows across the smooth sweep of her stomach. Adeline walks to Emily and puts her arms around her, running her hands down her lower back. 'Admit that you want me,' she says, kissing Emily's neck, and for a moment Emily is torn. She imagines the freedom of it, the start of something new, the release of the tension that is splitting her in two. She shakes her head and turns away. It wouldn't be the start of something but the continuation of something that she's spent too long trying to forget. She thinks of the time she's spent becoming strong and how even now she can feel the raw nerve that Charlotte exposed in her, her vulnerability too close to the skin. She'd like to inhabit Adeline's freedom, but she can't. So much for balancing things and clearing the air. They walk downstairs and skip the nightcap, parting ways on the pavement with an air kiss.

The next day Leo phones again. Her mobile this time. She speaks to him in the garden because for once the house is busy, Sam and Tom arguing incessantly and Ryan rallying for some peace.

'Did you think about what I said the other day?' Leo's voice is calm and measured and in control.

'Leo, the answer is yes.' She used to be a risk-taker, she used to be brave. She doesn't like the insecure version of herself that she's recently discovered. She's taking back control of something at least, and if she slept with him in the park already it's not such a big deal. Plus she'll do anything to clear up the mess at work, and Leo's promised to withdraw his allegations if she does this. She's well aware that she's breaking her and Ryan's long-standing agreement about repeat performances, but hell, he's breaking it too. She dismisses the thought that what she's about to do is paramount to prostitution, her name cleared in exchange for her body. The floodgates have been opened. There is a long pause and for a second she worries that she's being recorded. 'Leo?'

'Good. I'm glad,' he says finally. 'You won't regret it.'

She tells him that the rules are this. That it will be arranged by her, at her choice of location, time and date. That there will be no further contact after the event; this is a one-off arrangement. He will drop all allegations and make a formal apology to the dean, citing a crush as the reason for his perseverance. This is as much an experiment as anything else, and whatever they take from it, they take alone. They'll meet this evening, for it happens to be free for them both. 'Out two evenings in a row,' Ryan comments as she leaves the house.

She checks into the hotel she has chosen, close enough to be convenient, far enough away from home. At the arranged time of 8 p.m. she meets him in the bar. He offers her a mojito, but she turns it down in favour of a gin and tonic. 'It'll make you maudlin,' he tells her. 'Not a chance,' she replies. At precisely the time they agreed, 9 p.m. – not late enough for the alcohol consumed to dull their senses, but enough time for their drinks to seep into their veins, they make their way to the thirteenth floor, where she opens the door to room 133 and they enter. 'In Japan the hotels don't have a thirteenth floor,' he comments, 'they just skip it, twelve to fourteen, just like that.' 'We're invisible,' she replies, 'at least somewhere.'

Inside the room, she locks the door and they turn off their phones. She secretly checks for hidden cameras, though she knows this is paranoid behaviour and there's no way that he could have known which room they were coming to. She insists they shower separately, and she spends extra time applying moisturising cream and cleansing herself with baby wipes. It's just one evening.

Showered and warm from the steam, she sits on the bed and he faces her, standing. Light flickers from a candle on the windowsill. With one simple movement he pushes her back onto the bed and unravels the dressing-gown cord from around her waist. She feels a surge of power; she owns this; she knows how it works. There is none of the awkwardness that she felt with Adeline. She is at ease and in control. It is the antithesis of the previous evening, and even before he enters her, she knows that she needed this affirmation.

She'd been worried that he'd be too keen and ruin it, but

the reality couldn't be further from the truth. He is slow and considerate and she rises to meet him, equal. She thinks of Adeline as she does. Afterwards, when they lie together, he rests his hand upon her hipbone and, despite her insistence that they should sleep, she finds herself aroused again by his body, disproving Schopenhauer's theory beyond a shadow of doubt.

Rules of an open marriage #17:

Remember that fights are about feelings, not facts

Wales, Wednesday 20 July 2016

Ada climbs into bed during the night. The chill of her wakes him and she smells of earth and bracken. He cradles her gently, a wild thing prone to flight. Any thoughts he had of leaving are gone along with the policemen.

Early morning and she's still there, left arm flung sideways and palm upturned; hair strewn across her face. The shutter bangs on its hinges and rain heaves itself through the open window, a thin line of water trickling its way to the stairs.

She stirs in her sleep, unfurling. He pulls her closer and feels the warmth of her. Bending to brush his lips against her cheek, he tastes the salt of yesterday on her skin and smells the forest in her hair.

'Where did you go?' he asks her, and she shakes her head. He pulls her closer as if he can become her. He wants to see what she saw. He could not get any closer if he unzipped her skin and pushed his desperate face against her bleeding heart. It is not enough and never will be. The realisation is hollow. He lies back against his pillow and she turns, hair tumbling across his chest. The room is charcoal grey.

'You're hurt,' he says to break the weight of silence. He points to the shin of her left leg, where a long scratch drags itself from ankle to knee.

'A hazard of the forest,' she smiles. 'Too many trees.' He strokes her hair. 'It was inexcusable,' she says, 'my—'

'Shhh.' He presses his finger against her lips. 'We're both culpable.' He imagines her moving through the forest past where the dead walker had lain before. Among nocturnal animals; long limbs lean and glowing caught by the moon. The wild tangles of her hair as she snapped through branches and brambles. She is covered in scratches the breadth of a needle.

'That reminds me,' she says, 'I need to call a rescue centre. I found a fawn down by the water. It may be too late.' Pulling herself out of bed, she throws on her leggings and his T-shirt that's discarded on the floor. 'I won't be long.' He imagines her down by the quarry lake, skin goose bumped and icy among the slate heaps. The splash of her as she dives into the blue, sluicing him from her skin, pulling herself against the bottomless water.

He hears the creak of the cottage as the door opens. The brief wail of the weather as it attempts to enter. He tests his bad ankle. Today it is back to normal size and the ache is dull. Not broken. In the kitchen he makes a coffee and hums while he puts away the crockery. Maybe they can get out for a walk later, if Ada wants. He is uneasily calm and wonders if he is missing something. In the shower he turns his face to the scalding water and opens his mouth, feeling the water run through his hair and eyelashes. In the mirror his cheeks are pink and shiny and his eyes bright. Dressing quickly, he puts his jacket on and leaves a note for Ada on the table, *Gone to the shops, back soon.* Outside he puts the key in the key safe, snapping it shut with a click. The car revs into life beneath his fingers and he accelerates quickly through the gate, which she has left open, not wanting to lose momentum and skid against the new road, which streams with water from the mountains. A pool is forming by the gate.

In between the gates he drives with the windows open and the air whistling around his ears. Sheep graze the edges of the road and startle as he rounds corners; one refuses to move as he swings open a gate. For a moment he thinks that it might charge him, but it scampers away at the last moment. Six miles, but it may as well be triple for the time it takes and still he doesn't mind. The landscape is devoid of humans, as if he is the last man on earth. He doesn't see a single person until he reaches the town.

He wonders if Emily would like it here.

In the supermarket he pushes the trolley slowly, lost in thought.

'Hello there.' He looks up to see a middle-aged lady smiling at him. 'Gywneth,' she says by way of explanation. He scans her face and now he remembers. She is their second closest neighbour, a big old farmhouse on the bend of the road between the fifth and sixth gate, perched on the edge of the hillside where the forest breaks, revealing the estuary and Snowdonia beyond. A sheepdog that runs outside, barking as he passes.

'Of course.' He smiles and puts out his hand. 'Nice to see you.'

'How's it going down there? Are you in yet?' she says, shaking his hand. He remembers Ada saying that it was Gywneth who recommended the plumber they used.

'Yes, thanks for your recommendation – you'll have to come and visit,' he says.

'That'd be lovely, you're here for a while this time are you?' she replies. He is reminded again of what a small community this is, reassuring and unnerving in equal measure.

'Just a few days this time, but back in a month – we'll knock on your door.'

'Lovely,' she says. 'We never go far. I promised your wife some eggs. I may pop them by when you've left next week; she'll be glad of company, no doubt. Not sure I'd want to be down there alone.' Ryan starts to move away, then stops.

'What do you mean, alone?' Ryan asks. Gwyneth looks up from the eggs that she's inspecting. 'What do you mean she'd be glad of some company?'

'It's remote down there, poor love. I felt sorry for her when her car wouldn't start that time. She was drenched through by the time she made it to our house to use the phone.' He disguises his confusion, inspecting the sell-by date on a carton of cream.

'Yes, of course. Thanks,' he says quickly.

'What are neighbours for?' She smiles. 'Have a good day. The weather's supposed to break – could be in for some sun.'

The checkout lady recognises him too.

'Welcome back. Here for a while?'

'A week, but it's almost over.' Ryan puts the milk, wine and eggs on the counter.

'Horrible business up near you, wasn't there recently? That poor woman.'

'Yes,' Ryan replies, resisting the urge to run. If London is the city of anonymity, this is the rural antonym. He counts out his change carefully. 'Awful. I've only just heard.'

'Puts us back on the map, though not in a good way,' she says, smiling sympathetically as she places the items in the bag. 'It's not the first time that there's been tragedy round you, though the other stuff was before your time,' she adds, passing his receipt.

'I couldn't comment,' he says, knowing that he is being cruel by denying her this chance to gossip. He turns to leave, but as he does so she calls out.

'Some say it's the fault of the forest, you know.' It's inevitable that folklore and myth carry more substance here.

'Well, it is a dark and dangerous place; a hazard for lost walkers, for sure,' he replies.

'It's not just that,' she says. 'There've been lights and voices. The farmers have seen them. They stopped for a while but now they're back. They say the dead come back to claim the living.' Ryan clears his throat and reaches for his phone from his pocket.

'Is that the time? I must get back.' The woman stands upright and folds her arms, her smile back in place.

'Good luck with it all. Give my regards to your wife,' she calls as he pulls open the door. Outside he scuffs the dirt on the pavement, puts the bag in the boot. They've been careful to avoid too much interest, protective of their peace. Now the death of the hiker has flagged their presence all too strongly and the whole community is talking about them.

Halfway back to the cottage he realises he's forgotten the bread, the whole reason for his trip. He remembers a Texaco garage closer to Fairbourne; it's worth a shot. Branching right off the main road, he navigates a further four gates and descends a perilously steep one-lane road, berating himself for his forgetfulness. What did Gwyneth mean? They always come together, bar once when Ada came to meet with the builders. She hadn't mentioned her car breaking down, or walking to the neighbour's house. This time he remembers the bread and throws in some croissants for good measure.

'How was the land of the living?' Ada asks when he walks back in. She is in the armchair beside the fire, which is unlit. The sun that Gywneth mentioned is forcing its way through the window and creeps its way across the flagstone floor.

'Great.' He leans to kiss her head. This is how it will be, civility and smiles, tiptoeing around one another cautiously. It's no bad thing. 'Did you get through to the rescue centre?'

'Yeah, they'll send someone down to take a look, see if it's still there. I thought I'd take a shower and then we could walk – if your ankle's up for it?'

'Sure. I think I can manage a gentle stroll,' he says knowing full well that Ada has never taken a gentle stroll in her life. Ada stands.

'I'm going to shower,' she says, stretching.

'Ada?'

'What?' She turns.

'Have you ever visited here without me?'

'Why would you ask that? Of course not.'

'I bumped into Gwyneth and she was saying something about your car breaking down . . .'

'You know how the locals are, Ryan, always looking for something to talk about. She must have got confused.'

She walks over to him and drapes her arms over his shoulders. 'Why would I be here without you? I'd be so lonely.' She kisses him on the lips. While she showers, he unpacks the food and heats the croissants in the oven. Why would Gwyneth make something like that up? Why would Ada lie? He lays the table and is slicing through the thick shell of the farmhouse loaf when she reappears.

'I wouldn't mind, you know, if you had come here alone,' he says.

'Are you still going on about that?' she says, and now she's defensive. 'I told you, she must have been confused. What is this, a cross-examination?' She crouches down and rearranges the logs beside the hearth. 'Shit.' She throws the wood she is holding on the floor and squeezes her hand.

'Let me look.' He holds her hand to the light and sees the shadow of the splinter outlined beneath her skin, the size of a grain of rice. 'Wait here.'

In the bathroom he rummages through the cabinet for the tweezers that he knows she keeps there and finds them behind the pills. Back in the lounge Ada is pale and seated. It is unlike her to be squeamish.

'I'll get it out,' he says, crouching beside her, though his ankle has started to throb again. He digs the sharp point of the tweezers into her skin and she flinches. 'I need to break the skin,' he explains, 'it's in too deep to find the end.' She grits her teeth and closes her eyes and he digs deeper, a spot of blood appearing. He moves quickly and fishes into the now open wound, where he can see the dark point of the fragment. He pushes the tip of the tweezers into her flesh, feeling it give beneath the pressure of his fingers. She flinches.

'Got it.' He holds the tweezers aloft triumphantly. 'Ada?' She is leaning forward, elbows on her knees and head between her hands.

'Sorry,' she says eventually, all the colour drained from her face.

'What's going on? Are you ill?' He asks, thinking of the pills in the bathroom. He passes her a glass of water and she smiles weakly.

'I have a thing about splinters. The way they sneak under your skin.'

'Brave enough to face the Welsh wilderness alone but floored by a splinter.'

'Don't mock me,' she says. 'It's a real thing. It's got a name and everything.'

'Really? Well, it must be legit then!'

'We've all got our weaknesses,' she snaps and turns away.

'I'm kidding,' he says. 'What's going on with you?'

He's had enough of the tug of war. He's exhausted. Standing at the table, he continues cutting the bread. Ada walks over to the table and fidgets with the jams that he has laid out.

'I found out something when I was away,' she says. The knife sticks and he saws harder. The loaf deflates in the centre under the pressure and the air that took so long to expand it squeezes out. She continues. 'I was right – there was a fire here. Someone died here, a child,' she adds. He thinks of the neighbour who knows her better than he thought and the checkout lady in town.

'How do you know?' He asks.

'I felt him in the forest,' she whispers, 'along with someone else. Marlena.' A chill runs up his back. He hasn't told Ada about the walker they found dead. How could she know? Ada starts coughing, her face flushing and her body convulsing with the effort to breathe. He grabs her hand and pulls her to the kitchen. He tugs open the oven and pulls out a tray of crisp, dark shells, dumping the forgotten croissants onto the side. Smoke pours into the room. He turns the tap on and leads her to the sink. She turns her face sideways to the water and drinks.

Afterwards he takes her upstairs and she lies pale and diminished on their mattress, face turned away from him. How on earth did she know about Marlena when he hasn't even told her? Back in the kitchen he throws the burnt croissants in the bin. Breakfast is ruined. Sunlight retracts back across the flag-stoned floor like oil back from heat. *There's been lights, and voices. The farmers have seen them. They stopped for a while but now they're back.* The checkout lady from this morning. Did Ada really feel something?

She's still resting when there's a knock on the door. He opens it.

'Huw?' He remembers this at least, the man with the sheepdog who rescued them when they were lost all those months ago.

'You've settled in, then. Nice to see you dressed.' Huw winks at Ryan's trousers.

'Come in. I'm Ryan,' he says, offering his hand. Huw chuckles.

'Thought it was Ben.' Ryan recalls the names that Ada gave him back when it felt like a game. Huw grins.

'Don't worry, I get it. I'm good at keeping secrets.' Huw's hand is tough and dry, the lines and grooves folding around Ryan's fingers like roots.

'Can I help?' Ryan asks.

'It's Ada I was looking for,' Huw replies, stepping inside the door. 'I bumped into her a couple of weeks ago and she was asking about the history of the cottage, told me to swing by.'

He removes his jacket, throwing it over the back of one of the chairs. 'I didn't realise that you'd be here.' There's a scratching at the door that Ryan has just closed and he opens it, jumping aside as the sheepdog runs in. It growls at him as it makes its way to its master's feet, where it sits upright, staring at the ceiling.

'She's sleeping. Can I help?' She never mentioned bumping into Huw, and the last time they were here was a month ago. Still, Huw's elderly, could be his memory going. Ryan's irritated by the insinuation that there's something private between Ada and Huw. He's old enough to be her uncle.

'Don't wake her, there's not much to tell,' Huw says. *Then why come?* Ryan wants to ask.

'Huw, you're too sweet.' Ada appears at the top of the stairs and leans over the bannister. Ryan wishes she would go and put some more clothes on. Her shorts and vest seem insubstantial. Huw stands, removing his cap.

'Ada, did I wake you?'

'I was just waking up when you arrived. Ryan, I was asking Huw—'

'I heard,' Ryan says.

'Shall we go for a walk, Huw, and you can tell me what you found?'

'Well, I—' Huw says, and at that moment the sheepdog bounds up the stairs to the crog loft, his growls erupting into barks. 'Sorry, don't know what's got into him – he's not usually like this,' Huw apologises and the barking continues.

'Why don't I make you a cup of tea?' Ryan offers, 'I'd like to hear what you didn't find out.'

'Really?' Ada says. 'I didn't think—'

'That I'd be interested?' Why is it that Huw always brings out the petulance in him?

'Tea would be great,' Huw answers. The dog runs back downstairs and follows Ada. In the kitchen Ryan can hear her talking quietly to Huw.

'Thanks, Huw, I didn't expect you to remember.'

'How could I forget when you asked me so nicely,' Huw replies with a twinkle in his eyes. 'They were asking about you the other day at the Crown, wondering when you were coming round again.' Ryan stops pouring the water, his ears peeled. They've never been to the Crown.

'There's not much to tell,' Huw is saying as Ryan walks in with the teas. 'This cottage has been empty since I was a lad, and anybody who knew anything worth telling has gone. Some people think this place is haunted, but I don't believe in ghosts.'

'But something must have happened for them to think that,' Ada says, leaning in, excited.

'There's a rumour that they left in haste, but that's it,' Huw says.

'So there wasn't a fire?' Ryan asks.

'There were always fires back then,' Huw says, 'Fire regulation is a recent thing, but you'd know that as architects.' He winks at Ryan, who doesn't remember telling him that they were.

At the table Ryan watches the way that Ada nibbles at the bread, breaking it off in small pieces. He swigs from his coffee. Ada watches Huw, who looks around the room.

'You've done a good job,' Huw says looking around appraisingly, 'I didn't think you'd stick it out. But don't get too comfortable: the land has a way of reclaiming its own. Everything is borrowed for a short time. These mountains and lakes will outlive us all and our worldly sins.' With this he looks at Ryan.

When Huw takes his leave the sheepdog utters a final bark towards the ceiling. Ryan watches them walk across the field and disappear into the forest. He can hear Huw whistling long after they disappear from sight.

'So you're none the wiser,' he says, turning to Ada.

'It was nice of him to come,' she replies. 'But something did happen here. I sense it.'

'He's a character.' Ryan scoffs.

'Don't be mean,' Ada says. 'He's wise.'

'Outlive us all and all our worldly sins? Come on, Ada, he's a fruit loop. Don't try and pretend that he's not.'

'He saved us that day we got lost, if it hadn't been for him—'

'We'd have got a little bit colder but we'd have been fine. And if he hadn't rescued us then we probably wouldn't have found this cottage either,' Ryan says. Ada fixes him with a withering look.

'And that would have been a good thing because?' she asks.

'I'm just saying that just because he happened to be in the right place at the right time doesn't mean that we owe him a debt of gratitude, or that we should trust him,' he adds.

'You're such a cynic sometimes, you know that?' She grabs her book and marches outside, slamming the door behind her.

Later, they walk along the Mawddach Trail. They don't mention their conversation about Huw. They've been meaning to explore the trail for ages and the route, though flat, is beautiful, tracing the disused railway track along the southern edge of the estuary. Ada delights in discovering abandoned pieces of equipment now overgrown with bushes along the edges of the track, leaving Ryan alone with his thoughts. He is grateful. He thinks of the marble rolling across the floor. Dislodged from hidden spaces.

'Isn't it tragic?' Ada says, catching up with him, 'that once survival depended on this stuff?' She holds out an iron hinge. 'The railways would have been the arteries of the country and now they're forgotten and rusted.' She pulls a weed out from the rim of a wheel. 'All those people thinking they were building longevity and prosperity and their efforts ended up like everything else, damaged and redundant.' Ryan glances at her sideways.

At Barmouth they find a pub and sit outside it on a wooden picnic bench overlooking the water. The sun is warm, though there is a ripple of ice beneath the breeze. He holds Ada's hand across the table and she lets him.

'What are you thinking about?' he asks.

'I'm wondering what you're running from?' she replies.

'What do you mean?' he says.

'This. You.' She throws her arm towards the water and the sunlight catches her golden hairs, her arm strong and tanned from the summer. Ryan shakes his head.

'I could ask the same of you,' he says.

She continues. 'First me, then the cottage. What next?'

'I'll remind you that the cottage was your idea. The seduction too.' All those months ago at the awards ceremony, after Emily left. The sheer force of her energy as she touched him. He wonders if flesh loses sensitivity over time. Whether a body becomes weary with the same repeated touch.

'You didn't object at the time,' she says.

'I didn't have a choice,' he says. Feeble but true. He removes his hand from hers.

'You have everything you need. You're rich and successful. Two sons, a beautiful wife,' she says, exhaling her breath slowly through her front teeth, emitting a soft low whistle. Her sadness sweeps across the table.

'When was the last time you saw Emily?' he asks.

'Months ago,' she says, carelessly. He's frustrated by her alternately verbose and ambiguous statements.

'Did you two fall out?' he asks, biting his tongue to stop himself asking more.

'Not really.' She sighs. 'Sometimes you meet someone and you think they're really special, you know, that it could be the start of something, and then you realise that you were just seeing what you wanted to, and you start to wonder if you just imagined it all in the first place. Seeing things because I want them there – it's the story of my life.'

Her lengthy answer unnerves him and he fiddles with the zip of his coat and shifts position on the bench. He feels his pulse beating in his neck. She tilts her head back and squints at the sky, running her fingers through her hair. She twists it into a bun and snaps an elastic from her wrist onto it, securing it.

'What happened to you, Ada?' he asks. She inspects her fingernails. He's glad that they are out in the open and in full sight. That he is forced to measure his words carefully.

'I've given you everything I am capable of giving,' she replies finally. 'What more do you want?' she says finally, laying her palms open upon the table, facing the sky. 'Blood?' The honesty of the moment is usurped quickly by this, and he's angry.

'That's not fair and you know it,' he says, aware of a twitch flicking in his left eye. 'You're impossible. Every time I think we're getting somewhere . . .'

'Getting what, Ryan?'

'Every time I think I might be capable of understanding you—'

'It's all about you, isn't it? Why's it so important to you that you understand me? I'm not a fucking puzzle. You want to dismantle me piece by piece until there's nothing left of me. If you had your way I'd be reduced to fragments and then you'd what? Compartmentalise all your favourite parts? Get rid of the bad bits, fix them?' She looks straight into his eyes and he feels the filaments of her anger in the air. 'Guess what, Ryan, I am an accumulation of the smaller parts, that's what makes me whole. You don't get to play the martyr and come along and fix me. I don't need fixing. I won't fit in your fucking box. Sometimes I can't breathe around you.'

'That's not fair,' he says, 'I don't want to fix you.' He's had this conversation before with Emily. This is what he does. 'All

I want is some honesty,' he says. 'Have you been coming here without me?' He thinks of Huw referring to the Crown.

'If you wanted honesty you shouldn't have started an affair in the first place,' she says.

'I'm sick of the riddles. I don't know what to believe,' he says. He thinks of the Jammie Dodgers and the neighbour's comment. 'I have sacrificed my family for this. Tell me something that makes sense.'

'There is no big reveal, Ryan, no great dark secret. Sorry to disappoint you.' She is crying and it's the first time he's seen her do so. She brushes tears away with the palm of her hand.

'Ada, I . . .' He reaches for her but she turns away.

'I think we should have some time apart,' she says.

Across the estuary sailing boats cut through the water towards shore, signalling the end of the day. Sunlight skitters across the broken surface and vanishes behind a cloud. Bells clang in the distance. He wishes he were out there with the wide sea beckoning, the narrow mouth of the estuary soon behind. The distance between them is too great to cross. He sees it clearly.

Rules of an open marriage #18:

Be willing to reassess the open arrangement

London, June 2016

The rituals families create to reassure themselves. An annual holiday; a Christmas-tree routine; a Halloween party. Traditions that hold them together like determined glue. Since the boys were born they've had an annual family holiday and this year is no exception.

Emily chose Annecy in France because there is cycling and hiking and a huge array of water sports.

'We could go sailing in Dorset,' Ryan suggested. She always hated sailing. It made her feel sick. She had no aptitude for it either.

'There's something for everyone here,' she told Ryan, though now they're here it's apparent that the one thing that Ryan needs is not.

The journey was interminable, the four of them trapped in the car for eleven hours. The Channel crossing was delayed and they'd been held up inside the tunnel due to signal problems. She'd stood leaning on the car looking out of the windows of the tunnel into the black space that was intermittently laced with lights and fire exits. She tried hard to forget that they were boring through the ground with the mass of the English Channel above them. When she was younger she'd imagined the tunnel to be see-through, a supersized aquarium with fish peering in. A mass of boats above her. Now she's glad that she can't see a thing, finding solace in the invisible.

The apartment they've rented is up in the mountains and Cézanne's landscape sprawls out below. Lake Annecy stretches as far as the eye can see and beyond the small clustering of hotels and restaurants around the edge of the water the mountains rise majestically. She anticipates elongated days spent paddleboarding and swimming, cycling and hiking. Some, however, have a different view. 'Punishment,' Tom said yesterday, moping in Ella's absence. 'Solitary confinement,' said Sam. It's a forty-minute walk to the lake and they've done it once, giving up before they reached it. 'Too hot,' they said. 'Spoilt,' she commented to Ryan, who ignored her. Ryan is distracted. So much for the hours of board games that she'd envisaged, idling days spent reading in companionable silence. She's missing a past that they've never really had. It's a fabrication in her head. When did they ever play board games? Not even when the boys were small. Two days down and five to go and she's angry again because it's clear that though she has brought Ryan hundreds of miles away, his other woman is right beside him.

She proposed a no-screen rule for their time here, but the response from the others was as if she'd suggested abstaining from food. It's quiet when they're all occupied. She checks her email once a day in the morning with a sense of dread. The WiFi is slow and the sender's name appears before the messages. Leo Sawyer. Three messages since yesterday. She hasn't seen him since their night in the hotel, nor responded to his messages. Hundreds of his words she has deleted and committed to cyberspace. Their arrangement is concluded and Schopenhauer's theory proven, as far as Emily's concerned. It's over. Leo has withdrawn his allegations and her name is cleared at work. Officially. Her boss was surprised, though knew better than to ask questions. She thought that would be it, but then the emails started. They're all the same. Declarations of love and accusations of penance. An insistence that they had something true. Callous, he called her. Heartless. She feels weary. This holiday is her celebration of the withdrawal of his complaint and he is tainting it. Not that Ryan knows about it. She's doing a good job of pretending that she's having fun, at least. A far better job than Ryan is.

Emily thinks of Adeline. She couldn't have predicted the way that things have unfolded. Adeline was insistent that they meet again after that night in Peckham but Emily refused. She ignored her calls. Adeline is everything that Emily longs for: freedom and instinct, cold-blooded desire. She is the ice-sprung fist of lake water and the screaming of muscles up a trail. A few days later Adeline turned up on their doorstep when Ryan was at work. This time Emily was ready, and willing to fall. She knew what she wanted and she owned it. She explored every inch of Adeline's body and it felt like coming home. Afterwards she held Adeline close. No more guesswork. One foot in front of the other; Emily was writing this path. She felt free. Emily hadn't realised that she'd been waiting for this release. Adeline is the persistence of the sunshine reflected in the water.

'Come on, we're going to be late,' Emily calls as she throws the sun lotion and water bottles into her bag. She's persuaded them to join her for a family experience of paragliding.

'Hardly a family experience if we're each strapped to a separate instructor,' Tom complains as they set off in the car.

Driving is a thrill as they wind up steeply to the Col de la Forclaz, which they will take off from. On the right the hillside drops steeply away towards the azure-blue lake while the road grows steeper. In Montmin they park the car and weave between the tourists and cyclists. It's a fifteen-minute hike uphill to the Col and although it's not yet midday, the sun is warm on their backs.

'Where do we land again?' Sam asks.

'Doussard,' Emily replies, 'over there.' She points towards a barely visible area of flat land in the distance, on the west side of the lake. Tom shields his eyes and squints.

'What if they miss the landing spot?' he says.

'They're experienced, Tom, they know what they're doing,' Emily replies.

'An instructor died last year on a solo flight,' Ryan contributes. 'Forgot to do up one simple strap and whoosh, free fell to the ground.' Emily bites her lip.

'Accidents can happen at any time,' she says. 'Think like that and no one would ever do anything.'

'Or maybe they just wouldn't go paragliding,' Sam adds. The narrow path broadens to a wide, flat area cluttered with instructors and nervous-looking punters. Children and partners sit along the bank on the right. Intermittently the tension picks up as the next paraglider prepares to take flight. Emily watches carefully, memorising the technique. There's a lot of time spent on straps. Ryan is silent beside her.

'Could you at least pretend you're having fun?' she whispers.

'How are we going to get back from Doussard?' he says. 'Our car is here.' Shit. She hasn't thought that far ahead. Doussard is miles away.

'How about I skip the gliding and meet you down there?' Ryan grins, and she wants to smack him.

'We could get a bus,' she replies.

'Or I could drive to Doussard?' Sam offers.

'Absolutely not,' Ryan and Emily chorus together.

'Look, it's no big deal, I can go another time,' Ryan says. 'You lot have fun and I'll see you on the other side. Keys?' He holds his hand out. Emily slams them into his hand with more force than necessary. He leans forward to give her a kiss. She turns a cheek and receives it coolly, furious. She prides herself on her meticulous planning and now the whole experience is ruined.

'Anyone else want to abscond while they've got the chance?' she says. Tom opens his mouth to reply but closes it quickly. Sam shakes his head.

'I'll wait and see you off,' Ryan says, setting off for the grassy bank where spectators sit.

They are introduced to their instructors: all men, Emily notices. Why do men still dominate adrenaline-fuelled sports?

'Are you nervous?' her instructor, François, asks.

'Not at all,' she replies, irritated by his tone. She can tell that Tom and Sam are though, Sam by his paleness and Tom by his lull in complaining.

'It's okay, you'll be fine. You wouldn't be doing it if it were unsafe,' she says. Sam snorts in reply. 'It's an adventure – try to be excited,' she adds.

'There's got to be better ways of having an adventure than throwing yourself off the edge of a cliff,' Tom says. In the distance Ryan waves his hand and smiles, giving them a thumbs-up.

'I bet if Ella were here you'd do it gladly,' Emily says. She knows it's cruel.

'I can't do it,' Sam says, pulling at the straps that have just been adjusted around his chest.

'Sam, don't mess with those,' Emily says.

'I can't do it,' he insists. 'Get them off,' he snaps at his instructor, who looks to Emily for guidance. She shakes her head.

'Life is full of things that scare us. We're doing this. It's all paid for and you are committed.'

'Well I un-commit,' Sam says, stamping his foot. People are starting to stare and Ryan is heading towards them now.

'What's up?' he says to Sam.

'We don't want to do it and Mum won't listen,' Sam says. Ryan turns to her.

'Look, Em, this is supposed to be fun, if he doesn't want to do it then . . .' She takes a deep breath.

'We all do things that we are scared of. Don't pander to fear.'

'Fear is a safety mechanism in humans,' Tom chimes in. 'It's when we ignore it that we are at risk.'

'For God's sake,' she says quietly, just loud enough for them to hear. 'What's wrong with you all?'

'What's wrong with *you*?' Ryan says loudly, and the conversations around them fade.

Emily flushes. 'Get them out of this kit,' Ryan says to the closest instructor, gesturing to Sam and Tom. 'We'll see you in Doussard,' he says to Emily.

So now she's here alone on the edge of the mountain, 1,250 metres up above the lake that spreads below them with an instructor pressed against her back. He's telling her to run. Fear fists in her throat. Her claustrophobia is kicking in and the urge to shake him off is strong. She's strapped to him so tightly that the ropes dig in to her thighs and shoulders. There's nothing to do but follow his instructions. 'You okay?' he shouts in her ear.

'Never better,' she says, forcing a smile and running until the ground falls away beneath them.

They're waiting on the field in Doussard and as soon as her feet touch the ground Tom comes running over. 'How was it?' She is unable to speak, so nods her head and smiles.

'If it was that good then why are you crying?' Sam asks. Ryan approaches nervously, fiddling with his hat in his hands.

'Em?' he says. She clears her throat.

'All good,' she replies. There was a moment there when she was floating between land and air. She was weightless and free.

'I'm sorry, Mum,' Sam says after she's been released from the instructor. 'That wasn't fair, leaving you like that.'

'It's fine, Sam, really,' she says, and she means it.

Holiday over and back in England and the only good thing about returning is Adeline. First Ryan announces that he is going to visit his mother for a few days next month. Emily wouldn't begrudge this if it were true, but she knows that it is a lie, not least because the night before he tells her she accidentally picks up the phone to her mother-in-law and is subjected to a fully fledged rant about sons and the rapid demise of the mind with old age. Though it was not remotely coherent, Emily did sympathise with the essence of the complaint, which was neglect.

Next Emily spots Leo loitering at the end of their road one evening when she is walking back from the shops. She recognises the shape of his body and the slope of his shoulders. He is on the phone, head down. She's wearing Sam's sweater and pulls its hood up, walking faster, her heart pounding. She hasn't had an email from Leo for days, which is unusual. No text messages either. But the next day she spots him, and the next. Each time she leaves the house her stomach clenches.

Rules of an open marriage #19:

Look after each other in sickness and in health

London, Friday 14 October 2016

It's been three months since Ryan last saw Ada; not a phone call, not a word since they agreed to have some time apart. This doesn't feel like space, it feels like amputation. The days have dragged themselves forwards. There have been positives, though. He's been around for the boys through the summer and taken Sam to university in Durham.

Emily's moved into her sister's temporarily with Tom. No words of fire have been flung between him and Emily. He hasn't felt comfortable pushing for anything greater than small acts of civility: the occasional family dinner, a pub lunch in the sun. If she'd been around, Emily would have noticed that it's over between him and Ada, but he's barely seen her. He wonders if there is someone she's seeing, but he doesn't ask, unsure what he'd say if there was.

Everything is protracted and he takes each day as it comes, not allowing himself to be hopeful. Time apart. The dreaded words of doom. He tells himself he's better off without her. Sometimes he believes it, but then he imagines life without the promise of snow-laced mountain winters and wind-brushed lazy summers, without palette-defying turquoise lakes. The cottage visits him in a state of decay when he's sleeping. Buildings flex around empty spaces. He dreads what he will find there. He considers where he and Emily can go from these once familiar walls that now divide them. It's impossible to imagine how they could bridge the gap between them.

Ada calls when the trees have started shedding their leaves.

'Hey, stranger.'

'Hey, you.' He had forgotten what her voice sounds like. He's so shocked he forgets to ask questions.

'Fancy a road trip?' And even though he's told himself it's over and even though he knows that it won't work, he's already packing when she ends the call.

The nine gates are interminable and in a state of disrepair, rusting and many of them held shut with loops of rope where the metal catches have broken. The road is potholed and littered with sheep that have jumped the crumbling walls of the fields. The summer has been unkind to the order of things. It's dusk as he turns the corner of the road to where the roof of the cottage is exposed and he's forgotten how quiet it is here. He's been wondering if she would be late again, whether she would keep him waiting, but her car is there, parked neatly to the side. He thinks again how little he knows her, always failing to predict. He relaxes. From the outside the cottage has survived their absence. The new roof is intact and the path to the door is clear and weed-free. A thin trail of smoke comes from the chimney and as he opens the door the sound of Einaudi reaches him. As he steps inside, a wave of emotion catches him off guard.

His mouth waters at the smell of food. Signs of Ada are lying around: a cardigan on the back of a chair, her shoes beside the door.

'Ada?' He peers his head round the kitchen door and sees

the casserole bubbling, the bottle of wine opened and ready. 'Ada?' He considers briefly that the date is wrong and she is not expecting him. He dismisses the possibility that she is with someone else. To cheat on your lover would be quite something.

It's hard to get lost here. She must be upstairs. He takes the stairs two at a time and she is there, strewn upon the bed, sleeping. It is not the warmly charged welcome that he had hoped for. They have only two days together and time slips quickly here.

'Ada?' He bends and sweeps a lock of her hair behind her ear and she murmurs to imaginary companions. Downstairs the casserole bubbles. Does she want to cause a fire? It's careless to leave things cooking and to fall asleep, the fire burning in the grate and the front door unlocked. He wonders if she treats all her belongings with such disregard. What kind of welcome is this for him, who has driven through the falling dark to be here, each gate drawing him closer to his cottage that he yearns for, and all after she asked him for some space? He could have chosen not to come at all. Should have, perhaps. He walks back downstairs, his feet louder than they need to be against the floor. In the kitchen he turns the stove down low and pours himself a glass of warm white wine. He puts more logs on the fire and then, zipping up his jacket, he walks up through the field behind the cottage to the ridge, where his anger pales against the vista of Barmouth and beyond it the sea. The lights of the coastline pepper the grey evening with shots of gold and the sea reflects them back, sparkling.

'Sorry, I didn't mean to fall asleep,' she says behind him. She is translucent in the light, hair glowing and tousled down her back. She pulls her cardigan up around her neck and huddles against him. 'Beautiful, isn't it?'

'How was your journey?' he asks, kissing her forehead. He'd forgotten what she smells like.

'Fine. Long.' She sighs. 'Dinner's ready when you are.' Walking back to the cottage from the ridge, he scans the black-and-white patchwork horizon, the squares of forest pitted against the paler rectangles where the trees have recently been slayed. The cottage is already in darkness in the crook of the valley. The first place to lose light in the evening and the last to be touched by it in the morning.

He watches Ada while she moves from cupboard to counter, counter to drawer. There's something different, but he can't place it.

'Did you change your hair?' he asks. She shakes her head and her laugh is velvet deep. She serves casserole onto plates and places them on the table. 'Are you not hungry?' he says, noticing her small portion and the way she picks at it with her fork, sliding off tiny morsels piece by piece.

'Overtired,' she replies, clinking her glass against his. 'Nothing a good night's sleep won't fix.'

'How've you been?' he asks her. 'Good summer?'

'Not bad,' she says, her smile not stretching to her eyes. 'You?'

'Same,' he says.

She leans towards him to remove his empty plate and he notices the etchings of time upon her face, the tiny lines around her eyes. Her skin seems thinner. She balances the plates precariously, waitress-style, upon her arm and her hands tremble as she moves towards the kitchen. He insists that she sit while he washes up.

Beside the fire she lifts her feet onto his knees and sinks back against the cushion, putting her book down on the side table.

'Gwenallt,' Ryan says, reading the cover. 'Where did you find that?'

'In the attic where I found the photos,' she says. 'It's beautiful.'

Before bed they shower separately. The water drains slowly and pools around his feet, threatening to spill over the lip of the basin.

'We should fix those pipes,' he says as they pass in the doorway. 'I brought new ones.'

'Leave it for another time,' she says, 'there's no rush.' He watches Ada's back as she disappears into the bathroom. Ada who never delays.

Listening to the hum of the shower, he heats the kettle for the hot water bottles.

'We're old before our time,' she comments on her way upstairs. In the bedroom she climbs under the covers fully clothed and he hesitates, unsure. She turns away from him and he notices the softness of her rendered sharp.

In the morning she sleeps late and he brings her tea and an OS map. Sitting up in bed, it's like old times, just them and the mountain. After breakfast he wanders round the front of the cottage, facing the trees that sculpt the mountainside. He listens to the sounds of the wind coming in across Cadair Idris, which dwindle to a whisper as they creep across the clearing in front of the cottage. Morning frost spreads across the bonnet of his car like stale breath. He hears the sighs of the valley and the creaking protest of the trees as they adjust to the mist lifting. Banking around the side of the cottage and looking up towards the ridge he sees the back of Ada in outline, facing the estuary below. As he draws closer, he sees that she is staring at her hands. She doesn't see him coming and when he slips his icy hands up beneath her windbreaker she gasps.

'I didn't see you – you scared me.' He notices the edge of her phone, which she has thrust hastily into her pocket. Earlier he convinced himself that he was being paranoid, that it was just tiredness after all. But seeing her in the white light of morning, he is not so sure.

'Is everything okay?' he asks.

'It's fine.' she replies. He quells his reservations.

'Shall I get on with the pipes?' he asks her after he's finished unloading them from his car.

'I was hoping that we could go for a walk while it's not raining,' she says. He looks at the sky and frowns – in the distance grey clouds hang like puffed curtains over the tops of the hills.

'Don't be a spoilsport,' she says, pulling on her walking boots. 'Winter will be here soon. Come on.'

They've summited Cadair Idris many times since their first disastrous trip, but this is the latest in season that they have walked. Already in the distance they can see the mist swirling along the top of the summit.

'Are you sure this is a good idea?' he asks Ada as they park the car in Minffordd car park. 'We'll be racing against daylight.'

'Don't worry so much,' she replies. 'We'll be fine, we know the paths.' The mist has started descending and the summit can no longer be seen.

'Come on,' she calls restlessly as he leans against the car and pulls his walking boots on. As they start to walk, the paths are steep and the mist has made them slippery. Usually the slopes are covered with plants, but now the ground is bare and exposed. The landscape is punctuated unevenly with moraines and cwms. The walk feels longer, the stiles higher. He cups his hands into fists to warm his fingertips. She walks a few steps ahead, stopping now and then to inspect the ferns that cloak the trees. After two hours of walking his legs start to cramp. They're near the top now and he struggles to catch his breath, while Ada walks precariously close to the edge above him.

'Look,' she says suddenly, holding out her arms. 'It's like flying.' She has grown wings, her coat billowing out behind her. The clouds are heavy and lint-stained and he feels them pressing down, smothering. Below them a sea of mist carpets the view. Their voices are muffled. The final ascent is treacherous, and the damp ground icy. He's bitterly regretting his inability to say no. He catches up with her near the top and though her smile is jubilant, she looks exhausted. They haven't seen a single person the whole way up.

At the summit he sits on a rock and pulls out a sandwich. The bread is soggy and the cheese rubbery. He passes one to her and they share coffee from the flask. They're 2,930 feet up, but they may as well be two feet off the ground for all the views that they have. Standing abruptly, she peers into the swirling mist. He glances at his watchless wrist and readjusts his hood, pulling his zip to his neck.

'We should get going or we'll be descending in darkness.'

'Look,' she calls, and she is so close to the edge that he cannot make out where the ground ends and the space begins. She is pointing and leaning out and one simple gust of wind could end it all. He follows her finger and, on cue, sunshine forces its way between the clouds, splintering light above them. Moisture mingles in the air and a rainbow is born, spreading widely above them. Ada's in silhouette now, beneath the ribboned colours, as if she's commanding the mountain. Head back and motionless, palms upwards. He is suddenly afraid of what is to come.

'Ada.' He approaches carefully, his hand out before him. She turns and her face is torn with grief. She's inches from the edge. He's never liked heights and as he looks down towards the lake at the bottom, his stomach lurches.

'They say that Llyn Cau has no bottom and that a monster lurks beneath,' she says, pointing to the lake below. 'It feels like it's waiting.'

'Why don't you tell me about it later once we're home,' he cajoles, as if speaking to a child. He's had it with her volatility and proclamations of second sense. His fingertips brush hers.

'We should go,' he adds, 'the weather's turning.' As he speaks, the clouds close up over the sun and the rainbow vanishes. Slow drops of rain land heavily against his skin. They could be at the cottage in front of the fire, or tucked safely inside their car. They could be sharing a pint down by the estuary or making love in the crog loft. The only reason they're here is because of Ada's impulsiveness and now disaster trips in his chest. He steps forward and grabs her hand hard. He's not letting go. Locking his fingers through hers, he pulls her away from the edge and she falls towards him, plunging them both to the ground.

'You nearly broke my hand – what were you thinking?' she says. He has landed face down on the ground and he turns, pushing her back roughly.

'What was I thinking? What was I thinking?' he shouts into her face, and his spittle flecks her forehead. She lies back on the ground with an expression he has not seen before.

'I'm sorry,' he says, easing the pressure on her shoulder. 'You scared me.'

'You're crying,' she says, and he realises that he is.

'I don't want to leave,' she says, putting her frozen fingers against his face. He sees the indentations of his fingers on the back of her hand and imagines that he is capable of being his father. The lines between passion and pain are so fine he can barely distinguish between them. He leans forward, cupping her face in his hands. He kisses her eyelids.

'It's okay,' he says. 'It'll be okay.' He wants to believe it.

Halfway down he loses sight of her again.

'Maybe we should spend the night here.' Her voice emerges through the fog that lies across their path. Ten minutes ago visibility was three metres but now it's one. He peers through it and makes her out ahead of him, standing inside a shelter. 'It's a shepherd's hut,' she explains. Inside it is small and snug with the remnants of a fire and a bale of hay against the far side. 'Cosy, isn't it?' she says, pulling him inside. He steps back outside.

'They say that anyone who spends the night on Cadair Idris will awaken as a poet or a madman,' she says, laughing. He ignores the hysteria lacing her voice. 'Which do you think we would be?'

'I'm not sure that spending the night is necessary,' he replies. 'Come on Ada, seriously, I'm getting cold.'

'Can't we stay for a little longer?' He sees dark shadows beneath her eyes, her sallow skin. The sooner he can get her back to warmth the better.

'Another time,' he says, taking her hand and leading her back to the path. They descend in the diminishing light in silence. His relief when he sees the car is palpable. Inside he turns the heater up and the windows fog, and when their silence becomes too much to bear he asks her.

'So what is it, what's wrong?' he asks, but she shakes her head.

Bathed and beside the fire, they eat leftover casserole and drink a Sancerre that he's saved for the occasion. They read their books quietly. There's no music tonight, no cushioning for missing words, and when they have gone to bed and are curled up like mice beneath the sheets, he asks again, 'What is it?' and the thing that she will not speak of cements itself between them and will not budge.

In the morning she is up before him and he thinks that she has gone for a run, but when he goes downstairs he finds her sitting at the table, poised, elbows upon the table. Without saying a word he pulls out a chair and sits opposite her. So here is her reason, why she needed space, why she made him wait so long.

'Ada, listen ...' he says. Perhaps if he keeps talking it'll be okay. She puts a finger to her lips to quieten him.

'There's no simple way to say this ...' She takes a deep breath and he wants to exhale and blow away the unsaid. He wishes that they were back in the shepherd's hut. This time he would stay there, curling himself around her to keep her warm. They'd watch the sun rise above Llyn Cau and see all the rainbows that the sky could make. They'd wither and grow old. He wouldn't complain. He'd give up everything. He already has. It was madness to think that he could ever keep her.

'I can't do this any more,' she says. He feels himself crushing inwards, slowly.

'Don't do this,' he says. 'Please.'

'It's over,' she says.

'We've only just started,' he says.

'It's not working, I'm sorry,' she says. He opens his mouth to reply but nothing comes. He wishes that she would stop talking.

'You owe me an explanation,' he says, 'I don't understand.'

'I've met someone,' she says. He pushes back his chair and it scrapes against the floor. He walks carefully, as if his legs don't belong to him. Facing the wall and curling his hand into a fist, he plunges it into the wall, again and again until the pain obliterates everything else and fragments of his skin and blood smear the stones. His knuckles may be broken but the pain doesn't come close.

'What is wrong with you?' he says. 'I don't believe you. It must be something else. What is it? Tell me, we can fix it.' She shakes her head.

'I've never felt like this about anyone before. I'm sorry. I wish I could have felt like it for you.'

'You're a fucking psycho,' he says. His anger rises in his throat. 'All the shit that I put up with from you. The risks I took, everything I lost. For what?'

'You're scaring me,' Ada says, but he can't believe that anything would ever scare Ada.

'I've given up everything,' he says. 'Why did you bother coming here this weekend, what was the point?'

'I had to say goodbye,' she says, looking out of the window at the forest, and he knows now that it was not him she came to say goodbye to. 'I didn't intend to hurt you,' she says.

'What the fuck did you think would happen, Ada? I'm a middle-aged cliché. Jesus fucking Christ.'

'I'm sorry.'

'Well, that fixes it all. I'll just run home and apologise to my wife for betraying her. If she's as understanding as you expect me to be, then it'll be no problem.'

Ada doesn't say a word, doesn't move a muscle. The pause stretches.

'Don't underestimate Emily,' she says at last.

'I thought you were going to tell me that you were sick,' he says, 'then maybe it wouldn't hurt. But this?' He puts his face in his hands.

'We're all dying,' she replies. 'But there's no date.'

'Who is the bastard?' he says.

'Does it matter?' she replies.

He walks to the ridge, where the wind rips his hair away from his flesh, pummelling his skin back from his bones in fleshy pockets. He contemplates hurling himself from the top, towards the water. He looks back at the cottage that could be a postcard, a note from the edge.

In the end they sleep, Ada in bed and him by the fire. The next morning they say goodbye. He looks at the sign they've restored that now hangs on the gate. Cyfannedd Fach – *small inhabited*. She'll sign the deeds over to him, she says. Her way of an apology. He won't be coming here again, he tells her. 'You never know,' she replies. She packs her bag and carries it to the car. She looks out at the forest and she is crying.

'I really love it here,' she says.

After she's left, he packs and locks up the cottage carefully. Leaves a note for the caretaker.

In the car he drives quickly, and with each gate he feels a tightening twist in his chest. With every mile the knot gets larger. He turns the radio up, drowning out the images of the cottage and the feel of it against his hand as he touched the walls for the last time. He wants the pain to swallow him. He knows that he will not go back to the cottage, that the forest will grow between its stones and the wind will sweep between the sheets; the rain will wash away their taste of one another. It was never theirs to take in the first place.

Rules of an open marriage #20:

Accept one another's flaws

London, July 2016

When Emily leaves the house, she is smiling. The property she's seeing in Dorset later is her favourite, on paper at least. She throws her bag in the passenger seat and pulls out onto the road, her smile vanishing as she sees Leo loitering by the postbox. When was the last time she walked carefree down her own street? What does he want from her? The deal is done, concluded. He glances up at her and she pretends she hasn't seen him. He's giving her the creeps. Ryan's away again, his 'mother's' trip. He left two days ago. As if he would visit his mother for anything longer than a coffee – he hates the characterless care home and its soulless spaces, returning each time sullen and quiet. She turns the stereo on and presses play on the *Desert Island Discs* that she has downloaded just for this trip.

Three hours later she parks her car on the side of the road, a foot from the edge of the cliff. It's good to get away from London. As she climbs out of the car, a handful of stones drop off the edge and bounce down the cliff towards the sea. Consulting her handwritten instructions, she locks the car and sets off on foot. One hundred metres down the road she turns right down a narrow footpath overgrown with black-berry bushes. They arch over her head and she is plunged into darkness in spite of the clear skies. She checks her instructions again. Past an iron gate on the right and a twisted old oak tree on the left. The cabin should be just on the left. She looks to the left but sees nothing but bushes rising to twice her height. She walks further but the path soon peters out to a patch of grass, dropping sharply to the cliffs again. The sea is still and shimmering. It must be here: there's nowhere else it could be. She walks slower back up the path, squinting into the blackness of the bushes.

'Mrs Bradshaw?' She spins around, disoriented. There's a face poking through the hedge.

'That's me.'

'It looks impenetrable but it's really not. The trick is to look for the red ribbon.' Leaning in, she sees it, more like a string, faded and wind-torn. 'Just push against the growth and it'll swing open. It's an ingenious design of the owner. The ulti-mate privacy. He grew the hedge onto a hinge. You'd never know it was there.'

She pushes it and true to his word, it swings open, a hobbit hole of an entrance that she has to bend to enter.

'I'm Richard,' he says, shaking her hand. She brushes leaves out of her hair and offers her hand.

'Emily.'

'As you can see, it's an acquired taste.' She follows him up a narrow path flanked by piles of driftwood. 'He's quite a collector. Brought it all from the shore. He's too old now for the access and is moving into a care home. It's heartbreak-ing really.'

He's already opened up the cabin and he leads Emily into a narrow hall. It's dark, with no source of light as far as she can see. She stands for a moment, allowing her eyes to adjust.

'So here you have the first bedroom . . .' He turns left and she is in a room entirely panelled in wood. 'Sorry, electricity's out.'

There is a tiny window at the back. It's laced with mould and mildew and when she tries to open it the handle jams. Richard clears his throat. 'A bit of TLC is needed, for sure. But the window faces the sea. It could be stunning.' The room has a single bed and a chest of drawers. At a push she could squeeze in a double bed with storage above it.

'Second bedroom,' he says, opening a door on the right. It's smaller than the first. No furniture in here aside from a desk in front of a window. Emily peers through the smoky layers of grime upon the glass. 'He's an artist, you see. Or was, before his eyesight went.' 'And here's the lounge. Or, rather, the rest of the house. I know not everyone's into open-plan living but . . .'

Emily stumbles on the third step. *Play it cool when house hunting,* Ryan always said. She can see the outline of her future self here, imprinted against the view of the sea.

'People are put off by the dirt and access,' Richard says apologetically, attempting to wipe a mark from the window ineffectively. 'Usually a place in this location would be snapped up quicker than hot cakes.' Emily walks the circumference of the open-plan living space that's the size of her kitchen. She wonders if Adeline will visit.

'It's chain-free so you could move quickly if you wanted,' Richard says. 'Reckon he'd take a lower offer too. He needs the money for the care home.'

The tour takes five minutes.

'I'll call you as soon as I get back,' she says. Richard has given up his sales pitch and is staring out of the window mesmerised.

'I know it's not everybody's cup of tea,' he says, 'But there's something about this place . . .'

'I get that,' she says, 'I'm going to explore a bit.' Pushing herself back through the bramble hedge, she follows the cliff path down to the sea. The tide is out and there's no one around. A cormorant basks on a rock.

It's mid-afternoon by the time she gets home and there's a bunch of red roses on her doorstep. The boys are at friends' houses and she's glad they're not here. It's the third day in a row that flowers have been left there. She cuts them into tiny pieces and tosses them in the bin. She calls Richard.

'I'll take it.' Within an hour he's checked with the vendor and they've agreed a price. With a cash purchase she could be in within four weeks. All the weekends she will have there stretch out before her. She can't shake the images from her head. Long scrambling climbs, skinny-dips first thing in the morning. She always wanted a dog. Even in winter she'll swim. She'll build a deck out from the house and sit there in the summer. In the winter too, with a heater. The doorbell rings. It's her sister.

'Sarah?' She never turns up unannounced. 'Is everything okay?' Sarah walks into the kitchen and throws herself in a chair. She looks dishevelled and hot.

'Matthew's asked me to marry him.'

'What? That's great, isn't it?' Emily says. Sarah fixes her with the long stare that she's perfected since their youth.

'You know how I feel about marriage. But I'm worried that if I say no he'll leave. I wanted your advice.' Emily almost laughs out loud. 'You and Ryan are happy, right?'

'Wine?' Emily goes to the fridge.

'I mean, you seem like you've got it sorted. And if you can do it, surely I can too?' Emily pours two large glasses.

'Cheers.' Emily clinks her glass against Sarah's. 'Congratulations.' Sarah paces the kitchen, then dumps her handbag on the table and starts going through it, crumpling up receipts. 'Why do you keep so many?' Emily comments.

'I'm an inveterate hoarder of useless things,' Sarah says, opening the bin. Emily thinks of Matthew and is inclined to agree.

'Why are you cutting up roses?' Sarah asks, pulling a handful of stems out. Emily blushes. 'Emily? Have you got an admirer? Or did you and Ryan have a fight?' Emily presses her fingers against the edge of the table hard. She's deliberately kept Sarah away from the details of her marriage. She means well, but she's an intolerable gossip, even if she is her sister.

'It's just someone with a crush,' she says dismissively. How she wishes it were Adeline, but this flamboyant display of romance doesn't bear her mark.

'I'm not sure I believe you,' Sarah says, her tone wheedling.

'He's a little obsessed,' Emily mutters. Why does she feel like she's being told off? She takes a deep breath. 'I made a mistake, a while ago. Got too close to a student. He complained, formally I mean. It got nasty. But it's all sorted, apart from . . .'

'Apart from what?' Sarah says.

'He can be a bit clingy. That's why I cut them up.'

'You should report him,' Sarah says. 'That's not right. Most assaults happen from people you know.'

'I don't want to report him,' Emily says, 'He's not a bad person.' Sarah looks at her, waiting for her to say something else. She crosses her arms.

'Did you sleep with him?' she asks.

'No,' Emily replies. 'But I confided in him and he took it to mean something more.' Sarah's expression says it all.

'Does Ryan know?' Emily shakes her head. 'Then you should tell him.'

'He's not around much at the moment.' Sarah finally sits down beside her. She puts an arm around her shoulder. 'You know you can talk to me, right?' Sarah says. Emily nods. 'Why don't you come and stay with us for a bit, just until he's lost interest?'

Emily thinks of Leo and his determined persistence. The same determination that it takes to complete a novel. A stubborn, iron-hard constitution that doggedly pursues an outcome, no matter what. It wouldn't be so bad to have some time away, a break from this house.

'It's fine – we're fine,' she says to Sarah, 'but thanks.'

'What's this?' Sarah asks, picking up the details of the cabin by the sea.

'I'm buying it,' Emily says. Sarah raises her eyebrows.

'You know you can tell me anything, right?' Emily nods and looks out of the window. 'Anyway,' Sarah says. 'What do you think about Matthew's proposal?'

'I think you should run a mile,' Emily says. The truth feels like peeling off a scab.

The next morning Emily has three lectures. She struggles to inject enthusiasm into her voice.

'Make sure that you don't switch narrative perspectives within your writing: choose a viewpoint and stick to it,' she tells her first-year students. She pauses, watching their heads bend down as they scribble notes.

'Why, Miss?' asks a boy in the front.

'Because you need the reader to buy into your main character, to align themselves with their views. You need them to trust in what they're being told.'

A hand goes up towards the back. 'Why can't you have an omniscient narrator? Third person limited or first person are too restrictive: they only tell one side of the story.' The voice comes from the very back of the lecture theatre, where the room slopes into darkness. She can just make out the outline of a dark hoodie, but she'd know the voice anywhere.

'If it was good enough for Eliot, why aren't we being taught to experiment with different forms of narrative?' Emily's struggling to follow the questions and sweat is trickling down her back. 'You have read *Middlemarch*, haven't you, Miss?' Cocky shit.

'This is a first-year lecture and Eliot was an experienced writer. Of course we should all aim for her standard one day, but we need to start somewhere . . .' Her voice peters off as she loses momentum.

'But we all know there's more than one side to every story, don't we, Miss.' This time the students in the front rows turn towards the back, craning their heads. Emily walks to the table where her briefcase is and takes a sip of water. Say something. Anything.

'It's hard to pull off the omniscient narrative viewpoint,' she says, swallowing hard. 'The majority of books that get published now are either first or third person limited. With first-year students we focus on these two points of view. In the second year we encourage experimenting with form.' She stands straight and projects her voice towards the back of the room. 'As a student who has already graduated, you'll be aware of this.'

Leo stands and swings his rucksack over his back. He makes his way down from the back and when he reaches the front of the room he pauses. Up close she can see bags under his eyes and stubble lining his jaw.

'Sorry for interrupting your class,' he says, shrugging. Turning to the other students he nods at Emily. 'She does know what she's talking about. My book's coming out next year.'

'That's great,' Emily says, 'congratulations.' He tilts his head. She waits.

'See you around,' he says, and winks at her before sauntering out of the room, letting the door slam loudly behind him.

The heat of the underground spills onto the streets and she walks, not paying attention to where she is going. Her heels are not designed for speed walking and quickly her feet are blistered. She buys a pair of flip-flops and dumps the heels in a bin. She peels off her jacket. She'd like to strip off and plunge into cold water. She pauses to take stock of where she is, and seeing a bar, steps inside, grateful for its dark interior.

'A pint of water and a large gin and tonic please,' she says to the man behind the bar.

'That kind of day, hey?' he replies, putting them in front of her.

'That kind of year,' she says, downing the water. 'God, it's hot out there.'

'It's going to be an Indian summer,' he says.

'Good to know.' She swallows the gin and tonic and puts the glass down on the counter harder than she intends to. 'Another for the road?'

'This one's on me,' he says, filling the glass up to the brim. 'I hate to see a damsel in distress.' She drinks this one slower, watching the barman flit from tap to fridge expertly. Customers served, he returns to her and leans his elbows on the counter. 'You can tell me.'

She shakes her head. 'I wouldn't want to ruin your good mood.'

'It would take a lot to do that,' he says, 'I'm celebrating my divorce papers coming through.'

'I'm sorry,' Emily says, 'I didn't . . .'

'Don't be – like I said, I'm celebrating. Start of a new life and all that. So, what's your story?' She groans.

'No really, I can't . . .' She stops. Out of the corner of her eye she sees Leo, outside on the street. In spite of the heat she feels goosebumps spreading up her arms.

'Are you okay?' the barman says, following her line of sight. 'You look like you've seen a ghost.' He must have followed her haphazard route across London. It never occurred to her to look back. Perhaps she should go to the police after all. Emily twists on her bar stool so that her back faces the door.

'Just someone I wasn't expecting to see.' He could be coming in at this very moment, sidling up to the bar. Her skin crawls with the things that they have done. She pushes her empty glass towards across the counter.

'Thank you, you've been kind. I should go.'

'The pleasure's mine,' he says, and she stands to leave, ready to take her chances. She drops a note onto the counter.

'Keep the change.' Outside the heat has intensified and the alcohol spins to her head. Hailing a taxi, she winds down the window and scans the overcrowded pavements, checks her phone. Three missed calls from Leo.

She tells the boys about the cabin by the sea that evening. Sam's excited he'll have a holiday pad for his university holidays. Tom accepts the news as if she's updating him on what they're having for dinner, but as day slips into evening she feels better. Leo will lose interest. Adeline will be back in London soon. She can't wait to take her to the cabin. The boys disappear to their rooms and she's thinking about watching something escapist on TV when there's a knock at the door. She opens it, ensuring the latch is on. There's no one there. On the doorstep there is an envelope. Scanning the driveway, she bends down and picks it up. She opens it tentatively. It's a lock of her hair entwined with Leo's. He must have cut it while she was sleeping beside him all those months ago. The sight of it makes her feel sick. Anybody could have found it. This has got to stop.

She calls Sarah.

'I've been thinking about your offer and I think we should come and stay for a while.' The boys are done with college for the summer. They'll complain about the estate, but it'll be good for them. She throws away the envelope and closes all the blinds, giving up on the idea of TV. She goes to bed.

*

In the morning she knocks on the boys' doors.

'Tom, Sam.' Tom doesn't respond.

'Tom?' She tries the handle of his door and to her surprise it turns. Usually he locks it. She pushes the door open and peers in. His room is tidy for once, the bed made and the surfaces clear. She opens the blinds. He is not there. The last time she saw him was at dinner yesterday. He'd seemed okay then, as good as he ever seems. She rubs her eyes and squeezes them shut. As if she needed this right now. Perhaps he heard her on the phone to Sarah. He'd hate the idea of staying there for a while, not least because it's further away from Ella, who, unlike all his past girlfriends, seems set to stay for a while.

'Sam, do you know where Tom is?' Sam emerges from the shower wrapped in a towel.

'He isn't in his room?' he says. She shakes her head.

'Maybe he went somewhere early this morning?' They both know how unlikely this is. Tom has never left early for anything.

At 9 a.m. she calls Ryan. It goes to voicemail and she leaves a message asking him to ring her. She asks work to arrange cover for her lecture. It's too soon to call the police and too early to be scared. Tom would be mortified if she sent out a search party. She phones Ryan again and this time he answers. He's coming back to help look for Tom and should be back by evening. He doesn't even try to pretend that he's in Manchester.

'Try not to panic,' Sarah tells her when she rings her. 'He's probably getting stoned with his friends. I'm sure he'll come back soon. It's unlikely it's got anything to do with the student you mentioned.' Emily's stomach plunges. She hadn't even considered it could have something to do with Leo. She locks the doors and watches TV for hours, scarcely registering what's on the screen.

*

Her phone rings and it's Ryan. He's not coming back, claiming he's just as much use there as he would be in London. He sounds hammered.

'Where the fuck is there?' she shouts, and hangs up. The police tell her that Tom must be missing for at least twenty-four hours before he can be filed as a missing person. When Sam gets home he sits at his computer and logs into Tom's Facebook account.

'How do you know all his passwords?' Emily asks him.

'Someone's got to be responsible around here,' Sam says, shrugging. A few hours later and Sam has a lead, an email he found in Tom's trash. 'He's staying in a Travelodge in Dover,' he announces, 'with Ella.'

'Dover? Jesus Christ.' She unlocks the cabinet with their passports and Tom's is gone.

'He's really into this girl, you know,' Sam tells her. 'He doesn't even hang out with his friends any more.' How did Emily have no idea that this was going on? She grabs her keys and her coat.

'You're not seriously going down there, are you?' Sam says, 'He'll be furious.'

'He's a kid, Sam, not an adult. Despite what he may think.'

'I'll message him on Facebook,' Sam says. There's no reply, but then the phone rings and it's Ella's mum, distraught. It seems that everybody monitors their kids' social media apart from Emily.

'We're going down to fetch them,' she tells Emily.

It's late by the time Tom is home.

'Where on earth were you headed?' Emily asks him.

'To Paris,' he replies. 'I really love her. You wouldn't understand.'

'You're too young for this,' she tells him.

'I'm not you,' Tom says. 'I've had my fun. I'm ready for this.'
Emily reels from it but feigns calm.

'What about your A-levels, your education?' she says.

'I'm not Sam.' Tom shrugs. 'We don't even know if I've passed my GCSEs.'

Emily wants to reassure him but part of her knows this is a possibility. Could she have helped him more than she has?

'We can talk about it later,' Emily tells him, pulling him into her chest. 'I was so worried.' She blinks back a tear. While she's not been paying attention he's been growing up, but what can she teach him about love? She's still learning herself.

Rules of an open marriage #21:

Don't leave anyone in the dark

Wales, Sunday 16 October, 2016

Ryan drives fast and distracted away from the cottage, Ada filling his head. Laughing Ada, hiking Ada. She's everywhere, in the fleck of the sunshine, in the smell of his skin. He ploughs through the familiar twists and turns and waits for green lights without noticing. He arrives back in London with her words still ringing in his head. It's over and all for what? The house is empty and silent. The doorstep is covered with roses, dried out and dead. Fumbling with his key in the lock, the door clicks open and the air inside smells stale.

Leaving his bag in the hall, he heads straight for the kitchen and pours himself a large Scotch. The fridge is empty save for a half bottle of milk and some Parmesan. It doesn't matter – he's not hungry.

In the cold light of the next morning he ventures to the front of the house with a pen and a piece of paper, noting a tile slipped here, mould growing around a window there. The palm trees that line the front of the property are brown and wilted and the stones that cover the drive are strewn across the path to the front door. Out back has fared little better.

The pool cover looks worn, although it's only months old, and weeds have sprung up between the poolside tiles. The steps down into the pool are rusted and a pair of goggles have been abandoned on the side. Inside the house the catalogue of neglect grows; a broken window handle in Tom's room, a red-wine stain on the designer rug in the lounge.

He should go to the office; there's a new project coming up, an investor from abroad has commissioned an eco-house in a restricted planning area. There's a mountain of work to do and meetings to be had, but he can't summon any enthusiasm.

He rubs his knuckles where the skin is raw and sore from punching the wall. Ever since she told him that it's over he's been searching for an answer. Who were you in love with, the question niggles him. The woman or the cottage?

He walks back upstairs to his bedroom and lies face down upon the pillow. He inhales, hard. He rings his secretary and tells him that he is unwell, that he'll be in tomorrow. He throws away the list he has made of things that must be done. Shutting the blinds in his bedroom, he lies down naked among the dirty sheets, Emily's dead skin cells mingling with his own.

After some time the doorbell rings and he burrows down beneath the covers. It can wait. It rings again, insistently. 'Go away,' he mumbles. Then he sits bolt upright. It could be Ada. She knows where he lives. Perhaps she's changed her mind. He wouldn't put it past her. He leaps from the bed abruptly and the room spins with silver stars. Stabilising himself with one hand on the wall, he shouts out, 'Coming.'

Down the hall shot through with light and down the floating staircase. He flings open the front door.

'Hi.' The man standing on the doorstep is young, late twenties tops. A shock of blond hair falls across his eyes and is promptly swept back with the hand that is then offered to Ryan. 'I'm Leo.'

'Can I help?' Ryan asks. He shouldn't have answered the door.

'We have something in common,' Leo says slowly, then waits as if he's asked a question.

'I don't think so,' Ryan says, turning to shut the door. He never did have the tolerance that Emily did for strangers. Leo puts his foot out and wedges it in the doorframe.

'You're Ryan,' he says.

'Bingo,' Ryan says. 'Now if you'll excuse me, I have places to be.' He pushes the door and feels it press again Leo's foot. He pauses. 'How do you know who I am?' He opens the door and peers at Leo's face, taking in the intensity in his green eyes.

'We have a mutual interest,' Leo says, 'in your wife.' Inwardly Ryan groans. Of course.

'You're wrong,' Ryan replies petulantly, 'I have no interest in her,' though it's not entirely true. 'She's yours if you want her.'

'She was right about you all along,' Leo says, a tremor in his voice.

'Take whatever she has or has not told you with a pinch of salt,' Ryan says. 'You're young. It's not your fault.'

'Don't patronise me,' Leo says, taking a step forward. 'Can I come in?'

Ryan is about to say no when he sees a flicker of desperation in Leo's face. It reminds him of Sam when he last saw him. He opens the door and Leo walks in, heading straight for the kitchen. Ryan follows him in. It's not an obvious place for the kitchen, tucked around the corner. Leo's been here before.

'Drink?' Ryan offers. He opens the fridge and reaches for a beer, and holds it out to Leo, who shakes his head.

'Not for me,' he says.

'Suit yourself,' Ryan says. He snaps the ring pull. The fizz of the beer and the cold bubbles burst against his throat. He slides open the doors to the garden and leads the way to the rattan chairs that he despises. Emily insisted on them. 'Some comfort in this cold place', she'd said sulkily when he complained. It's chilly outside, but he'd rather be outside in the fresh air than inside with a stranger violating his space. 'So, how can I help you?' he asks.

'Don't you want to know where your wife is?' Leo says.

'We are not each other's keepers,' Ryan replies, kicking off his shoes and resting his feet on the table. 'She can look after herself.' He peers at Leo, who shakes his head.

'It's not about that,' Leo says.

'Come on then, what's it all about?' Ryan says. Gloves off, knuckles bared. The blood of his father rushes through him. Where has denying instinct ever got him, anyway?

'She loved you, you know,' Leo says. 'Some people want to be needed.'

'I think you might be confusing my wife with someone else,' Ryan says. 'Emily doesn't need anyone.' He's aware of Leo's eyes scanning his face.

'That's where you're wrong,' Leo says.

'Get out,' Ryan says, standing. 'How dare you come into my house after fucking my wife and tell me how to run my life?' Leo shrugs.

'Don't you want to know where she is?' Leo says. A prickle of unease runs down Ryan's neck. There's something not quite right about this man.

'How do you know where she is?' Ryan asks.

'Ways and means,' Leo replies with mock nonchalance. '"My love for her is a source of little visible delight, but necessary. As is my protection." Brontë, if you didn't know,' he adds, taking a step back.

'You pretentious little prick,' Ryan grabs his elbow. 'What do you know about love, running around stalking other men's wives?'

'More than you,' Leo spins round and he is so close to Ryan's face that Ryan feels the heat of his breath. '"I don't want to sit here and talk about why we barely make love any more, or sit here and not talk about it. I'm tired of it all." Sound familiar?' Leo says. Uneasily, Ryan recalls his words from an argument long gone. She told this kid about that?

'Nice place you have in Wales, by the way,' Leo says.

'How do you know about that?' Ryan says, remembering Ada's face when she saw someone all those months ago. He jumps forward, catching Leo's shoulder. Ryan's chest slams into his arm. Leo is large and strong but Ryan has caught him off guard and he falls backwards onto the floor with a sickening crack. Without a pause Ryan is on top of Leo's chest, knees digging into his ribcage. 'How the hell do you know?'

'I needed to see what my competition was,' Leo says through the blood that is running from his nose. 'Turns out it wasn't much after all, though your girlfriend's hot as heck. Great figure.' Ryan thinks of the man Ada claimed she saw, all those months ago, when she was naked but for her wellies. 'If I weren't in love with your wife then I'd be tempted ...' Ryan pushes his hand against Leo's mouth, longing to crush his fist through this beautiful boy's face. He imagines his nose breaking, the dull crack of cartilage as it snaps and shatters.

'GET OUT,' Ryan says, moving off Leo's chest and standing above him. 'Get out of my house.'

'Oh, I'm leaving,' Leo says, peeling himself from the floor. 'Enjoy your life of glass palaces. I came here to tell you where your wife is. You've always underestimated her.' He walks through the kitchen and into the hallway with Ryan following at a distance. By the front door Leo pauses, 'Believe me, you'll regret not wanting to know where she is.' He slams the door behind him so hard that the windows rattle with his threat.

Rules of an open marriage #22:

Never be with someone that we both know

Dorset, Monday 17 October 2016

'How much longer do you think we'll be able to keep swimming?' Adeline asks Emily as she emerges from the sea. Her lips are blue and her pale skin mottled pink. She links an arm through Emily's.

'We can get wetsuits for the winter,' Emily says. 'Neoprene, with hoods. People surf all year out here.'

'I can't wait,' Adeline says, smiling.

Back in the cabin Adeline showers while Emily puts the kettle on. She looks around the cabin. It's been two months since she got the keys. Tom's been spending weekends in London at Ella's and Adeline's been here every weekend apart from the one just gone, when she went mysteriously away. There was something she had to do, she told Emily. 'Very cryptic,' Emily had laughed, kissing her. Emily had been looking forward to her first weekend alone in the cabin since she got the keys, but late last night Adeline had rung her and asked if she could join her after all. She turned up in the early hours of the morning, smelling of woodsmoke.

Adeline comes up behind her and Emily leans back as she feels Adeline's arms around her waist.

'I love it here,' Adeline tells her. She burrows her face into Emily's neck and Emily feels her lips brush her ear. 'I love you.' Emily turns and meets Adeline's mouth. It's the first time that Adeline's said it. She kisses her hard, pulling her closer, moving her fingers down against the small of her back.

Later they sit on the tiny sofa looking out at the view. On the table in front of them is Emily's notebook. She's writing again.

'I think I'll move here eventually, when Tom goes off to university,' Emily says. 'It's only two years to wait. If he goes to university, that is.' Having scraped through his GCSEs, Tom's started studying for his A-levels, though she's not overly hopeful that he'll stay the course.

Adeline leans forwards and kisses the tip of Emily's nose. 'When are you going to tell Ryan that you're leaving him?' she asks. Emily sighs.

'Soon. It's bad timing, though. He's in pieces. I think his affair is over. He's living back at the house in London full time now.' Adeline walks to the fridge and pours herself an orange juice. Emily watches Adeline's throat as she swallows, still not quite believing that she's here with her. 'You've changed my life,' she tells her.

'It took some persuading,' Adeline says, laughing. That awkward night in Peckham feels like years ago.

'I always felt like I was giving up something by being married,' Emily says. 'Even with our open arrangement.' She's told Adeline everything now. 'But with you it doesn't feel like I'm giving anything up.'

'Maybe the secret to a good marriage is to marry the right person,' Adeline laughs and slips her hand up Emily's thigh. 'I really think we can make this work, you know.'

'What happened to you being a serial short-termer?' Emily laughs.

'I hadn't met the right person, obviously.' Adeline leans over and kisses Emily.

'Maybe. I never believed in *the* one.' Emily sighs. She doesn't want to go back to her sister's. The place is too small and Sarah's been fractious since Matthew left her. She hasn't exactly said it, but Emily's fairly sure that Sarah blames her for his leaving when she turned down his marriage proposal. Sarah's asked Emily if she can come with her to the cabin, thinking the fresh air and seawater is the secret to her new-found luminescence. Emily's aware that it must be hard for Sarah, watching Emily's happiness while her own life is scattering off its tracks. Emily's dreading telling her about Adeline. Dreading admitting to her that perhaps the secret to happiness can be found in one person after all.

Emily's phone rings.

'Ryan?' She pushes her finger to her lips as Adeline raises her eyebrows. 'I wasn't planning on being back in London until the weekend. Really? Can't we talk about it on the phone?' She hangs up and feels Adeline watching her.

'He needs to talk to me,' Emily says. 'He's really upset. I should go and see him.'

'But I only just got here,' Adeline says, pouting. 'I don't see why you need to run back to him after everything he's done.'

'I still care about him, you know,' Emily says, kissing Adeline on the lips. 'And he is the father of my children.' She pulls away. 'Plus I'm about to leave him, so I feel like I owe him this. And it's not like I am going to invite him to come here. Why don't you stay? I can be back by tomorrow. You can keep the bed warm.' Adeline laughs.

'Do you have to go right now?'

'If I leave now I can be in London before it's dark. I'll be back before you know it.

Rules of an open marriage #23:

Be loyal to one another in your hearts

London, Monday 17 October 2016

Ryan closes the blinds in his office and turns off the lights, nodding goodnight to the cleaner, who comes every day, even when there's nothing to clean. The summation of his progress is a pile of broken pencils and a pressure corn on his thumb. He was surprised when Emily agreed to come to meet with him. She must care more than he thought she did. Outside it's bitterly cold and he pulls up the collar of his coat. The reflection of Southbank breaks across the river, inverted. He considers visiting an exhibition at the Tate Modern and starts walking, he loves Georgia O'Keeffe's work. Halfway there he changes his mind though, racked with indecision. He doesn't feel like being inside, his head is too crowded to appreciate art, too jumbled for anything much at all. This city that he used to love feels empty, stocked full of a million different ways to use up time, as if it is not precious. He feels it ticking in his gullet and chasing at his heels. Below him the river looks tempting. Never before has he realised how transient life is, the present slipping to past in the blink of a moment. Pulling his coat closer around him, he walks faster, concentrating on his footsteps. The streetlights snap on and the pavements teem with tourists, all with somewhere to be. He belonged somewhere once as well. He hands a tenner to a homeless man. So what if he buys booze with it? Hailing a taxi, Ryan responds to the small talk of the driver with small gruff answers until eventually they travel in silence. He watches the streets flash past the window as if on a movie screen.

The lights are on in his house.

'Emily?' he calls as he lets himself in.

'Hey,' she says, coming out of the kitchen, cheeks flushed and a glass of wine in one hand. She looks great, positively glowing. He leans in to kiss her on her cheek and as he does so he catches a whiff of the sea on her skin. He recalls what Leo said earlier about her being away.

He accepts the glass of wine that she offers him. It's been months since he's seen her like this and he's reminded of the young woman he first fell in love with.

'Thanks for coming,' he says, 'I'm a bit of a mess. Have you heard from Sam?' Emily sips from her glass.

'Yes, he's having a blast. He's talking about trying to get a placement in Monaco during his second year of university.'

'On an English degree?'

'He's optimistic – you know Sam. There's pasta ready, unless you already ate?'

'Sounds perfect,' Ryan says. She pushes a bowl across the table and he sits in front of it. Under the lights her eyes are bright.

'Thanks,' he says. 'How are you? You look good.'

'Didn't you have something you wanted to tell me?' Emily asks. Ryan clears his throat.

'Leo visited earlier . . .' The colour drains from Emily's face and she puts her fork down on her plate.

'Look,' Ryan says. 'You should know that he's been following you. He wanted to tell me where you were.'

'And did he?' Emily says.

'I'm not your keeper,' Ryan says. Emily sighs loudly.

'He's been a problem for a while. He won't leave me alone. It's why we're staying at Sarah's.'

'Do we need to report him to the police?' Ryan says. Emily shakes her head.

'I don't think he's dangerous, but . . .'

'He's in love with you,' Ryan says. Emily nods. 'And you with him?'

'No,' she replies.

'If there's anything I can do . . .' Ryan pours himself another glass of wine from the carafe that she's set upon the table.

'Did you call me here just to ask about Leo?' Emily says.

'My affair is over. Done.' Emily takes slow, deliberate sips from her glass.

'What happened?' she asks.

'I ended it,' he says.

'Huh.' Emily doesn't move. She doesn't blink. He forces himself to continue.

'So I'm going to be around a bit more.'

'Good for you.'

'And if you'd like to give us another go, I'd be up for it.'

'Did you seriously expect to walk back in here to open arms?'

'Of course not. I just wanted to tell you.'

'Well, you know what? I met someone too.' It's too warm in the kitchen and Ryan stands and opens the doors on to the garden. He wishes he could walk to the ridge. Ada's gone. Emily's going. The boys started checking out years ago.

'Look, Emily. When I told you that I'd met someone, you said I could carry on discreetly, that it didn't have to mean the end of our marriage.' She is still sitting at the table. She doesn't move a muscle.

'I'm happy to wait for you,' Ryan says.

'That's generous,' Emily says.

'It's just – two decades of marriage: it might be worth fighting for,' Ryan says, struggling to hide the desperation in his voice. 'I'm just asking you not to shut the door.' She laughs then and it is a cruel serrated sound that clatters.

'Which bit of it do you think is worth saving?' she says. 'I've spent a lifetime trying to be everything. Mother, best friend, lover. I've curled and crisped and crumbled beneath the pressure. And now I've found someone who makes me feel alive, you want me to come back?'

'I'm just asking you to leave us options,' he says.

'Options are the curse of the modern human,' Emily says. 'All the options we had. We drowned in them. I was naïve to think we could break the mould and survive it.'

'You're breaking the rules,' Ryan says.

'I am. I AM?' she is shouting.

'You wanted them, remember? I was never enough for you.' he says. Emily stares at him.

'You really think that's why?' she says angrily, 'Really?'

'I didn't want an open marriage. I told you that.'

'It was to preserve us,' she says, 'and you didn't object.'

'PRESERVE us? What planet are you on?'

'Rules to protect us, Ryan. Parameters of safety.'

'Protect us?' Ryan says. 'Really? Last time I checked marriage was a monogamous commitment. It's the whole bloody point of it.'

'You're lecturing me on commitment when you've bought a cottage with someone else? And what, now that she's dumped you, you're ready to re-commit?'

'I wouldn't have *been* with someone else if it wasn't for your behaviour,' Ryan says. 'All the times you – every time – imagine knowing that you're not enough for the person that you love. Every argument we had, every time I went away, I knew. How do you think it felt knowing that you were out screwing another man, punishing me?'

'That's not how it was,' Emily says, 'and you know it. It was just sex. It wasn't ever about love.'

'Why couldn't we have tried to make marriage work the way it's supposed to?' he says. 'At least given it a shot. I'd prefer it if you'd had affairs behind my back than parade your exploits in front of me. It would have been nice to see you trying to commit.'

'I didn't parade anything. It was just an outlet.'

'Is it supposed to make me feel better that they meant nothing to you?'

'You know sex wasn't as important to you as it was to me,' Emily says. 'We knew that from the start. It would have become a problem . . .'

'You think it would have become a problem.'

'It's biology. You can't just shut it out.'

'Can't you? Isn't that what people do when they get married, adapt?'

'If you were so miserable, why didn't you say?' she asks.

'I did say: remember the time I threatened to leave? But you wouldn't listen and you gave me no choice. I couldn't leave Sam and Tom. I couldn't leave you.'

'You never tried to leave me,' Emily says. 'I'd remember that.' She presses her forehead against the glass of the doors to the garden.

'You thought you could control everything and you were wrong. You thought you could control love,' Ryan says. He looks at Emily. 'Okay, you win.'

'Really? This is about winning or losing?' she says.

'That's not what I meant,' he says.

'I'm moving out for good and I want a divorce,' she says, walking outside.

Rules of an open marriage #24:

Remember that love is not possession

When the boys were five and six he decided to leave. He packed a bag. Emily had stayed out the night before and when she'd kissed his forehead he could smell the other person on her skin. She'd gone straight to the shower and he'd paced the bedroom, counting how many people she had been with other than him. Sixty or seventy, at least. He was moderate in everything. They made love once or twice a month, and for him, it was enough. He wished it were enough for her. It was bothering him more and more, their arrangement. He couldn't stop thinking about who was last inside her. He wondered who she became with other people. He didn't believe that it meant nothing. Bodies are sandstone, etched permanently by touch. When the hum of the shower went silent he was waiting. She'd wrapped her arms around him as if she knew.

'I can't do it any more,' he'd told her.

'Why is Mummy crying?' Sam had asked, running in, followed by Tom. Then they were crying too, and Ryan was between them, holding them together like glue. Emily had leaned against him.

'I don't know what I'd do if you left me,' Emily said. 'You're my rock. I wish I found this commitment thing easier.'

'Me too,' he'd replied, and his resolve to leave had weakened.

Rules of an open marriage #25:

Above all, love one another

Dorset, Tuesday 18 October 2016

Adeline is woken by the gulls early. Emily will be back later. The day stretches ahead. Pulling on her trainers and running gear, she locks the door behind her. The beach is deserted at this time of year. She runs hard and fast, completing the route before the tide cuts off the cove completely. She's heading back to the cabin when she sees him. She'd recognise him anywhere. She considers turning around and running back up the beach, but there's not enough time, the water's too high. Anyway, he's already seen her.

'Ada?' She pulls out her earphones.

'Leo? What are you doing here?'

''I could ask the same of you,' he says, pushing his hair out of his eyes.

'Running,' she says.

'You know what I mean,' he says. 'Staying with Emily.'

'I didn't realise you two were in touch,' Ada says, a trickle of sweat running down her back.

'Where did she go?' Leo asks.

'What do you mean?'

'Yesterday. I've been watching you both.' Ada thinks back to when she saw him from the ridge at the cottage in Wales.

'Why do you want to know?'

'Emily is incapable of looking after herself,' Leo says. Ada shrugs.

'I disagree.'

'I have her best interests at heart,' Leo says. 'Is it love between you two or just sex?' Ada doesn't answer. 'I suspect you don't know the difference,' he says. 'People like you never do. Either way, when Emily finds out that you've been sleeping with her husband she'll see everything in a different light.' Ada kicks sand with her foot.

'*Was* sleeping with her husband. How do you know I haven't told her?' Ada says.

'I know Emily,' he says. 'One inkling of what's occurred would have her running in the other direction. Straight towards me.' He laughs.

'I doubt that,' Ada says.

'Shall we test my theory?' Leo says.

'What do you want?' Ada says.

'I want you to leave her alone.'

'I can't do that,' Ada says. Leo steps closer until Ada can see the pores in his skin.

'You're persistent,' Leo says. He chuckles to himself. 'We have that in common. So how's this? If you don't leave her I'll tell her about you and Ryan and then she'll hate you for not telling her yourself. If there's one thing that Emily values, it's truth.'

'I'll tell her eventually.'

'Not good enough. I'm asking you to leave before I blow this whole fantasy into pieces. You seem to attract escapists Ada, have you noticed?'

'I can't leave before she gets back. She'll be devastated.'

'Don't credit yourself too much. She's tougher than you think.'

*

Emily wakes up early at her sister's. She rings Tom to see if he wants to meet before she heads back to Dorset and they agree on Café Rouge. She takes a table at the back, away from the window, and orders a latte. Minutes later she sees Tom searching for her among the crowded tables.

'Hey,' he says, pulling out the chair opposite her.

'Hey yourself,' she smiles, 'Do you want something to eat?' She nudges her thoughts away from the bed he left this morning with his girlfriend. He virtually lives there. Tom nods and orders a panini.

'Are you staying at Aunty Sarah's?' he asks.

'I'm heading back to the cabin until the weekend. I can't wait for you to see it,' she says.

'Maybe.'

'Your dad and I are just figuring some stuff out,' she says, lowering her voice as the woman at the next table turns. She reaches for his hand and he pulls his arm away. She taps her fingers against the table.

'Why do you always pretend?' he says. She is aware of their proximity to the neighbouring table.

'I don't know what you mean,' she says quietly, tucking her hands back into her lap.

'That's it, right there.' He stands, pushing his chair back quickly so that the woman next to them looks up. 'So worried about what other people think. Always an act.' Emily watches him weave his way through the restaurant, her cheeks burning. She picks at the remains of her croissant and settles their bill.

She's knackered by the time she gets back to the cabin. She's too old to be driving up and down the country. She slings her bag over her shoulder and opens the door.

'Adeline?' There's no answer. 'Adeline?' It takes all of one minute to check all the rooms. She's not here and there's no message. She's probably gone for a run. Emily opens the back doors and goes outside to the crumbling terrace. Eventually she'll build a deck out here. The views are spectacular, straight out to sea and to the beach below. The path down is obscured. Sailing boats potter against the horizon. God, how she hated sailing. All the people she has tried to be over the years come back to her. It feels good to finally accept herself. If Ryan hadn't met someone then this never would have happened. He'd have carried on feeling hurt and she'd have carried on hurting him. What's happening with Adeline feels delicate.

There's movement on the beach below. A lone walker stops and looks up at the sky. Following their line of sight, Emily sees the arc of a contrail falling. There's something familiar about the walker, the motion of their stroll. Of his stroll. As he looks up towards her she sees his sand-coloured hair and the line of his jaw. Leo. She holds his gaze and he waves his hand in response. Suddenly it doesn't feel idyllic at all in this cabin on the edge of a cliff. Hidden from the road and tucked out of sight from the path, it's a trap that she's walked straight into. He must have followed her here. Where is Adeline? A thought solidifies.

Adeline's mobile goes straight to voicemail. Pulling on her Converse and coat, Emily walks through the cabin and out of the front door, leaving it open. She's at the gate when she reconsiders and heads back inside, emptying her bag upon the floor, trying to find the keys. By the time that she's found them the cabin is a mess, bags emptied and contents strewn upon the ground. Outside the gate she looks left down the path that leads to the beach, and right up the path to the road where the car is. She needs to make a decision.

Ryan gets off the train at North Dulwich after another unproductive day in the office. He thought they'd grow old in Dulwich Village, with peonies at their gate and grandchildren tugging them to the park. He stops at the Fox for a beer and inhales the deep musty smell of the place. Love ruptures more easily than he'd realised. He hasn't slept since Emily left yesterday. Ada is fading, a shadow glimpsed, then gone.

He stands and heads for home, suit jacket slung across his back, tie loose and twisted. Inside the front door he dumps his jacket on the floor and takes off his shoes. The landline rings and he picks up.

'Leo? What?'

'Emily.' She looks up and sees Leo.

'What the fuck are you doing here?'

'What way is that to greet an old friend?' He wraps his arms around her. He could crush her if he wanted. 'Nice place you've got here. Does Ryan know?'

'No,' she says. She instantly regrets it. 'Where's Adeline?'

'She has a habit of leaving. You've got terrible taste in women. And men.' He winks.

'What have you done to her?'

'Do you really think I'm that kind of person? I don't think you would have slept with me if you did. Or perhaps it was the fear that turned you on? Because let's face it, Schopenhauer was no match for you,' he grins. 'You were insatiable.' Bile rises in Emily's throat and she throws up into a bush.

'Anyway, don't worry, Ada's fine. I just came to give you this.' He pulls out a package from his inside pocket and passes it to her.

'What is it – a finger, a tongue? Leo, this has *got* to stop.'

'It's a proof of my novel. I thought you'd like to read it,' he says, and his smile turns her stomach. 'I modelled my protagonist on you; there's a lot of similarities. You even share the same name!'

'You've gone too far,' Emily says, thrusting the package back at him. He puts his hands behind his back.

'Read it: it might force you to face some truths.' She drops the package on the ground. 'I can't wait for your loving family to read it. Uh oh, hit a nerve, have I?'

'Why do you hate me so much?' Emily asks.

'It's the opposite of hate,' Leo replies, 'but the lines are fine.'

'I'll tell everyone that it's pure fiction.' Emily says.

'Isn't that the problem? Your word against mine. We all know how flexible your truth is. It's a nice place your husband has in Wales, by the way, you should go there sometime. See what you've been missing out on.'

'How do you know about that?' she asks. Leo taps his nose.

'Just keeping an eye on things. I like to have the whole picture.'

'What will it take for you to realise that we were a mistake?' She speaks slowly and calmly, as if to a child. 'Twice Leo, that's all, barely memorable.' It's a low blow and she hears his slow intake of breath.

'What do you mean?' he says.

'I know it meant more to you than it did to me and I'm sorry but—'

'What do you mean, twice?' he repeats.

'Do I need to remind you?' she says. 'The hotel, of course, and the time before, in the park.' He stares at her as if she has lost her senses.

'Hotel, yes, the park, no. I think I'd remember. Once is all I've got. The closest I've come to heaven.' He looks at her strangely and she remembers Adeline – *Oh honey, I told you not to go with him* – her hand on her knee, reassuring her. Reassuring her or something else? Until that moment in the bar with Adeline, she'd had no memory of what happened that night after the pub. She would never have slept with him to keep him quiet if she hadn't already done it once. Her decision to do so pivoted on it. It was easy to believe Adeline. Simple for her to fill in the missing hours. Emily should never have got so wasted. But why would Adeline have lied? Emily looks up again and can smell Leo's aftershave.

'Adeline told me that we - that you – that night in Dulwich Park, we—'

'Ada is a manipulative bitch,' he says.

'But I wouldn't have—'

'You don't know the half of what she's capable of,' he says.

'What's that supposed to mean?' Emily asks.

'Who do you think your husband has been having an affair with?' Leo asks. Emily looks at him blankly. 'Come on, who? You're smart. I can't believe you haven't figured it out.'

'Who?'

'The very same woman you've been practising your cunnilingus with. It was quite a turn-on watching. In different circumstances – well.' Emily throws up again and then sits down on the floor. She wipes her mouth with the back of her hand.

'I don't believe you.'

'Makes no difference.'

'Can you go now?' she says. Leo walks over to Emily and puts out his hand. She takes it and lets him pull her up.

'Are you going to be okay?' he asks, and he sounds like he means it. She runs through the past few months in her head. All the times that Ryan was away. Where was Adeline? 'On second thoughts perhaps you'd better not read my book, you might find it distressing.' He picks it up off the floor and tucks it back into his jacket. He starts to walk away and then pauses. 'You must have really loved her.' He smiles. 'At last you're experiencing some of the pain you caused me. That's something. The croaking raven doth bellow for revenge. I won't bother you again.'

'You're lying,' she says.

'I'm the only truthful one of the lot of you. If you don't believe me, then go to the cottage in Wales.' He scribbles on a piece of paper and passes it to her. 'Pretty sure you'll find her there. It's as untameable as she is. Also, I told Ryan that she's headed there and where she goes, he goes, so . . .' He holds his hands up in the air. 'You'll thank me later.'

Ryan is packing his bag when Emily calls him.

'Emily?' She's talking so fast that he struggles to understand her. 'Look, you need to go slower. What's wrong?'

'Did you know?' she's asking. Her fear crackles down the line.

'Know what?' he says. He presses the handset against his ear. 'Please, slow down. Did I know what?' He switches the phone to his other hand. 'What about Ada?' She's crying too much for him to make out what she's saying. 'Who's with you? Where are you? She did what? Of course it's not true.' Then, 'No, don't.'

He imagines her driving to Wales, knuckles white against the wheel. The phone cuts out and he places it on the table. He walks into the lounge and closes the blinds, adjusts the picture beside the door. *Captive* by Louise Pallister. Emily insisted on it dominating the room despite the fact that it unnerved him. Sketched in charcoal and chalk onto untrimmed paper, it's huge. Ryan saw a powerful bird tethered. It depressed him. But Emily felt it was full of hope. He looks at it again and he sees it poised and ready for flight. Shit shit shit. How much of Emily is unknown, and Ada too? He zips up his bag and runs to his car.

Emily goes to the sink and pours a glass of water. She puts her hands on the kitchen counter and leans her weight against them, willing them to stop shaking. She looks at the address that Leo has given her. It will take her five hours, at least, to get there. She shouldn't drive in this state. It seems unbelievable that only this morning she was in Dulwich with Tom. She wishes she'd stayed there and not come back to the cabin. She goes into the bathroom and brushes her teeth, then into the bedroom where she woke yesterday with Adeline, entwined. She's never felt so alive, so free. What if it was all a game for Adeline? The whole thing a web of manipulation designed to expose Ryan and Emily's marriage for the wreck that it is? The slightest wind and it collapsed at the foundations. She pictures Ryan and Adeline together. How often she has loved them separately. Why would Adeline have told her that she slept with Leo in the park? So much could have been avoided if she'd told the truth. She scoops the clothes that scatter the floor into a bag and turns the key in the lock behind her.

The A40 was slow but the M40 is clearer and Ryan drives fast, each mile pulling him closer. He tries to focus on the road. Ada and Emily? Rain hurls itself against the windscreen and his wipers struggle to keep up. He'd been hoping that he and Emily could work things out. That something might be salvaged. He would never have done anything with Ada had Emily loved him more than *plenty*. Had he been enough. It broke him. A truck cuts in front of him and he brakes sharply, feeling the car aquaplane. He eases his foot off the accelerator and drops his speed to seventy miles an hour.

The car is knocked around by the wind and Emily's struggling to stay in her lane. Not much traffic, though. At this time of night most people are tucked up inside. The rain is incessant and relentless, slamming against the windows. Everything is cause and effect. She searches for logic in Adeline's lie about Leo. The questions coagulate and pound inside her skull. Reaching for her handbag, she feels inside it for her phone.

She's forgotten to turn off her high beams and as she swings around a corner too fast she sees a truck approaching from the other direction. She grips the steering wheel and wrenches it hard left, but the road spins out from under her wheels. She is aware of the sound of screeching brakes and the horrified face of the truck driver illuminated by her high beams, his expression picked out in gruesome detail. Somewhere someone is screaming and perhaps it's her. She's slamming her foot down on the brake as hard as she can.

He forgot the key, he forgot the key, fuck. No, it'll be there where he left it in the key safe. *She liked the magic of arriving with nothing.* Thank fuck for fantasies. Ryan gets stuck behind a tractor and slows to a crawl, time ticking between his hands and the steering wheel. Finally the tractor turns in towards the mountains that flash with lightning. He winds his window down and thunder cracks against his eardrums. Snap, crackle and pop, Tom's favourite cereal when he was a child. Snap, crackle went the fire in the cottage, pop went his ankle. Into the woods went Red Riding Hood. Pull yourself together, he tells himself, forcing himself out of the car to open the nine gates as the wind grabs the door from his fingers. Gate five, four, then three. This time he leaves them all open. All the gates he has closed so carefully and where has it got him? As if nine gates could protect him. Each time he pulls away he sees the gates swinging wildly in his rear-view mirror. The world doesn't collapse. Two gates, then one. He drives slower, wary of the rain-washed road and his slippery brakes. Turning the bend, he sees the stone wall and the roof of the cottage. Smoke. He thinks of Ada and her claims about a fire. Of sensing things in the forest. She loves this place; she wouldn't destroy it. Would she? He can't be sure. He leaps from his car and has to jump back in to secure the handbrake. He runs up the path, pushing aside tumbled bracken, and tugs on the door.

Emily pulls over onto the hard shoulder and cries into her hands. That was too close; another second it would have all been over. She shouldn't have driven here, shouldn't have come. She thinks of Sam in Durham and Tom at Ella's. She thinks of their last interaction. Her longing to hold them close is so strong that it's painful. So many chances to fix things and she's blown it. Now everything is lost. When she's stopped sobbing she starts up the car again and pulls out onto the road cautiously. It's all been for nothing.

Ada sits beside the fire, smoke billowing out into the room. Ryan's eyes water and he marches to the window, throwing it open.

'Ada?' She looks up.

'I was always crap at lighting fires,' she says. Ryan bends down and opens up the grate, adjusts the vents, then sits down and reaches for the whisky. He forces himself to keep his voice calm. 'At any point during your seduction of my wife did you consider that it was a bad idea?' he asks.

'No,' she says.

'Not even when taking us into account?'

'It wasn't a bad idea, it's the best thing that's happened to me. I love her,' Ada says. Ryan feels like he's been punched in the gut.

'What a kick you must have got out of stringing us both along.'

'It wasn't on purpose.'

'Yeah, happens to me all the time, one minute I'm in a relationship and the next I'm falling into bed with someone else.'

'I really liked her. Did from the moment I met her.'

'Did you not consider it a conflict of interest – me, her?'

'It was unfair,' she says. He wasn't expecting contrition. 'Does she know?' she asks.

'Yes,' he replies. She mutters something under her breath and he catches a name: Leo.

'I owed you both more,' Ada says. She sweeps her hair to the side and a lock falls across her face. She tucks it behind her ear. Up close her eyes are glassy.

'Why didn't you end things with me sooner?' he asks.

'This place got under my skin,' she says. He remembers the comments from the girl in the shop, and the neighbour.

'Did you come here without me?' he asks. 'Alone?' She nods. He drinks from the whisky bottle and it burns his throat. He gags and drinks again.

Everything is black with no street lighting. Emily focuses on staying on the narrow road. She sees sheep gathered along the grass verges, illuminated by her headlights. She drives through one open gate, then another.

'You have cost me everything,' Ryan says.

'That wasn't part of the plan,' she says.

'Plan? PLAN?' He is shouting now.

'You always wanted more than I could give,' she says. 'Don't you get it?' She leans forward. 'Everything breaks when you capture it. Everything.'

'Apart from when you fall in love, apparently,' he says.

'You can't blame me for everything,' she says. 'You were involved in the decision-making too.' She reaches for his hand. 'What we had was special for a while,' she says.

'It was built on air and lies. It's make-believe,' he says. Her truth has wings. He shrugs her hand off and stands up.

'Why did you come, now?' Ada says.

'Leo called me and told me you were on your way. Emily rang too. She wanted to know if I knew. I couldn't believe it. I needed to hear from you what the fuck you were thinking. Emily, of all people . . .'

'I am sorry,' Ada says. He walks out of the cottage, slamming the door behind him and makes his way up to the ridge, pin drops of water lashing his eyes.

Emily peers into the trees and sees a glimmer of light through the boughs. This must be the turning. She drives down the road and in through the final gate, pulling the car up beside Adeline's and Ryan's. The cottage could be from a fairy tale with its golden-lit windows and smoke curling from the chimney. She stands for a moment, taking it in. She hears the wind in the trees and the roar of the sea in the distance. She places her hand on the door handle, then pauses. She could turn and get back in her car, drive back home and sort her life out. Get a divorce. She could give Tom some stability and stop the rollercoaster she's put him on. Or she could give things a go with Ryan. They could be stronger. Life can repair. Dinner parties and date nights and an inevitable return to before. It's hard to break a pattern. She stumbles forward as the door is opened from the inside by Adeline.

'Of all the people you could have picked,' Emily says. 'Where's Ryan?'

'He went up to the ridge. Please, sit,' Adeline says. Emily remains standing.

'Why did you do it?' Emily asks. Adeline sits beside her, pressing her hands together, leaving imprints of fingernails in her skin.

'I love you.'

'You should have ended it with Ryan.'

'We had this cottage by the time I realised how I felt. I tried to stay away from you but I failed. I ended it with Ryan two days ago. I couldn't tell you, because, well, then you'd know about us.'

'Did it not occur to you that I'd find out anyway, if we were to have any kind of future?' Emily says. Adeline flushes.

'I couldn't see that far ahead. I'm not used to planning,' Adeline replies. 'I wasn't thinking straight. All I knew was that I had to be with you.'

'Why even start something with Ryan if you were interested in me?'

'I didn't know if you were open to this, to me,' Adeline says. 'I was hedging my bets. It's a bad habit I have.'

261

'Why the hell did you tell me that I'd slept with Leo in the park? It was the whole reason I . . .'

'The whole reason you what?' Adeline says, moving closer and putting her hand on Emily's arm.

'The whole reason I slept with him again,' Emily says. Adeline looks at her in horror.

'You what?'

'After you told me what I'd done, I slept with him, to put an end to things. Don't you dare look at me with judgement.' Emily takes a step back and slaps Adeline hard across the cheek. Adeline puts her hands to her eyes and wipes the back of her hand across them. She takes a deep breath.

'I had no idea,' she says, and her voice is paper-thin.

'So why did you tell me I slept with him in the park?' Emily repeats, steeling herself against Adeline's tears. One step closer and she could hold her. She knows what it would feel like.

'Because I kissed you and you were horrified,' Adeline says finally. 'After you came out of the lake you were freezing. Leo warmed you up and I came to help. He went to find your shoes and you were lying in my arms and you looked so beautiful, so vulnerable . . . I couldn't help myself. I kissed you on the lips and you looked at me in horror. I thought I'd blown it. I was mortified.' Emily thinks back to that evening and the excitement she'd felt before they met, the thrill of the unknown, of what Adeline might become. Would she really have resisted Adeline's kiss?

'I told you you'd slept with Leo as it seemed plausible. He was clearly in love with you and I could sense the chemistry between you. You were wasted. I was jealous. I'm so sorry. If I had known what my lie would lead to . . .' She steps towards Emily cautiously and Emily lets herself be pulled into her arms. Adeline rests her forehead against Emily's. 'I love you,' Adeline says, brushing her lips against Emily's. 'I've never said that to anyone. No more lies, I promise. Forgive me?' Emily breathes in the soft scent of oranges and citrus. She pulls away.

'I don't know if I can,' Emily replies.

Ryan catches something moving swiftly out of the corner of his eye. A deer or a fox perhaps. In a space between the trees there is something lighter and he thinks it might be someone watching. As he peers into the darkness he sees that it is a boulder. Immovable and solid as the mountains that dwarf them. Ryan is soaked to the bone by the time he gets back to the cottage. He pours himself a whisky. He looks between Emily and Ada and without a word being said he knows. He shakes his head and goes upstairs.

They are leaving.

'What about your car?' Adeline says.

'I'll collect it later,' Emily replies. As Adeline drives, Emily stares out of the window into darkness, watching trails of raindrops as they streak down the glass. Adeline moves her hand onto Emily's thigh.

'We'll be all right, you'll see,' Adeline says. Emily doesn't reply.

Ryan comes downstairs and the cottage is empty. One car is gone. He throws a log on the fire and leaves the door of the stove open. He cups his hands to warm them. Upstairs the shutter bangs. The wind is howling up a storm. Perhaps tomorrow the sky will be clear and cleansed of demons. There are so many things to fix. Outside there is the crash of a tree falling. He lies down on the rug in front of the fire and lets the sounds of the forest wash over him. Somewhere an owl calls. His skin warms in the glow from the embers.

Acknowledgements

This book would not exist at all without my incredible agent Laura Macdougall. Thank you Laura for believing in me. You are an engineer of dreams and I'm incredibly lucky to have you in my corner. Huge thanks to Kate and Sarah Beal at Muswell Press for being willing to take a punt on me and for making my dream of becoming an author of a published novel a reality.

Thanks James Woolf for being the best writing buddy. Your integrity is inspiring. To my brilliant writer friends; Stephanie Hutton, Katherine Slee, Sarah Edghill, Chloe Turner, Andrew Leach, Astra Bloom, Laura Pearson, Laura Church, Jennifer Saxton and Janice Leagra along with many others, I love your words and am grateful for your support. Thanks Georgina Clarke for always making me laugh and I look forward to our island. I have been touched and humbled by the brilliant authors who agreed to read an early proof of my book and who provided endorsement quotes. The writing community is the best and I hope that I can pass on the generosity that you have shown me, to other writers going forward.

I wouldn't be writing this at all without the support of my wonderful friends, in particular Shirley Featherstone who shared this journey from the start and who has been there to toast the highs as well as to mop up the lows. I am blessed to have you. Thanks to Samantha Hyde for your wisdom on our walks and for never acting bored, and to Amanda Carroll for your faith in me. It's hard to remember life before writing, but before I'd ever written a word of fiction my dear friend Tammy was insisting that I should write books. Now there's belief. LUAAF Tams.

Thanks to my parents Martin and Jenny Spice, for being there for me, for reading everything I've written and for not hurling the computer out of the window every time I send a new story and immediately follow up with an email saying, 'ignore that one, read this one please,' just after you've started reading. Thank you for gifting me your love of stories from the very start. To the best sister I could hope for, Sara-Gwen, who read an early draft of this book. I love you to Proxima b and back. To my brother Will, thank you for being proud of me.

Thanks to my great love Arv for your eternal support, for letting me read you all my stories out loud even when you're tired, for putting up with half of my head being in a cloud, and for believing I can do anything I set my mind to. I'm so happy to be sharing this adventure with you and our surprisingly stable children Eva and Lucas.

Lastly, but by no means least, thank you to Lyra and Buddy for teaching me what unconditional love is and for our daily walks in the woods that remind me how beautiful our world is.